The Goose Mistress

A Dark Story

Conner McAleese

The
GOOSE
Mistress

A Dark Love Story

Conner McAleese

This is a work of fiction. Names, characters, organizations, places, events, and incidents are either products of the author's imagination or are used fictitiously.

www.darkink-press.com

Dark Ink Press

ISBN-13 978-0-9997016-4-5
ISBN 0-9997016-4-9

Cover design by Melissa Volker

Printed in the United States of America

For my Gran.

1939

November, *The Berghof*

"Unity Mitford has been shot."

I watched my sister speak, her lips curved around each word as if I was an imbecile and she my doctor. I heard the words.

Has. Shot. Unity. Been. Mitford.

But they didn't make any sense. How could that wooden, naïve English rose have been shot? She was at the Grand Hotel just a week or so before and then…

"Is she alive?"

Ilse's face looked relieved.

"Yes. She's critical. Stable. But she will never be herself again."

Lucky her.

"Why?"

Ilse shared a look with my mother, Fanny, and my younger sister, Gretl. My hand left the soft silk of my Italian dress from where it was pooled in a luxurious puddle in my lap, and traced the scar along my own neck.

"She did it to herself?" I said.

"A guard said he noticed a woman walking down the street, a gun in her hand. She walked into the *Englischer Garten* in Münich and…"

"I understand."

I stood to walk to the window; the green canopy of trees stretching down the mountains always made me feel safer, calmer, like I was trapped in a tower, surrounded by my own Alpine garrison. But I stopped midway across the room, preferring instead to look at myself. My chair before the vanity mirror was wide and its cushions plush. The creamy pallor of my pretty face was awash with grand swoops of skin that hung on the sharper edges that brought focus to my eyes and cheek bones. I picked up a hairbrush clogged with deep brown hairs, and ran it through my blonde curls, watching myself with every downward stroke.

"He visited her." I could see Ilse reach for our mother's hand, gripping it tightly.

She's scared.

I stopped brushing.

Good.

"Did he?" The acid bit my stomach, my skin broke out in a furious heat that pricked along my arms and shoulders.

It was a sweet pain.

"He instructed the doctors to give her the best care, that he would pay for it all." She was enjoying telling me. It was plain on her plain face. She wanted me to fall. She wanted me to be her little sister again. She wanted a dead girl back.

"He is kind," I said back. Monotonously.

"Are you ok, Effie?"

Gretl, my sweet, vacuous addition to the Berghof. She didn't listen, she was easily distracted – the perfect confidante. It was like bellowing into the void. It got *it* out of me. The anger. The dissolution. The despair. But it never went anywhere. Gretl would forget by morning when a charming young officer caught her eye. Ilse, however, was always watching, always noting with her eyes that which she would commit to memory. She watched me as I paused my brushing, she was probably the only one that thought it queer I decided to brush my hair at all. It made her dangerous.

She knew me too well.

"I'm fine. I'm sad for Fraulein Mitford."

"You never liked her," Ilse said.

"Did I not?"

"You know you didn't, Eva. You can't stand a rival."

"A rival? Is that what you think she was?" I watched my sister carefully in the mirror. "You think she was my rival? That silly slut that would let any

3

officer with a piece of information touch her, fuck her? You think a woman like that – a girl like that – could ever be my rival?"

"He spent a lot of time with her in Berlin."

"And tell me, Ilse, since you know so much, who exactly is it we are at war with right now?"

I was glad her face crumpled in confusion. *Stupid bitch.* Her eyes creased as she tried to better see the trap I was laying for her, the way of thinking that was twisting my mind around the obvious betrayal he'd lain at my door by entertaining that whore.

"France. England."

"Yes. Exactly. And poor Miss Mitford has lost her nerve right when she could have proved herself most valuable."

"Valuable?"

"For someone who came marching up those stairs with such self-righteousness, you seem to know laughably nothing, sister."

"I only wanted to make sure you had time to compose yourself." Her eyes glistened, but the tears welled in check by years of practice.

"What? Did you think I'd laugh when they told me? Or cry? No. Miss Mitford was a stupid piece of a larger puzzle, one that he won't get to play anymore."

"But...Berlin."

"You think a poor boy from Linz could ever be comfortable around an English aristocrat? Tell me, could he have risen in England and become Prime Minister?" Her mouth gaped, unsure of how to respond. *Who's the imbecile now?* "Exactly. She was a reminder of everything he must destroy. And now she's done it to herself. Let's hope her country does the same."

"Girls, stop this now. Come on, let's leave Eva in peace." My mother tried her best halt the growing anger, to suffocate the boiling hostility with her kind tone.

"She took him away. She took him from the Berghof to Berlin right under your nose. He never even said goodbye."

I looked back towards my own reflection in the mirror, away from my mother's gentle attempts to clear the room from me. I watched my lips as I spoke, admiring the way they parted and came together, parted and came back together, parted and always, truly, came back together.

"She'll never take him away again."

The air was temperate for November. Winter was approaching, as fast as it always did. I watched as the last Autumn sun of the year set over the Obersalzburg Valley. The yellow light poured itself across the pink. Honey blood. Like the sun had dared to tread too close to the world below and had pierced her own heart against his stony peaks. I knew she'd done it for love. For him. Maybe she loved the world so much that she couldn't stand to be so far away from him? Maybe she'd travelled across the heavens so that she could be with her love for all eternity, a perfect combination of life and fire, a coupling written by God himself.

I could understand that.

My ankles, my thighs, the soft skin on my pelvis, all yearned for me to stand up from the sun lounger and walk directly to his office. I could've sat there by the phone and known for certain whether he'd called or not; instead of sitting watching the sun bleed across the sky, praying that every scurry of a mouse, rumble of military boot on stone, was a messenger coming to tell me he'd called. But there, locked away in his hidden part of the Berghof, my mind would have run wild with fantasies and scenarios I couldn't entertain. Besides, I knew he wouldn't call. There'd be no soft sound of his timid voice. No squeal of delight from my own throat when I made him snigger at some small observation about the wives and how they'd made yet another day in paradise miserable with their jealousy.

I knew there'd be no phone call. He'd go to Unity, little vegetable Unity, and wish her well. The bullet was still lodged in her brain, or so Herta had heard from her husband. She was nothing now but a little English doll.

I smiled and then sipped my wine, enjoying it all the more now that I could relax.

It was the sixteenth anniversary of his Beer Hall Putsch, the path that thrust him to the pinnacle of government. Something more than a Kasier, far grander for sure than any president or prime minister. I wondered, as the wine lifted my head and seized the muscles in my cheeks, numbing them pleasantly, who I would be if he'd succeeded then. If he'd never walked into Hoffmann's photography shop.

No.

No.

No.

"No."

My voice became a wisp on the chilling air and I pulled a shawl around my shoulders. I was supposed to have gone to my little cottage on Wasserburger Street, but I was glad now I had not. Had I been in München, with him so close but at her side, I think I would have gone insane. Truly, madly mad. I took another sip of my wine, its taste bitter but steadying, and listened to the sound of the approaching night.

Heavy footsteps bounded along the stone beneath my terrace. Himmler must have had his men running drills, strange but not unheard of in the paradise of the Grand Hotel. I settled back into the soft lining of the lounger and listened to the crickets sing to one another. I let them sing for me. For my place in the world. And then their song became applause and I was standing on a stage in Los Angeles, the crickets the audience, and a glint of gold…

"Bomb," I heard someone say as they ran along the pathway.

I couldn't breathe. My heart daren't move. I pushed down on the soft flesh above it, but as I did my breath came back furiously and I choked on the wine that lingered in my mouth. The stone rushed up to meet me, its embrace hard and unyielding. The pain shot up my wrist and I felt tears surge and pour from my eyes as I spluttered and coughed.

"Eva?" Gretl rushed in and fell to her knees by my side. At once, she began to hammer on my back, her strength increased in fear.

"Bomb?" I belted at her between wheezy breaths, desperate to know. It was black around me; night had stolen the sky as I'd napped on the lounger. My wine glass shattered by its right-hand side. Stars twinkled down impassively which forced a humiliated scream up my throat.

"Father's here. He knows."

She must know. She must know something terrible has happened. Something awful has been done to my Führer and now he's dead. I knew this would happen. In my heart and soul, I knew he'd be taken away by the envy of another. His shaking hands that only I could still, the breath only I could bear, the tiny intimacies that turned him from their man to mine. My Addie…

I didn't cry. I couldn't. I became completely and perfectly still.

"Effie, come on." Gretl tried to lift me from the stone, using her old childhood nickname for me. "Come and see Baba."

I let her guide me, for, what did it matter? If he was gone, I would soon be too. Another little Unity in such a short space of time. My finger traced the scar along my neck as I saw my father, dust-covered but sober, sitting on the lime green of my chaise lounge.

I have to get out of here.

I turned to run back to the terrace. Maybe it was high enough that I could throw myself from it? *Romeo, oh, Romeo, where for art thou, Romeo?* But Baba was too quick. He caught me by the wrist and turned me back to him, violently. I was a young girl again. And this was his house.

And I'd just broken the rules.

"A bomb destroyed the podium at the Burgerbrau Keller. It was all over the radio. We couldn't cut the feed in time. The entire Reich heard it."

I wondered if it was his stupidity that made him cruel? Or the beer I could still smell on his breath? His eyes bloodshot and his cheeks smeared with dirt and grime. How was a man to look as he told a woman that the love of her life was gone?

What kind of life is this for a girl still in her twenties?

"He's gone," I said calmly; he'd have to let me go sometime and I could throw myself off the terrace then.

"Come with me."

9

I let him lead me down the simple stairs that tumbled in a rickety sort of way from my plain door. There were two guards there, instead of just one, and I wondered who had bothered to send another. A wide promenade that acted like the main artery to the entire complex ran the length of the Berghof. Paneled wood, stripped from only the finest German trees, stood tall over Swiss and French marble floors. Portraits hung with their dead eyes, watching the Führer's whore being lead along before them by her upstart father. I could have laughed – I wanted to – if it wasn't for the agony in my wrist from where my father clutched it so tightly.

I knew we were heading to Addie's office. I'd gone that way so often I knew that I could've sleep-walked to it. *But if we were going to his office then that could only mean...*

Goebbels must be here. He and his wife Magda would be assuming power over the Reich and she could finally be the First Lady of Germany in both title as well as deed. I didn't even care she'd won. I couldn't find enough strength to care. Any nerve endings that hadn't already been fried were in too much grief to be of any use. I knew they'd want me gone – if not dead – and I would laugh as I assured them that that would not be a problem.

Angela Hammitszch (neé Hitler) stood by his closed office door, her hands on her hips and her ugly face twisted brutishly with fury. That caught me up short. Surely, she'd be happy? Jubilant almost? That the little whore

– I – that had taken her daughter's place was now about to fall so heavily, so resolutely, that she'd be with the bones in the ground before dawn.

She said nothing as she flicked her wrist on the door handle and let it swing open. My father pushed me inside and shut the door behind me. A single lamp lit the spacious room and the muffled sounds of my father arguing with Angela battered at the wooden door.

Addie's huge portrait of Frederick the Great dominated an entire wall behind his desk. His cheeks sagged with ancient lines, beneath a pair of knowing eyes that followed me around the room. The red couch. I laughed when I saw the photograph of Chamberlain sat upon it, stretched lazily in the corner. A reminder of when I first gave myself to my Führer. This was a room of great men, men of history, and I never felt more like a little woman at the side of history than when I stood there.

It was like his voice was in the room with me. "Tschapperl. Tschapperl." I heard him whisper to me. The ghost of him, the part of his being that could never be blown away by some crudely made bomb in a cheap beerhall, was still with me.

"Tschapperl," I heard again.

I sat in his big chair, scraping its legs along the wood of the floor. He didn't like the American wheels that they put on newer chairs. He always said wheels where for cars, but when you sit that's all you should be –

11

sitting. I rested my cheek on the cool mahogany of his desk and waited for the shock to break so that I could weep until I died.

"Tschapperl?"

I jumped up, knocking over a cup filled with pens and pencils. They clattered to the floor, a rain of shrapnel. I knew I'd heard him. Not just in my head, but here, in the room. I looked up towards Frederick and wondered if he'd start talking soon too. Now that I was going mad. Surely that was it? I was going mad now. Truly, madly mad.

"Tschapperl?"

I looked to the phone, sitting off the hook. I don't remember knocking it over. I didn't remember feeling its smooth plastic edges beneath my fingers or elbow. I had spent so many nights, here, by this phone, that I thought the moment the shock would break was upon me until...

"Tschapperl?"

"My Führer?" I picked up the receiver and heard his voice so clearly, so vividly that I knew I'd finally broken and I was a mad woman ready to die.

1940

April, *Wasserburger Cottage*

I watched the dawn light tread softly across the floor, as if it believed I was still asleep. The air was warm, though not so much that I didn't need my blanket. I held it tight against my body, its soft skin reassuring my own. It had been a long night. This trickle of light, and my own gratitude at my blanket, was my reward for enduring another horrid night.

The stark reality of being a whore had taken hold of my body while I slept. My guard down, my dreams paramount, I had been struck with a wave of nausea that crested violently from my sleep into the bleak, dark room. Covered in a layer of sweat, my spirit broken by months of unanswered hostility, I'd wept as quietly as I could, fearful Gretl or

Gertraud might've heard me and come in to ask questions. Questions I had no answers to. Questions I dare not ask myself, for if I did, how would I ever console myself in the long nights again?

I'd left the Berghof in a flurry of pompous rage. Trunk hastily packed, a fact Gretl would hate me for when she realized all my fine, new dresses would be creased and thrown in the Mercedes, I had barely shot a parting goodbye to the smug face of Angela as she stood by the door, watching, waiting to report back to her brother. If she wasn't such a madam, then perhaps I would have felt sorry for her. Perhaps I could even have been her friend, for what was she, if not another woman trapped in his orbit? He would know I wasn't there by now. He wouldn't like that. I knew he wouldn't. Now, as I lay in the darkness, I realized how dangerous that was.

A gentle knocking came from the bedroom door. My skin prickled with fear, the sheets tangling around my feet and making me tumble from the bed. *What if it's the Gestapo? The S.S. come to snatch me?* How could I bear it? How could anyone?

"Breakfast," Gertraud's voice lilted through the door.

I breathed a sigh of relief that didn't quite steady my heart.

"Coming," I lied.

Two hours later, I descended the stairs to a messy kitchen filled with crumbs and fruit peelings all along the kitchen work tops and the hardwood table.

"Did you not wait for me?" I asked, incredulous at their lack of respect.

"We were hungry," Gretl laughed. "We aren't in the Berghof now."

I felt my anger simmer until Gertraud laughed too and pulled a fresh tray of crisp toast from the saucer cupboard behind her. A practical joke she was unsure whether or not to follow through on.

"Pass me the butter," I laughed with them, a weight falling from my shoulders like discarded armour.

I watched Gertraud as she played with Stasi and Negus – both Scottish terriers, both black – her young frame thin and boy-like. She had no breasts yet, despite being seventeen. Often, she would stop and pull at some fabric that cut into her armpit, hidden beneath the folds of her dress.

"So why did we have to rush down here?" Gretl asked as she sipped her tea.

"We didn't."

"Oh, Effie, we did. What happened?"

What happened? Something in me snapped. Something I once thought unbreakable. I was sitting at his large oak desk, the one that gazed down on the steep decline of the Obersalzburg mountains, papers scattered in front

of me like a snowy field in the countryside; like one of the ones Baba used

to take Gretl, Ilse and I to just before Christmas. As I scribbled notes on

what food to order, what guests to invite, the luxurious way I would have

the dining hall dressed up – reds, whites and blacks – something tore within

me. Those papers would still be there, I knew. Still scattered across the

table, unless Magda had spied them and thought to take them for herself. A

bold move, she knew that his birthdays were always planned by me. That's

how he liked them.

And I've left him to do it for himself.

"Nothing happened," I lied.

"She's a frightfully underdeveloped girl, do you not think?" Gretl

moved swiftly on, avoiding the hurdle of my silence as if it were a muddy

puddle on the trail before her.

"Some girls are late bloomers."

"Seventeen? How can someone be so late? And the way she walks, and

talks. It's like she's not even a person at all. She's a shadow on the wall. A

half-being. Don't you find that odd?"

"Our uncle is a stern man, bathed in the traditional ways. She'll be a

traditional woman." I felt my stomach turn as I said the words, the sickness

rose in me like a spectre growing from the flames.

"She won't be a woman if she doesn't get herself a pair of titties. Perhaps we should help her?"

"Help her?" I said as Negus tried to nip at Gertraud's ankles.

"You have some clothes and I have a great deal more," she jolted me with her arm, laughing, bringing a smile to my own face. "We could let her have some. Donate some to her womanly cause. Look at the horrid way that fabric keeps pinching her. Look." I looked and once again her fingers were digging into the soft flesh beneath her armpits, her face spasming in quick blasts of pain. "Poor girl's probably never even heard of silk. If we dress her like a woman, maybe her body will recognize that is what she is and grow accordingly."

"You really have no concept of biology, do you?" I laughed.

"Sorry, Fraulein Blue Hair, Blonde Eyes."

"Blue hair?"

We both descended into fits of laughter that drew Negus and Stasi away from Gertraud and yelping at our feet, as happiness so often does with the simple.

"But I don't need new clothes," she protested as we led her into my bedroom on the first floor of the cottage. "I have many lovely clothes."

17

"You have many clothes," Gretl conceded. "But let's have a few more, no?"

"My father, he…"

"Let her deal with your father," Gretl stuck her thumb towards me as if I had any authority to tell my uncle what to do this way or that.

I was about to say as much, tell them how negligible my influence was, until Gertraud's face broke open like the dawn that tread my floor that morning and I could see clearly that she was a trapped woman who believed I had the knife to free her from her bonds. So, I smiled back, nodded a lie and walked towards my wardrobe.

She was roughly the same size as me, perhaps a little thinner in the thighs and stomach. She was a slender girl, suited for reading and sinking into the background. *I'm a star.* A thick girl strengthened with muscles and talent. I didn't envy her lithe waist.

She fidgeted on the bed, her hands nipping at one another as if she were trying to wake herself from a dream. Her nails were polished but free of colour, her face soft and round, easily able to take a quick layer of French make up to straighten out her nose and give an alluring edge to her cheeks. Gretl sat by her side with her hands on her knees. "You're taking too long," she admonished, joining me by the wardrobe.

Gertraud let out an infinitesimal gasp at the wondrous colours within, as if I had shown her a world beneath the oak doors that she hadn't believed could exist. Her ankles clapped together and a tear filled her eye before tumbling down her cheek. Her practiced hand was quick to wipe it away as if it had never been.

"Here," I pulled out a floral dress swirled with purples and yellows. "This would suit you well."

"But the, er…the straps."

"What about them?" I asked.

"They're very thin."

"Revealing, she means," Gretl laughed. "You'll never get a husband if you're afraid to show some shoulders. There's a lot more men want from a young girl like you."

A memory crashed through my head like a train rushing through a cold forest. In the distance I could see heavy iron gates with big blinking yellow eyes ahead. Bright and blinding. I let the dress slip from my hands, my eyes so tightly shut that I couldn't see it ripple down to the ground like smoke falling instead of rising. A young girl, her blonde hair my envy, splattered with a gun's bullet.

"Are you ok?" Gertraud asked while Gretl tutted and kneeled down to collect the dress muttering about 'wrinkles.'

"Yes, dear. Yes. Sorry. Could you hand me that glass of water?"

I wish it was wine.

"All better, yes. Now. Try this on." I handed her a dress of baby pink made from fine English wool. "And this," an Italian leather jacket I had just got for Christmas. "Oooh and you will look fabulous in this too." A plaid dress of Scottish tartan. "Well, try them on then."

"Here?" she shifted her buttocks on the bed.

"Where else, silly?"

"I don't want to," she began to weep, her hands not quick enough to scatter all the falling tears.

Gretl's arm was around her in a moment, my own following more slowly.

"What's wrong? Tell us. You're safe here. What's wrong?"

"I can't."

Gretl and I shared a look.

"We need you to be brave now, ok? We need you to be brave and tell us what the matter is? Why won't you get changed?"

She buried her head in my breasts and I clutched her to me tight. Her own arms were snakes around my back, constricting like the flood was coming and they were terrified they'd be washed away.

"I can't," she sobbed.

"Ok. Ok. Don't worry. It's fine. We'll leave you in here. Would you still like to try the clothes on?"

Her eyes were red, her lips thin and blue. The despair etched on her face was like looking into the void, into the nothingness above heaven, and realizing how small and illiterate we all were. She nodded but didn't speak. Gretl and I stood up and left, closing the door behind us.

"She's terrified," I said.

"Bruises, maybe? Scars?"

"Scars? Bruises? From what?"

"Uncle? Herself? Who knows? There must be something making her so scared."

"You don't think she could be pregnant, do you?" my stomach turned. "And that's why she wears those baggy clothes?"

"Pregnant? She barely looks like she's had a period, never mind conceived a child. If she can't strip in front of us, Effie, what makes you think she could before a man? When would she even have the chance to?"

"Ok, ok. It was just a suggestion."

She looked at me with Ilse's eyes until a soft knock came from within the door.

She'd chosen the plaid dress with the Italian jacket. She looked ridiculous, like a mismatched school girl in her mother's clothes but I smiled encouragingly at her anyway. She needed this. She needed to believe she was beautiful.

She wore the clothes to dinner, her fork never outpacing a two-legged tortoise from plate to mouth. She sipped her drink with her chin jutted out, her fear of marking the clothes so terrible that she looked in pain to even be wearing them around such messy pasta – Gretl's only edible culinary creation. Dinner ended in fits of giggles as a dollop of sauce left her fork in slow motion and landed with a deafening thud on the hem of her skirt. Her eyes welling up, her mouth mumbling "but I tried," and Gretl and I falling to the floor while she sat still, unsure of how to react.

"What's it like at the Berghof?" she asked as we nestled into the fine American made couch that stretched the length of the cottage wall.

"What's it like?"

"Yes," she nodded. "Is it, you know, terribly fun all the time?"

Gretl was in the room next door, her voice warbling along with the old record player that sat by the wireless. She'd wanted to turn that on instead, saying my record collection was far too limited, but even there, in my own home, I was terrified he'd know I'd disobeyed him.

"It can be," I shrugged.

"And do you know Magda Goebbels? I mean, sorry, Frau Goebbels?"

"Yes, I know her," it was my turn to shift uncomfortably.

"Is she that glamourous all the time? I see her, you know, in the papers. She stands with such confidence next to her husband, such poise and the girls at school all say, 'That's the Reich's First Lady,' and I have to nod along, even though I know they are wrong."

"They aren't wrong," I said, sad. "They're very correct."

"But…"

"But nothing. I am a secret," I sipped my wine. *For now.*

"But, isn't that frustrating? Wouldn't you rather be the one at those dinners? In the papers?"

Would I?

"No. Not for that reason."

"What do you mean?"

It was hard to remember she was just a girl. We were similar in a great many ways – on the inside of course. We would run along the length of the garden outside, arms stretched out in front of us as our eyes were blindfolded. Gretl would laugh, guiding us with her voice, but out of all the ways we could run, so often, more than not, little Gertraud and I would run into one another. So, against ten years of habit, I opened myself to her. A fraction. The first bud blooming while ice still coats the world.

"I don't like politics," I admitted as if to a confessor. "It's boring. It is. I'd like to meet politicians, the Counts and Princesses of the world, but not to discuss politics."

"You mean, you haven't met them?" she asked with Ilse's wit.

"I am a secret," was all I said. All I could say.

"But you do want to be in the papers?"

"Yes," I smiled, sipping again. "Oh yes, I do."

"How will you get there?"

"As an actress," I said simply, as if it is the most normal thing in the world.

"Surely the Reich's First Lady may have her pick of roles?"

"Of course she could. But where's the fun in that? Being chosen simply for who I stand beside? I have talent," I said more to myself than her. "I am a talented actress. Day in, day out, I play the role of a beleaguered secretary at the most powerful home in the world. Day in, day out, I play happy at being ignored, of being a no one. There is no greater evidence of my talent than the life I lead right now. I will become an actress, have my face in the papers... but because I am Eva Braun, not because I am Hitler's Mistress."

Gertraud sat quietly, her eyes tracing the rim of her glass. I said nothing either, could say nothing, not after the filthy words I'd just spoken. "Mistress." That's all I was. A mistress. No wonder the Emmys and Magdas of the world had no respect for me, for what self-respecting woman could confide herself to a life of second best? Of solitude, as I had done? And, what's worse, how could she look to be enjoying it?

"Go and sing with Gretl," I commanded. "I am going to take a walk."

I pulled my wellington boots on over my bare feet. The anorak was green and crinkly, the noise quite loud in my ears, but I knew it would rain soon. April brought nothing if not showers and misery. If I were to guess the month in which the world would end, I would guess April without a second thought.

The darkness accepted me eagerly, pulling me along the carved dirt path from my backdoor. The S.S. men on duty looked on quizzically, the light of their cigarettes making their eyes blaze with a hellish glow. I waved them off and they returned to their cards. I should've been scared, I knew, I should have trembled in my anorak for the monsters that lurked in the night. But I didn't, I couldn't. I was exhilarated. This was not the high mountain of power, the peak of court politics that ebbed and flowed like a gaping wound atop the world, with a hundred different players all vying for the attention, not of a king, but of our Führer. No. This was the flat lands of Germany, the fields in which we grew our survival. There was something exhilarating about that. Most exhilarating. I could walk and walk forever. I could head towards Russia, past the satellites of the mighty USSR and towards Siberia. I could head towards Paris, if I chose. I could see the mighty Arc de Triomphe and then head southward for the Escorial of fascist Spain. I could circle the mighty Black Sea and turn back towards Egypt, cutting through the sands of Pharaohs and of Cleopatra, yet another

Kingdom once ruled by a powerful woman. I could do any and all of this –
all I had to do was walk.

The forest grew thicker and more menacing around me the further
along the dirt path I tread. I tried to remember how it looked in the
daylight, I'd been walking this way for so many years. A root, unseen
beneath the bracken, rose and snapped at my toes. I tumbled, my hands
shooting forward like I could push the ground away. The mud splattered on
my face.

The moon pulled itself out from around a dark cloud and
embroidered it with silver thread. The forest came alive, each branch a
wooden thunderbolt, each trunk a pillar of a ruined legacy, lost to the
advance of time. I could smell the thick, wet rotting of leaves and moss
even though it was April and all the world should be springing to life. The
wood must be cursed, I knew. I must have strayed from the path
somewhere, gotten lost in my fantasies of Queens and Tsarinas. This was
not the wood of my dirt track, this was someplace new. Someplace that did
not want me here.

I heard the wind rustle at the leaves as I scrambled to my feet. The
moon was once again taken captive by an onslaught of clouds, a battalion
of black fluffy air that had no idea the menace it was causing me so far
below them. A twig snapped to my left. I spun, trying to make out the

danger by prying free the tiniest details from the dark. I knew the wind seldom snapped twigs.

"Hello?" I asked stupidly, a young girl's response to imminent threat.

The darkness answered back with the sound of footsteps.

"Hello?" I repeated my folly. *Gretl come after me? Gertraud with more questions? Addie...come to take me home.* "Hello?"

"Henrietta?" the voice asked back. "Henrietta? Is that... who are you?"

A man stepped out from the trees.

His face was bloodied and dripping. Mud had clotted with the darkened blood and rusted on his face. Fresh and old wounds mixed into a great swelling mass that shut his right eye. A scarlet grin came from his left forearm, its yellow teeth seeping down his skin. He wore a basic shirt, so dirty and hidden in darkness that I couldn't tell what colour it was. His trousers so torn that they weren't truly trousers anymore.

"Are you ok? You're hurt."

He began to back away from me, his one good eye alive with hatred.

"Stay away from me. Stay back. You're one of them."

"One of..." and then I saw it. Sown yellow cloth on his right arm. A star that had fallen from the sky.

"Stay back. Stay away from me," the moonshine caught the tremble in his fingers, the sound of his thudding heart flooding the forest.

"I…" I *what?*

He turned his back and fled into the woods, continuing his desperate search for Henrietta.

I walked back to the house, the moon moving leaps and bounds across the sky, as best I could. Thorns caught my fingers and drew blood to their tips. The ground slushed under the growing rain and my boots sunk into the mud. When the first glimmers of the cottage came into view, I ran for all I was worth towards them. I could feel him behind me – the Jew – his bloodied arm outstretched and ready to grip at my coat. He'd pull me back and wrap his hand around my throat before I had a chance to scream, before I could get the attention of the S.S. men to come and save me. When I threw myself over the border between the forest and the neat grass of my own garden, I stumbled and let out a sharp yelp.

I saw Gretl first, her face aghast and pale.

"Where were you, Effie? Where? Why have you come from the wood here? You're so far from the path."

The two S.S. men drew their guns and began to poke around the trees at my back. Already I could hear the rumbling of car engines in the distance, meaning they'd already called my disappearance in.

"I was just going for a walk."

"A walk? But look at you! Are you ok?"

"Eva!" Gertraud came from the cottage to help me up, her eyes as wide as Gretl's.

"There was a man. In the wood. There was a Jew in the wood."

At once, the soldiers marched forward. I could hear their boots crunching against the fallen branches, the triggers of their weapons ready to click, click, click a hail of lead into the first thing that moved.

"A Jew? Oh my. Oh my, come in. Come in quick. What if he's still out there?" Gertraud said.

"What if there are more?" Gretl's youthful face whispered in fear.

"I promise I'm ok, my Führer," I said gently down the phone. "I was just walking, that's all. Just walking and I got lost."

The smell of lavender came in waves off my skin. Each movement of my arm brought forth a fresh bouquet of its aroma. The dressing gown was warm and cuddly, its thick hairs massaging the ache in my muscles. I was still a little damp, not having time to properly dry before he called me.

"You could have been hurt," he said, my heart leaping at the fear and anger in his voice. "He could have killed you."

"He was beaten up, weakened, I'm sure I could have taken him," I laughed, loving the feel of the sound of his voice on my ears.

"Not enough. You shouldn't have had to. Himmler is finding the man responsible for letting him go. He'll be dealt with."

"The Jew?"

"Yes, him too."

The phone crackled as silence singed between us.

"Why did you ever leave the Berg?" he asked, his last syllable breaking.

Because you're never there.

Because I'm trapped.

Because I'm a prisoner to my own love for you.

"Gertraud has been having a hard time lately. Gretl said she could do with some time away from home. Her father, you know..."

"Yes." *He knows all about mistreating fathers.* "Should I have someone speak with him?"

The thought was attractive. One word and a couple of S.S. men would be at Uncle's door, Gertraud could be free, never having to worry about whatever kept her so wrapped up again.

"No. I will speak to Baba. I think she just needs some time around girls closer to her own age. Family."

"Invite her to my birthday celebrations if you like," he said nonchalantly as I heard him rustle papers, his attention wavering.

I could have stabbed her then. If she was with me as he so carelessly invited her to my home, I could have stabbed her. She was young, far younger than I, and pretty too, in a shy, coy sort of way. Just the way he liked.

"No," I said.

"No? No matter. As long as you're safe. Get back to the Berg soon, Tschapperl, hm? Get back soon and I will be back in time for my birthday."

"You will?"

"How else would I want to spend my birthday?"

The line died, and I threw my head back in glee. He wanted to spend it with me. Me. I was important enough for him to spend his birthday with.

"How do you keep a man loving you?" Gertraud asked as she picked through my closet a little more.

"How do you mean?" I asked.

"How have you kept the Führer for over a decade is what she's asking?" Gretl laughed. "Isn't that right, Gertraud?"

The young girl blushed.

"I just mean that he sees lots of beautiful women and yet, he still sees that you're the most beautiful of them all. I didn't think men could do that."

"Most can't," Gretl laughed as I clenched the magazine between my hands and twisted. I couldn't be sure that she didn't know just how close to my inner agony she was treading.

"I walk with him," I said.

"Walk?" Gertraud asked.

"Yes. I walk with him. We watch films together. He naps, sometimes I do too."

"The Führer naps?"

"Of course."

"Even though he doesn't get up until noon," Gretl cackled, ducking as I threw the magazine at her.

"He works very late into the night. He likes to nap. And to read. I let him do those things. I join in too."

"That's it? You nap and read and watch films?"

I eyed her, taking in the way she held my chiffon scarf in her hand, running her fingers along its soft skin.

"You make it sound like it should be more difficult?"

"I thought men needed excitement."

"My Führer isn't just a man."

32

"Come on, Effie, she's asking how a girl from Münich could hold his interest when he sees stars and royalty and all the best women the world has to offer."

"You are?" I could taste the bitterness of rage on my tongue.

"Only because she's nothing more than a simple girl from Münich too, Effie. We all are. Nothing more," Gretl had stopped laughing and was watching me, her hand outstretched as if to calm me.

"Of course," I shook my blonde hair as if my earlier anger was just dust in my curls. "Do you know what those women do every time they meet him?"

Gertraud shook her head.

"Try to impress him. They dance and sing and laugh and talk about the power and follies of the world and how learned they must be for noticing. They try and dazzle him, as if he were a puppy and all they need to do was convince him they were a bone. It's insulting. I know him. Who he is. And I give him a break. There's no competition with me. I don't try and out know him. I don't try and out talk him. I just am. I sit with him and…we read. That's it."

"That's it?"

"Should there be more?"

"I don't know," she shrugged. "It just seems so…simple."

SIMPLE.

Simple?

SIMPLE.

Simple?

Simple.

It just seems so simple.

In that moment, that perfect clarifying moment, I saw myself through her eyes – through the world's eyes. My life was one of simple exuberance. One of sunshine and wine and wealth and power. My ego inflated as I sat there, my sense of utter control over how I was perceived. Simple? *I am the simple girl, who lives at the top of the simple stairs, who lives a simple life.*

The word lost all meaning.

"There's a lot more to being with a man like him," I whispered into my glass. "It's not as simple as keeping him, it's about *being* with him too. And those are two very different things."

"They are?" she whispered back, captivated.

"You have no idea, my little wide-eyed girl. But you will one day. Now, who would like to come and see the new gowns that arrived today for my Führer's birthday celebrations?"

"You had new gowns delivered?" Gretl asked as if she hadn't flirted with the S.S. officer that delivered them this afternoon.

"Of course I did," I smiled, "what else is a simple girl to do all day?"

Gertraud watched our breasts as we stripped in front of each other. Gretl's hung a little fuller than my own, their creamy complexion unhindered with the hint of a caramel tan. My own were perkier, though smaller, and had a touch of colour, kissed by the sun. I often enjoyed letting them embrace the cool mountain breeze as I sat on my terrace and listened to the world pass below. Every now and then I would pinch my nipple until it was pink and glowing, and then run my finger along its hardness, waiting for him.

"They're only tits," Gretl laughed. "You'll have them soon. Here, have this, it's yours, take it."

"I don't need anything new. I don't want it." She looked towards the ground and began to cry.

"You're crying?" Gretl asked. "But, I was only joking. A jest, see," she went to her, topless, and held her close. "Please don't cry."

"If I show you something," she looked up, her eyes ablaze with the fires of shame. "Do you promise not to tell my Baba?"

Gretl looked at me and I moved my head slightly, just the touch of a nod, as non-committal as I could be.

Gertraud surprised us both by standing up and removing her cardigan. Her hands trembled terribly as she undid each of the golden buttons down the dress I had given her the day before. She held it shut, even after all the buttons were loose, and took a deep breath.

She opened her dress.

"I've never seen anything like it." Gretl stood, appalled.

I looked over my cousin with cool detachment, trying to drink in what I was seeing and rationalize it before I picked up the vase by my bedside table and cracked it over my uncle's head when he came to pick her up and take her home.

Her brassiere was white and clean, tight but not unusually so. But wrapped in its cheap material were thick metal coils, wires and bars. A brace constricted at her chest and suppressed any inkling of her womanly curves and contours.

"Why?" was all I could ask. Tears in my own eyes.

"I do sports at the boy's school," she sobbed, barely able to breathe as she revealed her deepest shame. "Baba says it wouldn't be right to do it if I had wobbly breasts. And he says because I love science, because I think like a man, I should learn to look like one too," her voice wailed so loud at the last part of her sentence that the emotion broke over my head like a storm cloud ready for war.

"Gretl help me take this *thing* off. And call the guards, we are going to Palmers at once. Oh my sweet child, how could they do this to you?"

She came out of her shell before my eyes, as if the machine around her chest had been sapping away at her personality as well as digging into her skin – a bee that took too much nectar. As her mother's car approached, the sunlight just beginning to relax its hold over the long street, Gertraud stood by my side and gripped my hand. She didn't have to ask, I already knew. Her heart was beating so hard it was like I could feel it in my own teeth. She was nervous, but she'd never be afraid again. A genie freed from her bottle. And then, as I let her go and bade her inside, I wondered how I could have ever been jealous of her. She was a pretty girl, a young girl but she was a girl all the same. And I was a woman. The competition between us was brewed solely in my head and if it hadn't been for her father's monstrosity, I wonder if I would have been the type of woman to begrudge a young girl her youth, when I, still young, knew better than anyone the price all women had to pay for prettiness. Her mother stepped from the car in her high heeled shoe, her hand raised in hello.

April, *The Berghof*

"You look beautiful," Magda said as she swept into the reception room before Hitler's own bedroom. "As does this room. You've had it redecorated?"

"Yes," I said, busying myself by my vanity mirror – scared to look her directly in the eye. *Medusa.*

"I love the floral arrangements on the walls. And how nice it must be for you to be in a room that gets its flowers changed once a day. What were you before? Once every two days?" She sat down on a high-backed chair before a small coffee table. I had a glass of wine poured and she helped herself to a brandy, pouring it into a delicate Venetian glass. She took it all down in one swig, a python unhinging its jaw to swallow and antelope whole, before pouring another.

"Are you here for a reason?" I asked, not bothering to turn from the mirror.

"Why yes, to congratulate you, actually. Oh, don't look so shocked – I'm a nice woman, you know. The party downstairs is magnificent. Truly. So elegantly designed. The feast of treats you have, uh," she kissed her fingers, "delicious."

"Thank you," I said, speaking to the hair brush in my hand.

"Such a shame you have to pretend it wasn't you that organized it." Magda smiled into her drink.

"Those who matter know," I fired back; a quick retaliation to her opening salvo.

"And those who don't matter do not. Yes. We do. Are you over your little tantrum now?"

38

My cheeks blazed red, the blood rushing to them in furious shame. Still, I thought to my reflection, it gives them a nice glow. "Of course. It's so nice to be able to have them, you know. You should try it. You're getting wrinkles from frowning so much."

"Witty," she smiled. "So very witty."

"Why are you here, Frau Goebbels?"

"A strange thing, isn't it, curiosity?" she said as she walked towards me. With unquestioning authority, she placed her sure grip on the hairbrush in my hand. Like a mother to a daughter – *she's old enough to be my mother* – she began to brush out the careful curls I'd had set in my hair, lovingly, all evening, turning them into loose waves. I stayed seated, my hands unable to move. I let her. That was the worst part, the part she relished most.

I let her.

"It makes rational woman do the strangest things. It makes cats ally with mice, so that the mouse can squeeze beneath the door and unlock it from the inside."

"What are you talking about?" My hands were resting on my knees, which were bouncing up and down with nerves. I tried to look into her eyes, to see if she was already drunk and I was listening to the ramblings of a drunk woman.

"You have a very unique position here, you know that don't you?"

"An unenviable one if you were to be believed," I snapped back.

She tugged my hair with one sharp pull and I winced with the sudden rush

of white light that scattered down from my hair.

"It is. For me, anyway. It is. But you can do something I cannot.

Something those other pretty secretaries and servants cannot. There's an

aura about you, Eva – I don't know if you're aware of it."

I said nothing.

"But I am. I watch as the handsome young men of Himmler's S.S.

see you coming and yet – do you know what they do?" She toyed with me.

Her eyes shone like amber as she watched me. My breath hitched in my

throat, wrestling with the back of my tongue. I saw it. Clear as day. I saw

the horror in her eyes. "They avert their gaze," she said, her eyebrows

raising like the heckles of a cat that know it's been discovered. "It's not that

you aren't pretty – you are in a simple kind of way – it's that they know,

some instinct within them whispers it into their ears, that you are dangerous

because you are forbidden. They know it, they just don't know that they

know it."

Again, I said nothing, I just watched her hand rhythmically run

through my hair, destroying my evening's work.

"And that makes you powerful, in a way. No one notices you, no

one sees you. You glide like a ghost through these halls – when you're allowed." She let free a smile that bared her teeth. I watched it grow in her reflection.

"Why are you telling me this?"

"Because you can go somewhere I cannot. You can find something out for me that I cannot find out for myself."

"What?"

"You know Frau Hammitzsch, don't you? Of course you do. Your darling sister-in-law-not-quite. She has a key, have you seen it?"

"Half," I said in habit.

I had seen it, now she mentioned it. I'd seen her take it from her pocket and feel its weight in her hand. She would sit at dinner and stare at it as if it were the key to the Kingdom of Heaven itself. More than once, I had caught her polishing it with the hem of her apron or with the polish meant for Addie's silverware. She was his closest confidante, his own blood. She was the mother of his first love and a reminder of how far he'd come. She was the only one more assured of permanence there in the Berghof than Magda herself, whose overly ambitious husband could pull the rug out from her wonderful life.

I nodded.

"Do you know what it hides?"

I shook my head.

"No, neither do I. Do you see, little mouse? Do you see what I need of you?"

I felt the rough touch of my hair on the heel of my palm as I walked to Addie's birthday celebrations, Gretl's familiar weight comforting in the crook of my arm. Mother had taken Baba home to Münich, scared that he would get drunk and cause offence. Addie wouldn't stand for it, not in front of so many on his birthday, if Baba were to cause offence. It was too dangerous. The way Addie craved and loathed the attention of those around him, a nuisance like a drunk would take my family too close to *undesirable*.

The tinkling of crystal glasses acted as a droning note beneath the light hum of the violins playing in the corner. I had set them up as a double rouse. Addie would think that the violins were all the music provided for the evening, but when the party moved out to the terrace, he would find a selection of harpists, cellists and even a grand piano, all waiting for him in the garden. A grand masque would be held just out of reach of the terrace and everyone would be given a mask to wear so that they could dance. Addie would get one and everyone would know it was him, but they wouldn't recognize another blonde German girl as anything other than that. Then. Finally, then, I would dance with him on his birthday.

"Will he put it on, do you think?" Gretl asked as she bounced into the room, her eyes ablaze with wonder though she'd helped me oversee preparations this afternoon.

"I don't know," I answered honestly as I grabbed a passing flute of French champagne from a passing servant. "I hope so."

"I hope so too," she said absentmindedly as her eyes scanned the room. "A lot of new officers and generals here tonight. Look how handsome they are. This war is simply marvelous for us single girls." She prodded my side with her elbow, smiling as if I would appreciate the joke. I didn't. "Misery guts. It is, though – look how dashing they all look. All of them brave and courageous. All of them men in the very truest sense of the word."

"You're like a pup in heat. Calm yourself, Gretl. Don't make a show of us."

"As if I could." She rolled her eyes. "When does he arrive?"

"Do I ever know?"

Gretl said nothing, but for once, I knew she'd been listening. She, too, plucked a flute of champagne from a passing gentleman and drank it.

"Oh no," she finally said, her brain not used to holding onto guilt for awfully long. "Frau Himmler is here."

"She is?" This surprised me.

"Yes, see. She's over there by Frau Goebbel's eldest children. How many does she have again?"

"Six," I said. "Oh, she looks terrible."

"Another black eye."

"I wonder if he broke a bone this time?"

"Surely not," Gretl objected. "Before the Führer's birthday? Never. You know how he feels about wife beaters. Should one of us go over and speak to her?" Gretl asked, even though I knew she'd be severely disappointed if I asked her to. She'd do it, but she wouldn't be happy about it. She was loyal, and she'd asked because her heart was in the right place.

"I might. Later. Not now though."

I couldn't face being near her – the old Frau Himmler. She seemed like a portent, somehow. Maybe it was the rumours about her husband, his practices in the occult and newly formed Knights of the Round Table, or the truths about his temper, evident all over her face – either way, she was the shell of a woman, all her greatness scooped out by her husband and fed to the dogs. Even Unity, pathetic as she was, was at least *Unity*, Frau Himmler was just a nicely dressed vegetable.

Anytime I saw her, was near her, it raised the question I tried so desperately to quash inside my own head – how much will I have to pay to be his wife? The answer scared me, especially as the rough handed nurse

paid to stand next to her scraped at her chin with a dirty handkerchief,
removing an embarrassing trail of drool.

"Fraulein Braun." Angela's voice jolted me from staring at Frau
Himmler any longer. "It's impolite to stare."

"I wasn't," I lied.

"This is a marvelous party; my brother will enjoy it very much."

Half.

"Thank you, and where is your husband this evening?"

"He couldn't leave Dresden." She smiled but I could see a glint of
resentment reflected in her eyes, mirroring the bitter diamonds in her ears.
"Very important ministerial work to do, you know."

Eugh, it was sickening. Those conversations. Those long, drawn
out effigies of dialogue, devoid of any meaning other than ego-building. I
could've screamed, though I don't think any of them would have heard me.
A hornet's nest of rich, spiteful bitches high up in the mountains, too high
for anyone to bother. And its seclusion, the isolation of the nest, made the
hornets turn on one another. Their restlessness became rotting flesh
beneath their skin and turned them into angry, petulant women. I was sick
of it. Sick of the second guessing and the endless sparring of what these
ladies considered wit.

"Am I boring you?" she asked.

"Yes, immeasurably."

Her eyes narrowed. Her already thin lips became squeezed so hard that they vanished completely from her wrinkled face.

"A joke, Frau Hammitzsch. A joke and nothing more. Excuse me."

I knew I needed her. She was a powerful ally to have. The way she walked, the way she ran the household staff that kept the floor clean beneath our feet, made her powerful. Along with the blood in her veins. But I couldn't, not that night. I just wanted to have fun. And what was wrong with that? What was wrong with wanting to dance and laugh and drink and just be merry?

"Eva."

"Ilse," I said as my eldest sister strolled towards me in a gown of beautiful, shimmering ivory. "What are you doing here?"

"I came from Münich, I…" she began to tear up.

"You're crying." I didn't reach for her, my hands were too stunned to do anything but fidget with my glass. If she was crying it had to mean something terrible had happened at home. "Is it Mother?"

"No." She shook her head, the pearls in her ears making her lobes wobble. "No. It's…I'm sorry about how we left things. I don't mean to be…" Her dingers flexed once, twice, "I'm sorry."

I wrapped her in my arms, hugging her tight to my body. She hugged me back and my feet – which so often felt like they were floating above the void, barely keeping their distance from the black hands that

46

wanted to drag me into the nothingness – felt like they were on firm ground once again. *It's a rare thing to have an older sister like Ilse.* And in that moment, I was grateful for her like I hadn't been in a very long time.

"You came all this way?"

"Of course. You need it."

I didn't have time to ask her what she meant by that. The room had erupted into the peals of polite applause. I turned towards the grand entrance way that I'd garlanded with red roses, all their thorns taken off – my own special way to twist the knife. Then the cheers began. Magda stood resplendent, a pale vampire composed of ethereal beauty beyond mere mortal women, by the door. She was clapping and stomping her feet far harder than anyone else in the room. I may have loved the man more than anyone else in the world, but she truly loved the Führer and everything he stood for within the party more than any other being possibly could. She was the first to embrace him, the first to wish him congratulations on his birthday – if she hadn't sent a special telegram that morning or even the night before – and I wasn't ashamed to grip my elder sister's hand in jealousy. She squeezed back and I took a breath.

He was here. That mattered more than anything else. He was finally here again. And he was more beautiful than I had remembered him.

It was queer how the mind could do that to a person. No matter how many years you spent being with someone, being around their subtle mannerisms, the unique twitches of their mouths that make them *them*, our memory can never properly hold them to that rigorous level of detail. Things always slide. Memories are always blurred. And the gleam of perfection is always dulled with mediocrity.

He commanded the room's attention. His arms by his side while everyone else's – including my own – were raised in salute. He wasn't a beautiful man. The edges of his body were soft and flabby, his midriff swollen like that of a duck. He walked like a bullied child trying to make it from one end of the park to the other and his eyes – those misty eyes – clashed with the darker features of his distinctly *un*-Aryan face. But he was a lighthouse on the greatest shore of the richest land. He was taller than his body suggested, brighter than the quiet way his eyes scanned the rooms would allow you to see. A true lighthouse, standing tall over the violent tides of the black seas beneath him. And I was his ship. Only his light, that essential light, could draw me out of the storm that raged across the water. He was a lighthouse. And I was his ship. And so I loved him like a ship loves that stream of golden light, pulling it out of the darkness.

He smiled at me while he moved towards Heydrich and Himmler, both of whom were standing by the high table, waiting to offer their own congratulations. It was just a small smile – too polite to have any meaning behind it other than that of a boss to his employee – but it was something far grander to me, and he knew it. My heart swelled in my chest. I dug my nails into Ilse's palm to stay calm.

"You're hurting me," she said.

"Come on." I ignored her. "Let's go get a drink."

I never let him out my sight. It was almost as if it were a dream that he was here at all. I maneuvered around men in tuxedos and their beautiful girls in golden dresses. I dodged servants with clumsy grace and stood by tables draped in fine cloth. The music lilted round the decorated room and perfumes mixed with cooked meats and the smells of seasoned vegetables. Each day, I lived in constant fear I would open my eyes one morning and find myself still nothing more than a girl working in a photograph shop, alone once again.

As he walked from person to person, he would look up, though not as often as I would like, and smile when he caught my eye. He knew, I knew. He knew that I was watching him and it gave him immense pleasure to see my need, my wanton desire, etched plainly on my face.

"Come along, ladies." Gretl came bundling through a local mayor and his wife who were slow dancing to the violins. "This is Officer Gustinchan…ly? Oh I don't know." She looked up at his young and startled face and winked. "Officer Somebody, and he has cigarettes. Come on."

"No, Gretl. No. You know fine well that my Führer…"

And there he was. He raised his eyes to look at me again, and this time his smile was far from polite. It stretched across his face from beneath his Chaplin moustache like a poisonous army sweeping across the plains of Russia. With careless cruelty he took her hand and brought it to his lips while Heydrich and Dr. Morell both began to clap her on the back and rain compliments down on her sleek, red gowned body like she was a siren from the sea. And maybe she was. I was the ship. He was the lighthouse. She was the storm.

He pulled his eyes away from me and let them rest on Leni Riefenstahl, her pert lips arranged into a dazzling smile.

"Yes. Ok then," I said to their shocked expressions. "Before they're all led outside."

I dragged on the cigarette like it was the devil's dick. The smoke fell in lavish layers down my throat, like honey coating an open wound. For the first time in months my throat didn't itch and scratch. My lungs swelled, drinking in the potent nicotine of which it had been starved for far too long. Of course, I'd smoked in Wasserburger, but it felt different somehow, up here in the glory of the mountains.

"Stop hogging it," Gretl said. "He's only got two. Greedy bitch."

"Gretl," Ilse laughed. "Whipping dogs shouldn't talk to their masters like that!"

"Jealous cow," Gretl laughed back, taking a lazy drag on the cigarette. "Oh, come now, Effie. It's only a joke. No need to put your angry face on."

I smiled at that and snatched the cigarette back from Gretl's fingertips as she tried to hand it to Ilse.

"Hey!"

"Be careful," I said calmly, "or I'll make you my dog too."

Her face fell for a split second before she began to laugh like I'd never seen her do before. Great guffaws racked through her petite frame so violently that Officer Somebody looked ready to call for help.

"I wouldn't if I were you," I warned.

"Yeah. Who do you think we'll say this cigarette belongs to if someone catches us?"

I had never thought of Gretl as spiteful because she so rarely exhibited anything other than playful mirth. A juvenile propensity for amusement and gratification – though never spite. The drink in her hand could only account for so much of how she was acting and I watched as Ilse came to the same conclusion.

"Do you two know each other?" I asked as the glass doors of the patio were flung open to great fanfare and the party spilled out onto the terrace overlooking the grass that would soon be open to dancing.

I stepped into the shadows, quick to avoid the stares of anyone that might be looking for trouble. There was a side door just a little way up. I knew because I'd been smuggled through it often enough like a shameful concubine. I inched along the brickwork; if he saw me here, or anyone else did, and they told him I was smoking... *I just don't need the argument.* The handle slipped easily beneath my hands. My sisters stood with Officer Somebody and clapped as the piano I had moved out onto the grass began to play. The first few notes lingered in the air as panic tore at my throat with its dirty fingernails. The door was locked. I jiggled the handle, once, twice, three times and then...it opened. I slipped into the warm belly of the Berghof and shut the door tight behind me. I needed some perfume. Something to disguise the smell of tobacco.

I stood in my own simple rooms, without guard for now, and looked down from the pink tiles of my bathroom onto the spectacle I had conjured from thin air below. He wasn't dancing, though I hadn't expected him to. He was enjoying a glass of water beneath a canvas marquee lit up with lights. I couldn't see the men and women around him, but I could guess who they were. I squeezed the pouch of my Parisian perfume and let its floral aroma decorate my shoulders and mask my betrayal. As the scent settled, I realized how tired I was. How hopelessly and wholly exhausted I was. My ankles ached. The balls of my feet burned. My head was sore and my stomach was cramping. I rested my hands on my belly and wondered if

I could stomach a night with them all, just out of his reach. With him just out of mine. He laughed at something someone whispered in his ear and then caught sight of Gretl dancing with her cigarette mule. It may have just been the shadows of the growing night playing tricks with his face, but I wondered then if he was sad he couldn't see me. Certainly, the laughter stopped immediately and his pale, blue eyes began to search the grass, as if he'd dropped a golden watch of great value and had only just realized.

It was poetic. Sort of. Like Shakespeare. *Addie, Addie, where for art thou, Addie?* I was his Juliet, his Eva in the tower. Though he could never be a Montague, for that would imply there was a family of Capulets out there, somewhere, that rivalled him. And no one rivalled Addie Hitler. The Poles had found that out well enough last Autumn. But there was a tragedy there somewhere, lurking, I just couldn't see it. My eyes couldn't adjust well enough to the dark to pry it out from all the other shadows and shapes that lurked.

I turned back to my bathroom and climbed into the bath tub. It was clean, the smell of bleach light enough not to burn, but potent enough to assure me it had been freshly done today. I was safe there, I knew. Safer than safe. Utterly obscure. I was crying. Hard, actually. Harder than I had in a while. I wanted to stand up and shout at my reflection, tell the girl to grow up and act the woman she was. But my muscles wouldn't move. The shame burned too dimly against the rain of loneliness that assaulted it. I was all alone.

Truly, madly alone.

I heard a baby cry. Probably one of Magda's. Or maybe Hanni's. Or Emmy's. All the wives had babies. Most of them, anyway. They had other little beings to remind them that their injustices were worth it, because they didn't go to sleep at night and wonder if their children would be there in the morning. They had a reason to soldier on when the battle seemed all but lost. I didn't have that. I never would. He said that he was a fluke, a freak of nature. A genius born to mediocrity which meant any child would more than likely suffer the same disease as his family. An heir would be an embarrassment — not a sign of stability, so he said. I didn't care for stability, at least not for a Reich without him. There could be no Reich without him, at least not one I could see. I chanted the nonsense about a thousand years, of course I did. But I didn't believe it. He was my lighthouse; without him I would flounder on the rocks. I would sink.

But a child? That could maybe make the years between then and now a little more bearable. And perhaps, once he saw his boy, he'd be so in love with him that he'd do all he could to educate him up to a standard befitting of his name. Maybe.

My stomach cramped once again and then I was glad I was sitting in the bath tub.

My thighs were thick with what despair had brought.

Loneliness and blood.

The messenger he sent was a stocky little boy, far from the standards of beauty he usually demanded of his soldiers stationed in the Berghof. With a sweaty face and blood rushed cheeks, the boy bid me to the Führer's office at once.

The dread was ice on my skin, a slimy, congealing feeling that dripped inward.

Drip. Drip. Drip.

I hadn't returned to the party the night before. I'd listened to the band outside, to the revelers squealing and cheering in their masks – but I hadn't returned. I knew he was angry. He'd felt like I'd left him. Even though he wouldn't have spoken to me anyway, he'd have felt betrayed and I knew I'd suffer for it. As we walked along the wide corridor that led from the bottom of my simple steps to the grand promenade at the Berghof's heart, I used the stocky boy's pounding footsteps to regulate my breath. To stop the fear from making me scream out loud until my lungs exploded in my chest and my blood was spattered up the wall.

Step. *Breathe in.*

Step. *Breathe out.*

Step. *Breath in.*

Step. *Breathe out.*

And then I was there.

The boy knocked on the door before turning the handle and letting me inside. I stepped over the threshold as he shut the door behind me. It was dark. The curtains weren't drawn and only a dim amount of the noon light came trickling in. The gloom played tricks along the walls; tugged at the rug and made it quiver as I stepped on it. He wasn't here. His chair was empty and papers were scattered along his desk. I moved towards the red couch we'd first made love upon and saw only fleeting words leap out from the Führer's private papers. I didn't understand them. **OPERATION OTTO.** Surely he wouldn't hurt my father? **FINAL SOLUTION.** Was his intention to kill me? Was that the solution to the Eva Braun problem? Murder? No. No. I ran to the curtains and threw them open. The light poured in but the room was still dead with claustrophobic air. I tugged at the window lock, my fingers sliding with sweat along their smooth, metal bodies. It gave way only a fraction as I heard the door knob twist and his voice boom from outside. I left the window and ran back to the sofa.

"Ach, too bright," he said as he covered his eyes with his hands.

My muscles were serpents coiled around white trees. Tighter and tighter they constricted, as fearful of his anger as I was. I wondered how much it would take for my bones to turn to dust?

56

He yelled something behind him. The rigorous way the blood flooded my ears meant I couldn't hear what he said. He slammed the door shut when he was done. With great strides, he walked over to the window and closed the curtains. His back to me, I saw him take in a heavy mouthful of breath as he reached into his pocket.

"No. No, my Führer, please…"

He turned.

I was so confused at first – startled – that I barely recognized the mask on his face. A long black feather jutted up from the left eye and black sparkles adorned the eye piece. The nose was tipped with subtle ruby sequins and a tassel of matching red hung from the right eye. It looked like he'd been shot in the face.

"You look terrified." His hand hovered around the mask, unsure whether to take it off. "You don't like it? I thought it was you who bought them?"

"It was," I stuttered. "I mean, I did. I just didn't expect…this."

"Ah, my little Tschapperl, but that's why I have done it. You were not at the party for very long last night. I thought I'd bring it to you."

The words didn't make sense. Bring. I'd. It. You. To. He was going to kill me. Wasn't he? Isn't that what the papers on his desk said?

"You aren't angry?"

The pale blue eyes beneath the mask creased as his mind processed the words that were so different from what his ears were expecting.

"Why would you think that?" He tossed the mask from his face and came closer to where I was sitting. I tensed up in fear. He noticed. "Why are you scared?"

My eyes betrayed me and looked towards the papers littering his desk. His own eyes followed, understanding dawning brighter than the light allowed in the room.

"You read these?" He was smiling. "I'm sorry, little dear. I am. I shouldn't have left them out. You needn't worry. Germany will be safe. You know something only a very few men do. Not even Magda knows."

He knew that would catch my attention. And it did.

"She doesn't?" I played along.

"Of course not. This is far too sensitive to be shared with just anyone. Especially a woman that spends all night laughing at my jokes, which, if I am honest," he winked, "were not particularly funny. Now come here. There's no need to worry. Absolutely no need at all."

His open arms were a drug that purified the fear tainting my blood. Elated, I floated over to my Führer with an easy heart and light feet. He wrapped me tightly in his embrace and began to hum into my ear. The steady vibrations from his lips made my lobes quiver, made my body shake. He was quiet. So quiet that no one would be able to hear him outside the door. But to me, it sounded like a thunderstorm crackling around my ears, a symphony bursting from his throat.

"Sit," he commanded after he grew tired of gently swaying with me around his office. "Would you like some tea?" I nodded and he strode to the door and called out for Angela down the hallway. He tidied away his papers as I lay strewn across the couch, my skirt raised along my thighs as Angela shuffled in with a silver tray filled with tea and biscuits. She noted the creaminess of my thigh but said nothing. Addie gave her a gentle smile, which she returned, before she left the room and shut the door behind her.

"Come here, Tschapperl," he bade as he sat behind his desk and poured as each a mug of tea. "Would you like to see what I've been doing in Berlin?"

At once, Leni Riefenstahl was in the room with us. Her smile practiced and perfect, her camera on the window sill by her side. I had forgotten about her. As soon as he'd began to hum I'd forgotten her, but at the mention of Berlin, where I was rarely permitted to go, she was back in my mind and standing in the room with us.

I nodded.

"I am going to build the greatest city Europe has ever seen. It shall rival New York! It shall." He pulled out a large map from behind his chair and grandly rolled it out along the table with wide arm movements. He held one side down with a paper weight shaped like a cannon and the other with one like a train. I recognized Speer's work at once.

"Albert?"

"Yes. You have such a wonderful eye." He patted my head. "This is to be the new Berlin. As old as London or Paris, but as modern and grand as New York. See?" He pointed to a spot where South Station sat. "New South Station shall replace the old. It will hold 180,000 at any one time, can you believe?" I shook my head. "And here." He pointed to the map again, nearly knocking over his own tea. "This shall be the Hall of the People. Twice the size of Mussolini's St. Peter's Basilica! Twice. Can you guess how many it will hold?"

"180,000?"

"Exactly! Exactly. I have a name for it. I will change the name of Berlin to something more fitting of our new Reich. Would you like to know it?"

His eyes were ablaze with gunfire, his steady presence scolding to be around. In front of dinner guests, visitors, his passion was only ever a flickering candle, a barely-there glow of orange. But in private, here with me and when he spoke directly to the people, he was destructive in his enthusiasm.

I nodded.

"Germania. For all of Germany. For all of history. People in one thousand years will sift through the ruins of Germania and speak of the wonder race that created it. It will be a place where the arts can flourish, where new philosophies and sciences can be birthed and hatched. It will be wide and grand, with pillars and amphitheaters greater than anything in Ancient Greece. We are building the future, Eva. Together. The people. We will conceive a city so large, a metropolis in true name and being, that will surpass anything ever again built on our Earth. Do you see?" His arms once again swept across the hundreds of lines and rough sketches of what he planned to be the future of city planning. "Do you see the scope we are able to harness when we work as one? How can the world say anything against us when this is complete? When this is the station they see when they arrive in Germany? When this is the spectacle at the heart of our Reich?"

"They couldn't."

"Precisely." He grinned at me like I was his daughter who'd just brought home a good grade from school. "Precisely, Tschapperl. Precisely."

I was a fly caught in his web. His ardor was infectious and as he held his hands over my eyes and described the marble work, the stone pillars and the ambitious arches – I saw them. He whispered words of summer sunshine melting an ice cream down my wrist; of pianos on every corner on my birthday, all playing my favourite songs; of butterfly gardens in every park from here to Moscow; and of one colossal theatre in which I could finally be the woman he knew I was.

"It must mean he wants children," my mother said as she poured herself another chilled glass of water.

"You've been saying that for months now, Mother. It was one conversation. He's barely spoken to me since."

"He was conquering France, dear," my father said as he let the warm air moisten his chest hair. "Blitzkreig they're calling it in the papers."

"Not that she'd know that, Baba," Ilse said sharply.

Something had upset her. I didn't know what and I didn't care either. She'd been supportive at Addie's birthday party and then *poof!* All her sisterly love was gone in a flash.

"At least you're talking to me now," I said back.

"It really is a shame he doesn't let you read the papers or listen to the wireless." My mother looked at me, concerned. "It's very controlling."

"He doesn't want me to be bothered with all that stuff." I shook my hand as if it were nothing. "I'm his oasis of calm in an otherwise volatile world."

For now, Ilse's look implied.

"For someone so bratty, you seem to be making a nice little profit out of all this."

She had the decency to blush as she clutched at the diamond watch on her wrist.

"It was for my birthday."

"Still," I laughed with Gretl.

She looked ready to take it off until my mother intervened.

"Ilse, be more grateful. And Eva, you should be kinder to your sister. You know how hard it is for her to be here."

The mood instantly deflated, as if it were a balloon popped by the needle of Dr. Martin Levy Marx.

Ilse looked sullen. Her deep red lips fell into an unhappy rainbow of blood and she wrapped her arms around her breasts as if she could squeeze herself into oblivion. Her watch was carefully hidden beneath her arm – out of sight, out of mind.

"Gretl, will you take the dogs for a walk with Ilse, please?"

Gretl got up from her sun lounger immediately, much to my mother's dismay. Ilse, however, seemed grateful and quickly wrangled Negus and Stasi into the Berghof to find their leads.

"I wish you wouldn't boss her around like that," my mother began at once as we watched my sister's retreat along the manicured green lawns towards the myriad of mountain paths. "And why don't they take Blondi? Is she not here?"

"That mutt? No. Addie has her in Berlin. I can't stand to have her here."

"You are too sweet a girl to hate a dog."

"Am I?" I said back.

"So why did you send your sisters away?"

We both checked at the same time to make sure Baba was asleep. The steady snore coming from his throat confirmed that he was.

"I want to ask how to get pregnant."

Mother said nothing for a moment, choosing to collect herself with another sip of water. I helped myself to more wine.

"You can cut that out for a start," she said. "Do you really think this is wise?"

"Having some wine? It's after midday."

"No. I mean having a child without speaking to him first. I wouldn't want him to get...*angry*."

"He won't. He wouldn't. I'm not saying I will get pregnant. I'm just saying that it would be nice to know how to."

"When the time is right, God will send you a child."

"Mother, please."

"Just because you don't believe in my ways doesn't mean I do not. God has his plan for us all. He does."

I saw then, in her piety, how desperately she clung to that notion and how that may very well be the reason I still had a mother. She didn't like Addie, not in the beginning and maybe not even as she drank her water on his terrace. But she was with me, she was supporting me and if that came from a belief in 'God's Plan' then I wasn't about to start pulling at that thread.

"Would you not like a grandson to play with?" I said as I watched a red spider crawl slowly along the rough grey stone of the wall that separated the terrace from the garden.

Her eyes were watering before I had a chance to finish my thought.

"Of course, I would. Of course. A little boy or a little girl, so long as they're healthy. Do you think he would come around? Truly?"

"Weren't you just saying that his conversation meant that he must want children? That because he opened up to me, it meant he might want to start a family?"

"Yes." She dabbed at her eyes with the hem of her lavender coloured shawl. "But is that why you want a family? To open up?"

Her question drew me short.

"What do you mean?"

"I've known you since before you were born. You were in my belly and I knew you then. I've watched you grow, Eva, into a charming and talented young woman. But, also…" She looked away for a moment before meeting my gaze., "…A selfish and stubborn one. I know you want to be married more than anything in the world – is that the right reason to have a child?"

Wrong. Wrong. I don't just want *to be married, I* need *to be married to him.*

"I was only asking your opinion."

"No. Eva, no you were not. You were asking me how to catch a man with a baby. To trap him. And not just any man. No. A man that has conquered half of Europe. You want me to be an accomplice in something that could anger a dangerous man like that?"

"You're being too serious. I love him infinitely, and he loves me too. You have nothing to worry about."

"Oh, don't I? Don't you?"

"Mother don't, please," I said, not realizing I was scared until I heard my voice break.

"I'm not trying to panic you. Eva, stop scratching yourself," her fingers were a comfort on my own. Her warm touched soothed the red marks I'd trailed along my skin with my fingernails. "Stop. Don't get anxious. Just think first. Think before you act. Before you speak. You never know who is listening to you. Not here, not anywhere. All it takes is one

wrong word to be taken out of context and whispered into his ear and…"

"And what?"

"And I won't get to warm my old bones in such a lovely part of the

world," she tried to smile, but it was stunted and heavy on her lined cheeks.

"Would you like a glass of water?"

"You're a fearful old woman," I said. "He loves me."

"He does," she conceded while wiping her brow wearily. "But

where will that get you? How long will that protect you for?"

August, *The Berghof.*

He was late. He was always late. It had been a weary few days, the simple

steps becoming all I saw of the Berghof as I was smuggled in and out like a

fugitive Jew by S.S. men, terrified I would be seen. I gave thanks I was

allowed out for walks at all but since I wasn't a criminal, to be treated like

one felt wholly unfair. Countless princesses and dukes and lords and counts

and even some kings and queens of ancient European houses came in a

steady stream of diamonds, crowns and self-importance. I laughed when I

saw the first few, that they thought the name given to them at birth held

sway over Addie. That he would stop his invincible Wehrmacht from

spreading the Imperial Eagles any further – because they felt inconvenienced – was laughable. So, I laughed. But as the stream grew thicker, more putrid and more desperate, the cabin fever sunk in and I began to feel like a caged hound waiting to be kicked.

He promised me this day. He promised me that we would all have lunch together, me at his right-hand side. I wouldn't have to be hidden. It was a small lunch away from the prying eyes of those who would gossip. But Magda would be there, and Emmy Goering, Gerda Bormann and Erna Hoffman. The wives all sat together, down the table from myself and with eyes of pure delight that he hadn't shown up at all.

"We would be on to our main course by now if this was you hosting the event, Magda. You've done so well entertaining the courts of Europe this season," Christa Schröder said loudly across the room.

Gretl placed her hand on my knee as Herta Schneider looked at me with her make-up-less face and gave a reassuring smile. *She's infuriating, she could have at least tried to look presentable.*

Margarete Himmler gave a little laugh as if she understood what was going on around her before picking up her knife and slipping it into her handbag.

I was furious. Furious and heart broken. I had been a very good whore. I had hidden myself away, caused no problems and let him come up to my rooms whenever he pleased. I had been patient and kind and understanding of the strains that were placed on him, wrapped around his body like belt loops. But he had sworn on the grave of his mother that I could have today.

"Where is he, Magda?" Gretl asked, unperturbed by the hostile way the wives' eyes all snapped around to glare at her.

"In a meeting with Ribbentrop. Didn't you know?" she cackled and the other wives followed suit.

I stood from the table, all their eyes following. Emmy smirked; she thought I was nothing but pomp and hot air. They laughed like witches around a cauldron in the forest. Gretl's eyes begged me to sit down, Herta even reached out and tried to grab me but I shook her off. It wasn't fair. None of it was fair. I left the room at a march, my skirt swirling around my ankles.

I took the light-filled corridors along the western edge of the Berghof. The lake was far away from here but I knew from experience that if I stood still long enough and the day was clear, I could just about see the shimmer of the water in the distance. Today the lake would watch me shimmer.

It was one day; one out of 365. He had promised me one day and by God I would have it. It wasn't even a whole day – but a luncheon with his friends. I had put up with his departings, his silent games, his horrible teasing – I had put up with it all and smiled. Maybe in the past I hadn't been as careful, had been more selfish – I reached my hand to the scar on my neck and traced its familiar lines – but that was a long time ago, and I was a woman now. *He promised me today – he swore it.*

He would keep his promise to me.

The guards outside the meeting room door were at attention. One of them recognized me from his duty at my own room door and a smile spread his face. It was charming and friendly but I didn't return it, my eyes set on the gold handle by his gun. Neither of them knew what I was there to do, which is why neither of them tried to stop me. I was a simple blonde girl; what bother could I be? My hand was on the handle, pushing it down before they'd realized what happened. The smell of the room – like old books and freshly cut apples – hit me as I stuck my simple blonde head around the door.

Time froze. Ribbentrop and my Führer were pacing up and down the long room, a map curled in Ribbentrop's hands. Panic fluttered in my chest as I realized the terrible mistake I had made. The flash of fury rippled down the eyes of each man at the stately table, like a stone had been dropped into a very powerful pond. My breath left me, deserted me in shameful retreat. Only his eyes, those pale blue eyes, looked at me with anything other than anger.

"Oh Adolf, please, we must go have our luncheon!" were the words that left my lips. I instantly regretted them. They sounded childish, immature and unwomanly. Like I was a daughter aggrieved over her choice

of dress. I knew that half the men expected me to stamp my foot.

"*Oberführer.*" A man called Spitzy leaned over towards Ribbentrop

from his chair. "Who is that woman?"

In that second, with those words, his eyes turned to ice and Hitler's

mouth quivered with the same fury I had polluted the room with.

"Get out of this room at once!" he shouted, his left arm trembling

terribly. The guards needed no second telling. Their hands bit into the soft

skin beneath my dress, their boots deep thuds on the Berghof floor as they

marched me away.

"You promised me." I looked up from the pillow in my lap. I knew my eyes

were puffy and terrible looking, that I seemed pitiful for weeping but it's all

I'd done all day and there was no point pretending otherwise. "I wasn't

wrong to interrupt, you promised and you lied."

He looked at me from beneath his furrowed brow as he took the

military jacket off from his white dinner shirt. I'd had enough sense to have

some stewed fruits available for him, in case he did come up. Though, the

good Lord knew he may well have been too angry to even bother to do

that. I had decided to grovel for forgiveness but when I saw him standing

there, I opened my mouth and only indignation came out.

"I did promise you," he admitted, taking a seat on the long couch opposite me. "But it was a promise I had to break."

I said nothing, looking back at my pillow instead of him.

"Do you not understand what I'm doing?" he spoke to me like he would to his stupid bitch, Blondi. "You don't do you? And that is perhaps why I love you. That meeting was too important to be cut short, too vital to be ignored. My promise to you had to be broken."

"Why? Why did it have to be broken? You have all evening to talk war and politics. You have the rest of the year to discuss battles and plans. You have the rest of this war to talk about whatever nonsense you want to talk about. This was one lunch. You could have made time."

"I couldn't..."

"Yes you could you're the FÜHRER!" I shouted back at him. I tried to breath in to calm myself, scared at how close to danger I was treading but it came out as a pant, my breasts heaving with ire.

"I made a much greater promise to Germany," he said calmly. "I won't apologise for that."

It was like a bullet. He'd pulled the pistol from his belt and aimed it square at my face and squeezed the trigger. It blew away everything from nose to ear, the other half dripping in brains and blood. All the Riefenstahls and Mitfords in the world would have been preferable right then, rather than what he'd said.

"To Germany?"

He nodded. Again, like I was his mutt.

"It was one lunch, Addie. And Magda and Emmy, they laughed like you don't care. Like I'm nothing to you."

"Is that how you feel?" He rubbed his temples as the beginning of a headache took hold behind his eyes. "Do you feel that you are nothing to me?"

Do I?

"No," I said, unconvinced.

"Then what does it matter what they think?"

"Angela tells them..."

"She tells them what?" He sat up straight. I'd struck a nerve.

"She laughs at me too, I mean. She encourages them," I said, even though it was only half true.

"She does?"

I nodded.

"So, Angela is the one that is bothering you? I will talk with her."

"Were you terribly angry I interrupted?" I pushed the pillow aside and scooted forward on my chair.

"Yes," he said, smiling. "Furious."

"Should I make it up to you?" I slid further forward until I was on my knees. He opened his legs wider, a devilish smile taking hold of his lips.

"Yes, my Führer." And I slithered towards him like the serpent did to Eve, and undid his belt buckle as I felt him hardening beneath my hands.

He sighed as I took the tip into my mouth, just enough to tickle the sensitive underside with my tongue. As his length grew, I let it travel along my lips, my head passing down, down, down until my nose was by his testicle. I flicked my tongue across it softly, helping him hide his discomfort.

"Oh, my Führer," I gasped in delight as I took it into my mouth. He loved it best when I did that, and then licked just behind his sack. He let out a moan as I took my mouth from his testicle and swallowed his manhood whole. It was a quick job – it had been so long after all. And with a few practiced moans from myself – a gag to seal the deal – he held my head back and finished himself off, grunting with every pass of his hand.

"Beautiful," he murmured as he sat back and gladly watched me clean my face off with my fingers, showing him how eager I was to taste all he had to give me.

"You can't keep letting him treat you like that," Gretl said. "You're a lady. No wonder he isn't marrying you."

"You're sitting where he did it." I took joy from the disgust that marred her face as she jumped to another seat, recompense for her marriage jab. "And besides, after what I did, it's a small price to pay to not be banished."

"You really think he'd banish you?"

"Who knows? But he hasn't. Probably because I give him some relief. Showed that I was contrite."

"Contrite, loose, same difference, right?"

"Stop being such a ninny pants. You're the biggest flirt in the Berg."

"Yeah, but that doesn't mean I go around letting them stick their dicks in my mouth."

"Ah, but you're playing for cigarettes, I'm playing for a much higher reward."

"A reward not best got by slinking over on your knees and acting like a street whore."

"No, you're right. I should be a Berg whore, shouldn't I? That's what I am anyway, isn't it? That's what you're saying. That I'm a whore in deed as well as name? That it's my fault he won't marry me because why buy the cow when the milk is dribbling all over the floor?"

"Over the floor. Jesus in heaven you're not doing it right if it's all over the floor," she said, curving my growing temper. We laughed together, perched on a one-seater chair which only made the situation more hilarious.

"What's it like?" she asked as any younger sister would.

"Surely you've done it. I know you have, you've told me."

"Yes, but, with him, I mean."

"You want to know because he's the Führer?"

"Are you kidding? Of course, I do! What you know is worth a Queen's ransom to any paper willing to print such smut. Don't make me feel like a nosey parker for asking what any person in their right mind would."

"I've been with him for years; you know all this. I've told you before."

"Yes, but," she lowered her voice to a whisper, careful the walls couldn't hear her. "How can he…you know…with only one…you know."

"It works," I said. "I don't know the biology."

"Is it…less? Than a normal man, I mean."

"He is normal." I pulled back from her. "And how would I know what another man's stuff was like? Whether it came out in quarts or litres?"

"There was…" I heard the name before she said it. I slapped my hand across her face before she could breathe any life into him here

"Don't you ever mention his name. Not ever. Do you hear me, Gretl?" I was shaking her so hard that her teeth clattered together in her skull. Her eyes wide enough for me to stick my hand in and pluck the name from her memory. "You don't ever mention his name. Get out. Are you listening? Get out!" She pulled my hands from her shoulders and ran towards the door, not daring to look back at me, not daring to see if I was sorry for scaring her.

I wasn't.

There was a down side to her vacuousness. Coupled with being my best friend for so long, it meant that she often forgot when something was so vitally important, so horridly shameful, that it should never be mentioned again.

I remembered the warmth of his touch most of all. The languid way he would run his fingers along my arms, my legs, as he spoke to me of the country house he would build for us. My stomach was still tender then; the sleeping tablets had almost burned a hole right through. But he always had water nearby, always a slice of bread – anything to stop the acid building too great. He smiled kindly, I remember that too. Great white teeth that smelled of nothing but mint. His body was lean, his forearms strong and he had a military precision about the way he dressed. His shoes, belt buckle and even his buttons were always polished and gleaming.

The water of Lake Constance was pleasant enough. There was space, too, so that I could show him my cartwheels, could roll over and hold myself upright with only my hands. He'd clap and whistle, drawing the looks of passersby to me. Then he'd tackle me, softly, but enough for me to tumble and nuzzle his lightly stubbled chin into the soft flesh of my neck. All memories of the scar there gone as if it'd never been.

He was what a man should be. He was kind, caring but he was stern, too. He was aggressive. Not behind generals or clerks or a fancy lectern that made his voice boom like that of God. No. He was a man in his own right, a stubborn, rowdy man that saw his fists as the only protection he needed. We got drunk on cheap wine – "Why pay for the good stuff when it all tastes like piss compared to you anyway?" – and sang on the banks of the lake. The bottle was cold and heavy but he'd taken his scarf off from around his neck and wrapped the bottle in it, sealing it with a tight knot so I could hold it without losing a finger like a soldier in the frozen tundra. He was singing high, high and out of tune, when a pair of drunken boys walked past and laughed. I'd never seen a human move so quick, more viper than man. He was on them in moments, their laughter choking their screams. Each punch was met with a returning squelch, each kick with the crack of bone. They hobbled off after he stopped. And he stopped so suddenly that they couldn't believe their luck. He stopped and immediately began singing again exactly where he left off. He came back to me and laughed as he watched them hobble down the beach. I kissed his knuckle, took his finger in my mouth before lowering it to show him how grateful I was to be sitting on the beach with a man.

"Aren't you worried the police will come?" I asked in a fervent whisper as he worked his finger in and out, swirling it delicately.

"Let them," he growled. "What officer would believe I would leave you to beat on some barely aged men?"

"What if…"

"Let them." He bit my ear. "And I'll fight them off too."

I came over him twice before he entered me right there on the beach.

She called me over as soon as I walked into the room. She was an old woman with a heavy brow. Her cheeks were softened with age, much like Frederick's in Hitler's office, except, it didn't suit a woman quite so much. A bruise extended upwards from her dress and her hair had streaks of grey — more every time I saw her — as it coiled up into the bun lazily perched atop her head.

"Frau Himmler." I felt as if I should curtsey.

"Sit with me a moment, Fraulein. Here, please," she patted the space beside her on the bench.

The conservatory was by far the most magnificent room in all the Berghof. Light streamed in through panes of glass so large that they could have been glaciers of clear ice. Benches and seats were interspersed amongst long throws that made walkways between the wicker nests. The light illuminated it all but drew the eye outward towards the vast landscape that sat just beyond. It was a privilege to sit here, I knew. We all knew it, I suppose. No one came without his explicit consent and that was a power akin to God. For the Berg was heaven perched above the splendour of the world beneath us.

"How are you today?" I said, making careful consideration not to look at her neck. The purple and oranges were like a sunset falling beneath the horizon of her neckline.

"Cold," she said, irritably. "Cold and bored."

"Is that why you asked me to sit with you? You'd like some company?"

"You're his mistress," she said as if it were as simple as pointing out a cup of tea.

"Are you ok? You seem…"

"I'll take that as a yes. I'm not a simpleton you know. I am not yet doted. I visited Poland this year. Did you know that, little Fraulein?"

I shook my head. I thought of her as always being there. As trapped in the Berg as I was.

"Yes. The dirt is indescribable. The rabble of them. I was there to help, you see. I run the hospitals in Military District III. The Red Cross, you know."

"I didn't," I said as I shook my head.

"No." She looked me square in the eyes. She gave off no warmth. Neither emotionally, for her eyes were hostile and sharp. Nor physically. It was as if she was sucking in the heat around her and making the room colder for it. I shivered. "You did not."

"Why are you telling me this? Are you going away again?"

"You don't like Magda, do you?"

I said nothing, wondering if this were all a trick. A way for them to catch me out and have Addie send me away.

"Frau Goebbels. Surely, girl, you must know her name? You cannot be so dotted as to not know who your biggest rival is."

"I have no rivals," I snapped.

"Ah, there's the girl I thought was in there. You do a good job of acting like your sister but I knew there was something more. And I used the wrong word. I meant threat."

A breeze ran down my spine. She noticed.

"You're right to be scared. She asked you to do something. Didn't she?"

I thought to the key, to Angela and her secret room.

"She'll be plotting for you to fight against another."

"Fight?"

"Testing your strength. It means she sees you as I did when I first laid eyes upon you. It means your charade is crumbling. At least for those who are looking. You've grown tired of your act?"

I said nothing, my hands fidgeting by my side. I wished Gretl was there, she'd have told this woman to shut up, to hold her peace and keep her poison to herself. Gretl always said she was a witch.

"Do you know how I met my husband?"

I was thrown by her change of topic, so I stayed silent. Still.

"He was my *landsknecht* and he had a proclivity for parsimonious living and the power of plants. He believed, like I do, in the potency of leaves and berries. How they can be mixed together to create medicine. How incense smoke and candles and willful thinking can change the world. We bonded because of our mutual love and it made us strong. Once. What is your bond with him? With the Führer?"

"Bond? What concern is that of yours? How dare you speak to me like this? Like I am some simple girl and you a witch in the wood? You know of my life with the Führer, of his desire to keep our love secret, and yet you ask me to reveal the intimacies between us over breakfast? Look how well your 'mutual bond' has served you, Frau Himmler." I tugged at her dress, revealing the full extent of the horrific bruise that did little to hide the root-like scars along her body.

"There's the woman. Hello, Eva. It is nice to see Fraulein Braun has gone away. Sit down, sit down. Don't make a mockery of yourself." She began to cough, a high-pitched wheezing that made my skin crawl. She pulled a handkerchief from inside her sleeve and held it to her mouth. "I'm not as old as I look," she smiled, a trace of phlegm still clinging to her lip.

"Homeopathy doesn't work as well as you'd hope then?"

"Make your jokes. Make your jokes."

"About you? Or about the Knights of the Round Table your husband is trying to rebuild like we are in Avalon?"

"Watch yourself, he is still a powerful man."

"Unless my Führer says otherwise."

"Where is this woman when Magda makes you look foolish? Where is this woman that storms into the Führer's meetings as if she were a Queen and he a King only in consort? Why do you not act like this always?"

"Why should I? Strength invites challenge."

"But your position already does that. So why not show that you will protect it?"

"Because I don't have to. Now, Frau Himmler, why did you really ask me over here?"

"I told you. I'm bored."

And then she began to cough again.

"Why were you talking to her?" Gretl asked as we basked in the sun. "At all? You should have just walked right past her."

"Her husband is Reichsführer. Second only to Rudolf Hess. That's not a woman you walk by."

"You're scared of her, aren't you?" Gretl asked as she peered at me from behind her sunglasses.

"Of course I am, she'll cast a spell on me." We both laughed. "She asked why I wasn't more forceful around the Berg."

"She did? Nosey so and so. What's it got to do with her? Doesn't she have a hospital to run?"

"You know about that?"

"Of course I do. Everyone does. It's why Emmy hates her so much. She thinks she's just a nurse and shouldn't be allowed up here. She has work to do, so Emmy says, that should keep her away from here."

"She told me she went to Poland this year."

"Poland!" I relished watching her face light up. "I didn't know. Oh my. What did she say it was like?"

"Dirty."

"Oh no. Really? Dirty? Does that mean Danzig is dirty too? Will they clean it now we've taken it back? Oh, I would hate to have a dirty city in the Reich. Why would the Poles let their country get so horrid? Why would they, Effie?"

"I don't know," I said, leaving back into my lounger.

"Well, thank goodness for the Führer, then. Such a shame when a country falls into ruin. They needed a good clean up. Thank goodness for the Führer."

"Do you think so?" I asked.

"Do you not?"

"I don't care," I laughed.

"Ilse would," Gretl said. "You should call her. Make amends."

"Amends? I did nothing wrong. It's her. She has a poor attitude."

"You said some mean things about Dr. Marx."

"Wouldn't you?"

"He gave her a job. Do you remember those shoes she bought with her first wage from him? The straps?"

"She let me wear them," I conceded.

"She did. And me. Remember how furious Baba was when he found them."

"I do. And how furious she got right back at him."

"It's my money, I'll do what I want with it!" we both shouted together, scaring a flock of doves from the trees nearby.

"It was though," I said. "Her money."

"Those were great shoes."

"I'm sorry I hit you last night."

Her bright blue eyes dimmed as she peered into my own.

"I'm sorry you did too. But I'm more sorry I upset you. I shouldn't have…well, you know. I won't ever again."

"I dreamt of him," I breathed.

"What?"

"A dream."

"Was I in it?" she smiled. "I'm sorry though. Truly. I promise I won't ever again."

"Never, Gretl. Never. I can't afford to think of anyone else. Not anyone."

"I know," she said, but I knew she didn't.

Not really.

1941

May, *The Berghof*

"Oh Addie, I'm so sorry," I wrapped my arm around his neck and breathed through my mouth, careful not to grimace at the smell of his breath. "You've been betrayed."

"How could he? How could he do this to me? To the Reich?"

"He isn't a clever man. He can't be."

"That's quite enough, Fraulein Braun," Himmler said from behind his narrow spectacles. "You're making a scene."

"I'm making a scene? My Führer has been betrayed by one of your own, Herr Himmler."

"You let her speak this way, Adolf?" Angela said as she laid down a tray of tea and whisky on the table by her half-brother's shoulder. "It's not right."

"I won't be accused of causing a scene when I am doing nothing but consoling my Führer."

"Our Führer," Angela corrected. "Now come with me, you silly girl." Both Angela and Himmler shared a smiled at that. "And let's have no more of this nonsense."

The doors to Hitler's office were thrown open by an incandescent Magda and her husband, Herr Goebbels.

"The swine. The treacherous leech," Magda raged as she stormed into the room, thunder crackling across her face. "To betray us all – the party – like this is…"

"Hush now, wife," Goebbels said, his earlier appearance of anger simply fallout from his wife's. I watched him walk towards the tray Angela had just set down and help himself to a whisky. "This is a time to be calm. Herr Führer, are you ok?"

He'd said barely a word since the communication had been received. A quiet, sullen look of anger had been simmering across his features as the Nazi party converged on the Berghof to rally themselves for action. His hand was trembling immensely and so I tried to disguise it by sitting very near to him and holding it as steady as I could.

"He's held prisoner. One of our own is in the clutches of the enemy and what have we to show for it?" No one dared mention that half of Europe was under the German heel, nor that Britain was all but isolated on her island, her empire prostrate before her. *Before us.*

"We can get him back," Bormann said easily. "We will send in…"

"We will send in no one." Goebbels was firm. Hitler turned to him, his mouth hanging agape enough to look as if he'd had a stroke. I squeezed his hand tightly, worrying that that was what happened. "Führer, we cannot allow ourselves to follow folly with folly. If we look desperate to clutch him back, then they'll believe what he says."

"You think he would betray me? Us? And speak of it?"

"I did not think he would leave us as he did. For peace?"

"If he tells the Bolsheviks..." Goebbel's hand silenced his wife with a slap. I gasped aloud, terrified of what I'd just seen. She clutched her face, the rings on her fingers sparkling in the firelight. I could see the white coating on her tongue, the black spots of decay in her mouth, too. Her lipstick was smeared along her cheek, three fingers creating pronounced trails across her face, trails that mixed with the blood that dribbled from her nose. Her face flushed with shame and looked red hot to the touch. Her eyes met mine, the only safe place to rest them in the room. My spine went cold.

"The Bolsheviks will never believe him. Never. They want to believe that we are their friend. Besides, the British have been warning them since October last year. If you can't keep your hysteria in check, wife, then I will ask you to leave."

Seeing her humbled should have made me glad. I knew it should have. Addie would never lay a finger on me, his beloved; would never dream of inflicting pain like that on me before everyone. I swatted away the memories of being bundled up stairs and ignored for weeks on end. *Surely a slap on the face before the most powerful men in the country was worse?* And for Magda, surely. She was the most powerful woman in the Reich and that counted for nothing if a man could lay his hands on her so easily. My fingers twitched to reach out to her and pull her hand away from her face. Humiliation was a feeling best served internally. She had to stand up straight, her back still arched from the blow, and take her hand from her face. It made us all uncomfortable to see her so weakened by her husband's anger.

But her lips turned into a snarl, her nose rising as if she could smell manure on a farmer's field, and I knew that her anger wasn't to the man that struck her – but the woman who'd watched it happen.

"I gave him everything. He had power and money and respect. From the old days, he'd been by my side. And now…this. Now he has betrayed us to England. Has fled – like a coward – on one of my planes, one of Germany's planes – and hidden himself in Scotland. Why? To create a peace we do not need? To establish an ally that could do nothing for France?" He stood up, his monologue just beginning. "The North Sea should have swallowed him alive. The engines should have broken away and let him tumble into the choppy waters. For a Duke, too. Some entitled aristocrat buoyed on his own sense of purpose. I will have no peace I have not brokered. I will cease no war until I have London beneath the eagle or in ruins along the Thames. Tell Heydrich I want him slaughtered in his sleep. Silence him. Steal his voice. If that Red Bear can do it to Trotsky in Mexico, then surely my grip can extend across the Channel?"

Himmler nodded but promised nothing.

"How could such a fool be second to you, Herr Führer?" Goebbels asked, boldly. Had his wife had asked the same thing, I wondered how hard the slap would have been across her face then. And whether it would have stopped with one. "That is what the German people will be asking themselves. How?"

"The people love my Führer," I bit back.

"Goebbels is right. Tell them…" Words betrayed him. I could see the cold war going on behind his eyes. The desire to punish coupled with the instinct to remain loyal to his friend. Neither side quite opening fire on one another. Simply circling. "Why did the British not shoot him down? Radar? Tell them… Tell them he was mentally disturbed. Paranoid. Broken. That he…what?" He looked around the room. Everyone waited expectantly on his word, on whatever he had to say, but the shock ran so deep, the betrayal a wound so large that he didn't know what to say. He had no answers and no one was giving him any.

"You're right, Addie. He was an ill-minded man. Have Herr Goebbels here tell the Reich and all of England and her empire that he is deranged, insane. No one could believe the words of a mad man, and that's what he must be – surely – to have flown solo in the middle of the night."

"Yes." He clutched my hand back, desperate to stop himself from drowning in the catastrophe. I didn't know what they meant when they spoke about the Bolsheviks, but even I could see a map and what it would mean. "Yes, darling Tschapperl, yes. Do as she says, Goebbels." I winced at how he'd phrased it. I saw Bormann smile and try to hide it by turning to get another drink. Something had most definitely gone his way.

"Take your leave of us, ladies." Goebbels waved his hand towards me. "We need to discuss things that wouldn't interest you."

Hitler stood at his second in command's words and walked away, cruelly not looking back, letting me be ordered around by a man I could barely stomach. There was no victorious smile on his odorous lips as I stood and followed Magda from the room, but I knew in his spiteful little heart, that he would be gleeful at my expulsion, and how readily he had achieved it.

"Magda, are you…"

"Am I what, little whore? Am I what?" She gripped my wrists in her fingers and squeezed them so tightly that I felt the bones crunch together. I wriggled, trying to pull myself free but she was possessed by a wildness that only demons and wolves knew of. I caught the deep green eyes of an S.S. man standing guard at Hitler's door, but he made no move to help me. "That's right, look at the officer and bat your eyelashes so he will come running. You think I don't see you, little whore, the way you dance down the gardens, those mutts by your feet, and steal the gaze of every man around you? That I don't see the way you show off at the lake, doing your handstands and holding your breath for so long under water that the soldiers dive in to save you? You're an ordinary little girl, Eva. Ordinary, plain and simple. There is nothing spectacular about you. Nothing. You're a chew toy he uses to relieve stress, a whore for expensive perfumes and new dresses. You're no woman. You're nothing." She threw my hands back at me but she didn't move. Her eyes were devoid of any life, only hatred and malice swirled there. Her cheek was still red and swollen. I rubbed my wrists carefully.

"I'm not ordinary," I snapped back. "He makes me something other than ordinary. He is mine and I am his and that makes me far from ordinary. So, you can hurt me all you want, Frau Goebbels, but at least I won't simply be the wife to second place."

It was a physical blow to her. The breath left her mouth so quickly it whistled and she clutched at the muscles spasming in her stomach. Tears raised in her eyes but didn't have time to fall before she wiped them away.

"You'll regret speaking to me like that," she whispered.

"You'll regret not becoming my friend when you first had the chance to," I said back.

July, *The Berghof*

"He looks like a villain," my mother said as she looked at the picture I had thrown on the table. She'd been playing cards with Herta, their game now spread across the table like broken glass. Herta shot me a disapproving look but did not interrupt my mother. "Though I hear he is a fine Catholic. I'm proud the Führer has put him in charge."

"So he can pray for victory?" I said spitefully.

"Don't you make fun of God here. Not in front of me, Eva. I swear it. I won't stand for it."

"Sorry, Mother," I said as I went to sit with Annie, Dr. Brandt's wife.

"He does look like a villain though. Very bald head. The Russian winter will make him very cold," she chuckled to herself.

"They won't still be there in winter, Mother. Do you know nothing about war? The Bolsheviks live in a house of cards no stronger than your own on the table in front of you. One good kick is all it will take for them to come tumbling down." I kicked out my leg for emphasis. Gretl laughed.

"Napoleon thought the same thing," my mother said. The room sobered. Each of us warily appraising the other, wondering if even here, in a room full of friends, there could be a spy that would whisper back.

"I have polished your broach, Eva," Annie said, pulling out a small gold badge wrapped in a silk handkerchief. "My husband said that it was his greatest pleasure to give you it, and I was to make sure that it stayed clean."

"As long as your husband keeps Dr. Morell from injecting anymore poisons into my Führer then he will have my eternal gratitude. Thank you."

It was a four-leaf clover, one half shaped like an 'E', the other a 'B'. I adored it. Though Gretl so often called it a butterfly, it felt like an amulet of honour, a ward against the spectre of obscurity. I pinned it to the material above my breast and gave it a quick rub with my finger.

"Mother, will you take Negus and Stasi for a walk. Please?"

She looked as if she were about to say no, her hand raised like she would hold back my words from reaching her ears. But Herta stood quickly and hushed her with a look. Agreeing to take the dogs, she pulled my mother along with her, both terriers yelping at their feet.

"I'm worried," I admitted as I felt my stomach clench. "This is too big."

"But you said it yourself," Gretl reminded me. "It will be over soon. No need to worry."

CONNER M^cALEESE

"But what if it's not? He's just about mastered the continent, fought off everyone but England and then…"

"And then he undertakes a campaign that will keep him from the Berghof," Annie guessed.

"Yes."

"That's his nature."

"And what about my nature? I need to be with him. I have to be."

"Why?" Gretl asked, as if she didn't already know. "Why?"

"You know why! I love him. I love him deeply."

"You love yourself more."

"Why are you asking me this in front of Frau Brandt?" I picked up my glass of water and threw it across the room. It shattered, like a thousand stars had broken free of the evil hold of the night sky, and tumbled to the floor. Annie let out a little scream.

Gretl didn't look at me.

"Because maybe she can convince you more than I can. You're stronger than you know, Effie. Stronger than any woman who has ever lived, perhaps. What other woman could endure the feelings you feel? What man for that matter?"

"When the war is over, he'll come back to me." I slumped into my chair. Folding under the weight of my loss.

"Russia is the last enemy," Annie reasoned. "There's no one else when they're gone."

"I don't want to talk about Russia this or Bolshevik that," I said. "As soon as he has somewhere to put the people that aren't German then he can stop."

"Aren't German?" Annie asked. "He talks to you about the war?"

"Eugh. Not that I listen. And only a little. He prefers that I don't know. So do I, actually. But he mentions little things here and there. I don't even think he means to. But when we walk, he likes to talk. And sometimes we talk about things like that."

"Does he mean the Jews?" Annie asked.

"Did I speak French a moment ago?"

"Sorry, it's just odd."

"Odd? What could possibly be odd about needing more room? There's a lot of people in the world."

"But who is not German?"

"Italians, Spaniards, Greeks."

"They all have their own countries," she said back.

"Well then, Jews, yes. I suppose he means the Jews."

"What if they don't want to move?" Gretl asked suddenly. "What if they're happy where they are?"

I shrugged. "Maybe he'll let them stay where they are. Maybe he won't. Does it matter? Plenty of Germans will have to move when he starts rebuilding Berlin. I'm sure they won't mind."

"Eva, I don't know if I want to be alone up here anymore."

I turned to my sister, the hollows of her cheeks pulled tight by the downward fall of her lips.

"Don't be silly." I hugged her. "We aren't alone. Look – we have Annie."

I dreamt I was on a train. It was so packed I couldn't move. Rough slats of wood scraped my forehead and I could just about make the light outside. It stunk. The smell of cows and pigs and other people filled my nostrils like obnoxious gas, choking me until I couldn't breathe. There was a baby crying. I wanted to turn to try and find it, to see if I could ask its mother to make it be quiet. The train was miserable enough without listening to the agony of a baby while we jittered along. But I couldn't turn, couldn't move. It wasn't so much because of how crowded it was, though that would have made it difficult, but because the thought struck me like a bullet to the temple – what if the baby's mother is dead?

I knew then that I was right. I was riding a train of death, one that would stop only at the gates of hell. It was on a single track, a snake of iron and wood that coiled its way beneath the soil and through the rock until it tasted the fiery brimstone that promised its reward. All it had to do was drop us off, give us over to Satan, and the snake could slither back to the surface and hunt for another train filled with the living dead.

I woke up with a start. The sheets were moist beneath my buttocks and my hair was stuck to my face like seaweed. I pulled it free and tried to steady my breathing.

"Are you ok?" Addie asked. He was standing in his dressing gown, no slippers on his feet. He looked tired, weary, but alight with victory. He was the beginnings of a ruin, only just starting to crumble. I shook the thoughts from my head as I began to cry. I was just overtired, over anxious – my Führer could never crumble.

"I'm sorry I woke you," I wept as he came and sat beside me. The smell of his breath was unbearable, a horrid combination of chemicals and rotting vegetables. It reminded me of the gas aboard the train and I buried my head into his chest to hide my nose from it.

"Don't be silly." He kissed my head. "What's wrong?"

"I was on a train. A train bound for hell."

"Has your mother been citing the Bible to you again?"

"No," I lied. I knew how he hated her piety. "I was on a train full of dead people. I was made to leave my home and stuffed on a train like a sardine. It was terrible, Addie. Just terrible."

"A train? That doesn't sound so awful."

"Oh it was. It was, Addie. It was. It was filled with a stink like gas. And a baby was crying, its mother was dead. I think. And they were all dead. Except for me and the baby, they were all dead."

"Hush now, it was just a dream. Just a dream. No one is going to make you leave here."

No one is going to let me leave either, are they?

"Come sleep in my bed. Come on. You can't sleep in this mess."

"In your bed? Addie, are you sure?"

"Just for tonight," he said, as if he suddenly regretted the offer. "Just to get you over your bad dream."

His sheets were warm and fresh, barely slept in at all. He wrapped his arm around my stomach and pulled my body closer to his. I felt like a jigsaw piece, neatly slotted into my perfect mate. What a picture we must have made! If only I could have been an angel looking down from above, I'm sure we would have been a picture. He smelled my hair and took in its clean scent before blowing it back out over me in a putrid plume of his own breath. The room began to stink of it and his arm now felt serpent-like on my belly, constricting. His breath was the gas now, swirling up my nostrils and making me choke. My skin bristled at the hard scratch of his arm hair and his heartbeat began to slow from the racing pulse of a steam engine to the steady thrum of a marching army. *Pull yourself together, Eva. Enjoy this moment while it lasts. You don't know if he'll be gone again tomorrow.*

He wasn't, thankfully. He woke me up with his erection prodding my back and I kissed him, eager to move things forward when his door was knocked on. Loudly. I heard Angela's voice on the other side bidding him to get up, it was almost midday. She couldn't have known I was in his bed, she simply couldn't. But inside I knew she did and that's why she was waking him up.

He walked with me after lunch. There were no visitors and most of his generals were somewhere out East fighting his war for him. He'd come to me after lunch and asked me if I would like to take a stroll down to Teehaus further down the mountain. He liked to read there best of all and didn't fancy walking himself.

I accepted at once.

"You keep me sane," he admitted as he strung his hand through my own. "These walks are what I think about when work keeps me far away. When I am pacing up and down the chancellery, I think of these lanes and plot my way to getting back to them."

"You sound like a hero in one of your books. Plotting to get back to his princess."

"Princess? Oh no, Eva. You do yourself a dishonor, you are a Queen. I am a knight, a gallant knight, plotting to get back to my Queen."

He was being flippant. His boyish mood had been caught by just the right wind and he was talking in light fairytales, not meaning what he said. I knew that. I knew he didn't consider me his Queen. But hearing the word leave his lips made my chest dense with butterflies.

"You've been reading too many children's books, Addie."

"They keep my mind grand – open. If all I heard was generals' talk and all I read was field reports, then I wouldn't be half the man I am today. I wouldn't have had half as much success. What general would have said France could fall in six weeks? None. But I have the mind of a genius, the childish wonder of a boy that believes in Saint Nick."

"And the body of a man through and through." I let my fingers trace light circles in the crook of his arm.

"Hardly important, but yes."

I felt wanton. Like a whore so wet with lust that she felt like she was the centre of gravity, a force beckoning in all around her. I hated him most when he did this, when he brushed off my attraction to him as if it were no more than a toy train I repeatedly ran into his arm. He wanted me too, in those beautiful moments when he held me and entered me, I knew that we were on the same frequency, connected by more than habit and words. Those moments were so fleeting, so unlike the men that Gretl attracted, that I felt coated in a layer of filth.

"You love me, Addie, don't you?"

He stopped walking. His back was to the majesty of the swirling pine trees that cascaded down the mountain face like a veil of thick green leaves. A bride ready to be married. Birds, I didn't know which type of birds, swirled in sloping hoops high above us, cawing to one another as they lunged and retreated in a game of tag and catch.

"I need you to stop asking me this." His words stole the heat from the air.

"Why, Addie? Why?"

"Because you cheapen it every time. I will tell you I love you when I feel it most. But you…you goad it from me. It weakens it. Tarnishes its specialness. You have to stop asking me to constantly reassure you."

The birds flapped away, sensing the sadness that pulsed from my desperate heart. What bird, with wings that could fly so easily, would want to stay around someone as sad as I was then?

"I'm sorry. I am. I'm sorry. It's just difficult."

"I know," he said as he took my hand and placed it back in the crook of his arm. "I know it is. But it is what it is."

We spent the afternoon just sitting with one another. I tried my best to battle away the pain he'd inflicted upon me so easily. I read my magazines with careful eyes, forcing myself not to look up at him. He sat across from me in an armchair wrought with wooden roses. His book on his lap, he fell between quiet reading and light napping until the sun began to set. I kept his tea warm, and the room sealed shut so that he might have no temptation to entice him away. He looked far older when he slept and I couldn't help but look at him then, when his eyes were safely closed and my own were free to roam. His jaw open, a trail of drool falling from his curled bottom lip to the lapel of his military uniform, the wrinkles on his face looked more pronounced than ever before. He rubbed his arms while he slept and I knew that the incision points of Morell's syringes were making him itch.

When he was here, with me, I could scarcely believe he needed the cocktail of drugs and potions that Dr. Morell was only too eager to provide. A cabinet of clanking bottles, an apothecary's bag with herbs and pills, all looked too reminiscent of a wizard's collection of malicious maladies. I knew he shook. His left arm trembled when he was nervous, or scared, or angry or anxious. It was pitiful to watch. I hated the way his eyes would look at anything but his hand as it spasmed. I told him, over and over, I told him that it could be Morell's concoctions that caused it. But he ignored me. Choosing instead to place his faith with a faithless man.

His trousers were hiked up above his ankles, the way he was sitting stretching the material. Soft, pale flesh peeked out from under the hem. Swirling patterns of raw, flaky skin coiled like long maggots beneath the thin, fine hairs that decorated his ankle. They'd grow redder and redder when he scratched them, tearing his skin in places that would then bleed. When I saw his bedsheets, I would see the blood dried to them.

"You're thinking too hard," he said when he awoke. At once my muscles relaxed so that my brow was smooth and my lips in a gentle smile. It happened so naturally that I didn't even have to decide to do it.

"Just about how much I miss acting," I said. It was manipulative but still.

"You know how I feel about that, Eva. The guilt, please, not today."

"Of course, Addie. Of course. Read your book. Gertraud said it was very good. She'd love to know what you think of it."

Winter, *The Berghof.*

"She berates me at every turn," I raged to Gretl and Herta who stood side by side avoiding the fragments of flying china. "And they laugh. Himmler. Heydrich. Göring. Only Goebbels doesn't, but that's because he hates his wife almost as much as I do. It wasn't my fault I saw what he did. And now she's taking it out on me."

"Didn't Hitler just by you a trunk of new dresses?"

"How has that any relevance, Gretl?" Herta asked.

"Well, if I had just gotten a new trunk of dresses, I wouldn't be worried about a few bits of sniggering from people who didn't just get a new trunk of dresses. You see?"

"Has the sun addled your brain? Eva, I know this is hard, but you saw her at her most vulnerable, of course she's going to beat you down. She wants to see you vulnerable too," Herta said as she scratched her make-up-less nose.

"She sees me vulnerable. She does. Every time Addie leaves without saying goodbye, or…"

"No, she *knows* you're vulnerable then, but she doesn't see it. And worse, no one else does either. No one except Gretl and I. That's infuriating for her."

"But I'm ordinary. She said so herself. I'm just an ordinary girl, so why does she care?"

"Because ordinary girls shouldn't see First Ladies being slapped by their husbands."

"Please don't call her that, Herta. She's not the first anything, she's just an over glorified hostess that certainly does not have the most-ess." Gretl laughed as she spoke, trying to unstifled the air around us.

"Claws out, Gretl. Where did that come from?"

"I don't like it when people make Effie upset. You don't deserve it do you, Effie?"

I let them talk amongst themselves as they sat back down on the loungers, safe in the knowledge that there was nothing else for me to throw and injure them with. I did feel calmer. I sat beside Gretl and let her play with my freshly dyed hair.

"You just got it styled," Herta leaned over and swatted Gretl's fingers away.

"Leave her be. I can get it redone tomorrow."

"Wasteful. So wasteful, Eva. We're at war. You shouldn't be so gluttonous."

"So we're just ignoring the face that Magda has every secretary and the cook they let fuck them laugh at me?"

"You've got a new trunk of dresses," Gretl helpfully reminded.

"It's a war. We're at war. You think getting laughed at is as bad as that?"

"How would I know? Humiliation – pain – is all relative. I've never been to war. This is the worst thing that's ever happened to me. Surely that entitles me to moaning? Or should I tell the Wehrmacht not to complain too much about the winter approaching them in Russia because at least they have food in their bellies, unlike the witches in Africa?"

"You're being glib. Facing starvation or freezing to death is not the equivalent of…Frau Hess." Herta stood up, raining down the crumbs from the biscuit she'd been nibbling between lectures on the stone terrace. "You're looking well."

"Frau Hess." I nodded but didn't bother to get up.

"Angela said you'd be here," she said quietly, as if she was scared Angela would hear her and come marching out from the shade inside and beat her around the head with a rolling pin screaming 'liar!'

"Oh did she? Well you can go tell her…"

"Effie, don't," Gretl warned. "How can we help you, Frau Hess?"

"Please, call me Ilse, we've known each other for long enough now."

"Our sister is called Ilse," I said. *And knowing of you is significantly different from* knowing *you.*

"Hessie?" she offered to avoid confusion.

"Why are you here?" I asked.

She fidgeted on the doorframe, half in and half out of the Berghof. Her hands were wrapped in gloves but the winter sun was warm enough that she didn't need them. Her lips trembled. Each spasm no doubt a word, a sentence, she was desperate to say. In the end she chose to put a knife in her belly and open herself up. "No one speaks to me anymore."

"Your husband did betray the Reich," Gretl said as flippantly as if she were talking about a stolen hairbrush between sisters.

"He wanted to make peace. He thought that the Duke of Hamilton could…I know he did. Whether rightly or wrongly, I know he did. But I didn't."

"You kind of…"

"Gretl, hush," Herta interrupted her. "Come sit with us, Frau He- Hessie. Sit here by me."

"I know about you and the Führer," she said as if that would make me like her.

"Great. What a lovely thing to say."

"No. Sorry, this is all coming out wrong. I mean you don't have to hide it. Everyone hides everything from me now, I don't want you to feel like you have to, too."

"You really didn't know?" Gretl asked. "Really?"

Hessie sighed. "I knew he was planning something – I told the Führer that – but to fly on his own? From Münich to Scotland? You think I would let him do that?"

"He was falling out of favour," Herta said what everyone had been gossiping about for months. "You could have known and wanted him to, so you could stay here."

"I'm lucky to be here now." She looked at her lap. She'd have cried if she could, I knew. But she'd done so much of that for so long since her husband had left that I doubted she could have ever cried again. "He must be so scared. I don't know what they're doing to him – but I can imagine. No. I didn't know. He kept it from me. If only for his own safety I wouldn't have let him."

"I bet you didn't say *that* to the Führer."

"Gretl, enough. Go and get us some drinks. Now, Gretl, or I'll send you home to live with Ilse. Our Ilse." I smiled at Hessie so she wouldn't think I was planning on sending her away.

She rose without much grumbling, a murmur perhaps of having just gotten warm. We listened to her footsteps go down the stairway to the kitchens in silence.

"You take pictures, don't you?" she asked me as she fiddled with the hem of her dress, her eyes looking anywhere but my own.

"I do."

"They say Hitler only lets you take photos of him here. That you're the only person in the world that gets to portray him at peace."

"I guess so, if you say it like that."

"I bet that annoys Leni." The first smile she'd worn since her husband had abandoned her crossed her lips. "Can I see them?"

It was lucky, maybe, or fate even, that I had an album tucked away in the service room just two doors away from where we lounged. I had meant to send them to my mother, to let her see both Addie and I together. I didn't like that she worried, nor that the only person she could confide in was Ilse who hated Addie more than most. I placed the thick mahogany binding on Hessie's lap and opened the album to my favourite photo. He was leaning against the wall of the higher terrace that overlooked the cliff face we were perched on. I'd taken it just before war had broken out. His ill-fitting blue suit was bunched around his midsection, a mug of tea placed precariously on the terrace's edge. It was a peaceful white mug and as I'd taken the photograph I remembered worrying that his elbow might knock it over and it would fall away and shatter into a million pieces on the soil below.

"He looks so *normal*. Even here, I never see him this relaxed. Though I must, of course. But your skills, they make him human." She may have been over-postulating but I didn't care. The ego within me inflated itself on the breath from her words and filled my head with dreams once again. "You could do this for a living."

"I only like taking them of him," I said honestly.

"And yourself." Herta smiled. "You're in most of them."

"She's right," Hessie said like she hadn't noticed. And I was, but why shouldn't I be? If I had to hide from the public, well then that was the price I had to pay. But here, in the Berghof, or rather, in my photos of the Berghof, I didn't feel I should hide. I didn't feel I should let myself be swept away from the historical narrative that I was creating. "Will they ever be published, do you think?"

"One day, yes. They'd have to be, right?" I looked to each of them. "I'm the only one allowed to take photos like these. Surely he'll want them published when the war is over. Look." I flipped the pages desperately, snatching the album from Hessie's lap. "See, here he is here with Magda's children. See how at peace he looks? How fatherly? Goebbels will want these when the war is over. Won't he? To show my Führer in a fresh, fatherly light? To add to the war hero? What? Why are you all looking at me like that?"

"Just calm down, Effie. Calm. Put the album down and let Hessie see some more of your work, ok?"

"Sorry." I turned to Hessie. "Sorry, I just get a little agitated sometimes."

"No, I understand. Please don't apologise. It's a hard burden you bear."

"What do you mean?"

"No, see, I didn't mean anything by it. Oh God. I'm sorry. Look. Maybe I should go." She stood up and walked back inside, her skirts trailing along the stone without so much as a wave goodbye.

"What did she mean by that?" I asked.

"You know fine well, Eva. All the wives know how hard it must be for you. You know that. You'll apologise to her later, won't you?"

I said nothing, my feelings still stung.

"You will," she continued on. "She was only being nice."

"Maybe she should get on a plane too then, if she's only going to whine about no one speaking to her. I didn't see her coming and sitting with me for dinner when Magda and Emmy told the wives to ignore me. Did you?"

"Where would she even go, Eva? You're being silly. And besides, this is her home."

"Somewhere sunny. South. Hitler always says you should head South. Caucasus, I think he means. That's in Russia, right?"

"I'm sure he doesn't mean there," Herta said to me unkindly with that make-up-less sneer on her face. "You should show magnanimity in her defeat, Eva. You really should."

"Fraulein Braun," Angela said from the shadows.

"Am I on Berlin Boulevard? Selling tickets? Why must I be interrupted by every woman who wants a chat?" I said as I turned back into my sun lounger and rested on its pillowed back. "Yes, Frau Hammitzsch, how can I help you?"

"Rude." She stood in front of my sunlight, casting her ugly silhouette upon me. "You're a very rude girl."

"Do you bring news of the war?" Herta asked, aghast.

"There is no war here," I interrupted Angela as she began to speak. "War is a far-off thing that need not concern us. Isn't that right, Frau Hammitzsch?"

"My brother will keep it as far away from you as possible, I'm sure."

"Half," I reminded her.

"Rude. I am here." I watched her from beneath my hand, not trusting her not to move and let the sun blind me. "...to let you know I have invited Fraulein Riefenstahl up for Christmas."

"You've what?" I was on my feet and quivering as soon as I heard the letter 'R.' "You've done no such thing. Tell me you're kidding, you wicked old witch."

"I have. I thought I should let you know. So you can compose yourself, of course."

"You needn't look so smug; I mean it — you needn't! I'll make sure she doesn't come. You cannot do this to me."

"Eva, why are you so terrified of Leni coming here for Christmas?" Herta asked.

I thought of her slim legs, of that perfect way her teeth gleamed as she smiled. I imagined her sitting by the fire in his study while they discussed a new movie to buoy up the German people, yet another thing for her to be fawned over for. I thought of the new cameras she would

114

bring from Berlin and Paris, how they might eclipse my own Rolleiflex. I thought of the careless way she would laugh, they cruel way she would laud her success before me. Not overtly I knew, she wasn't so foolish as to do that. But when a guest tells you they've won this award or that accolade, what host could be so rude as to scoff? Certainly not me. And that's what I imagined hurting most of all, a hot bullet in my gut, how happy she'd be when she spoke of her new projects. While I languished by a sun lounger, she was out there following her heart. It would be unbearable.

"She's not welcome here. Not while I'm here."

"Then leave, Fraulein Braun. Just leave." She smiled at me sadly, with those same Geli eyes I could see watching me in my dreams.

It was just supposed to have been a silly love letter, a character I had created to show Addie how much I adored him. When he'd first seen me up that ladder, my legs on full display, I hadn't recognized him. And, even if I had, a politician was not an attractive mate.

"Herr Wolf is here, Eva. Smile at him," Hoffman bade me.

"Pleasure, Herr Wolf." I didn't bother to smile as I took his hand and curtseyed. I don't know why I curtseyed, it was so out of place. But I did.

"Who was that?" I asked, feeling like Little Red Riding Hood, basket in her arms.

"Herr Hitler. The Austrian. Surely you have seen him in the newspapers?"

It felt stupid to admit that I only read magazines, and found the newspapers to be depressing and boring. But I was young then, barely seventeen. It would have been forgiven. As I walked home that evening, the rain just beginning to fall from the night sky, I stopped by a corner stall and purchased the cleverest looking newspaper I could see. I opened the pages, the ink beginning to run, and hunted for him. I found him standing in front of an old building, his face very austere for a man who had apparently been to prison. I thought criminals were supposed to have a bit of life about them, a cocky attitude and jolly walk. But this man looked moody and unfulfilled, I thought no more of him.

Until I did.

The letter was hastily written. It had been almost two years – a teenage lifetime – of half courting, half being ignored, when the idea struck me to write him a letter. Chicken scrawl, Ilse called it as I showed it to her before I slipped it into the mail box. Two days later I read of the death in the same paper I had been buying for almost two years to try and catch a glimpse of him. *She's shot herself.* I didn't believe the monstrous scandals they published about their relationship. He was kind. Soft spoken. I didn't care much his niece was dead, only that I now had a chance to console him.

"You need to convince her to change her mind," Gretl urged as I got ready for bed.

"I can't. She won't. I am done for. I can't bear it, I can't."

"Eva, please, don't say that."

"Stop looking at my neck." I traced my fingers around the scars again. "Just help me think of a way to stop her."

"You could speak to the Führer. He might say no."

"Addie? Are you joking? No. He'd probably like that I was jealous. Forget I said that," I said as her cheeks blushed. "No. I have to stop her. What's to stop her doing this whenever she likes? She should go, Gretl. She must. This is my home."

"This is dangerous, Effie. Don't think like this. He loves you, I know. But she's his *sister*."

"Half."

"Yes, half. But still by blood. There's nothing he values more than that. Don't go against her, Effie, don't. It's not like Magda. Magda is all huff and puff. Besides, she needs the Führer's approval too much to go against you while you make him happy. But Angela? She would have you hanging from the gallows as soon as she'd have breakfast with you."

"You have a lot of thoughts for strategy for a girl who spends most of her day flirting with...oh, you haven't. You've called her, haven't you?"

"She'll be here tomorrow." She had the decency to at least look ashamed of herself. "I'm worried about you, Effie. You've been out of control for a while now."

"What would you know of out of control?" I said as I threw myself under the linen sheet and wrapped myself up warm, a caterpillar nesting in its cocoon, safe from the world.

"Christmas is so long away, Effie. Maybe she'll change her mind. Angela doesn't like the way Leni flirts with the Führer any more than you do."

"Go to sleep, Gretl. Go to sleep and I will see you in the morning. Hopefully before Ilse gets here, that is."

"Whatever Angela throws at you, you take, ok?" Ilse said as soon as she stepped from the long black Mercedes I had sent to collect her from the train station. Not even a thank you. I should have made her walk.

"Hello, sister."

"Oh don't play the madam with me, Eva." She pulled me into a deep hug so tight that I couldn't hold the frustration I had for her in my heart.

"Is Mother not with you?" I peeked into the dark interior of the car, hoping to see my mother's smiling face. Even if that meant smelling the drink from my father, too.

"She couldn't come," was all Ilse said. "She'll be here for Christmas though, if you invite her."

"Well apparently, it's not up to me, is it? That's why you're here," I said as we all crunched up the gravel driveway, careful not to tumble in our heels. "Angela does the inviting. I just have to take it."

"Don't be sarcastic. He'll never make you his wife if you act like a child."

"Maybe he will," Gretl said, not understanding the look of disgust that adorned both my own and my elder sister's faces.

"It's unladylike and exceedingly unattractive."

"So because you're on your second husband I have to listen to everything you say?"

"Don't start that with me, Eva. Does he know I'm here?"

"Who?" I asked, even though I knew fine well who she was referring to.

"You know fine well who I'm referring to, Eva. Does the Führer know?"

"He's not here just now. He's dashed off to Berlin. Again. I don't know why you're so scared of him. Marx is gone. I stood up for him too."

"Only on my word though, and he knows that. It's dangerous out there, Eva," she gripped my arm and her face looked pained, like she'd just stubbed her toe. "You don't see it up here. But the streets are scary.

Families go missing in the night. Businesses are sacked and looted at will. This isn't what he promised us."

"Give over, Ilse. Don't be so fretful. If you are scared I can have Himmler send over some S.S. men to keep you safe?"

"You don't understand. It's not about me feeling safe. Why should this be happening at all? These are good people."

The understanding dawned slowly across my mind, like a late morning in deep winter. I said nothing as I let what Ilse said run through the valleys and peaks of the inner workings of my brain and smelled the danger they brought with them. A fox fearing the hunt.

"Don't speak of this here. Not with me. Not ever, do you understand?"

"But, Eva…"

"Eva nothing. This is his Reich. These are the beginning of the Nazi regime. We are just Münich girls. We don't question them, ok? We don't."

"How can you be so obtuse? So frightened?"

"How can you not be?" I blurted before I controlled myself. "These are war times. Assurances must be made."

"Dr. Marx fled before the war."

"Don't you ever mention his name again. Understand? Never."

"Effie, stop shouting. Come on. Let's go up to your rooms. Just don't shout anymore ok, Effie?"

We traipsed up the simple stairs in sullen silence. There was no guard at my door today. I threw myself into the bath tub beside the pink tiles and curled my knees up to my breasts, staring out the window.

"So Angela is making moves against you?" Ilse said as she took the wooden chair by my vanity mirror.

"You make it sound like a game of chess. She's trying to get me kicked out. Worse, maybe. She wants me to act like a brat so that my Führer will leave me. She wants me gone, Ilse."

"Now, come on, don't cry," Ilse said as she left her chair and came to hug me in the waterless bath. Gretl was huffing as she brought through a chair from next door when she saw the one Ilse had just vacated and gave a sigh of exasperation. "Don't cry, Eva. He loves you. He does."

"You really think so?" I could still smell my mother on her clothes. The smell of honey and cinnamon in the hairs that tickled my face.

"I know so. I know so. How many years has it been now? Oh, twelve?"

"Since I met him, yes. We've been together for ten."

"A decade. You've been together a decade, since you were no more than a young girl, he knows you Eva. He knows you and loves you. Tantrums and all."

121

"But she's blood. She's his sister. She was the only one there for him when the art school in Vienna rejected him. The only family he had to come back to after the war. The mother of…"

"She's gone now. You don't need to worry about her anymore. You hear me? You don't need to worry about her. Angela is only acting like this out of fear. She's scared of you, Eva. Surely you can see that? She's scared that you've eclipsed her as the most important woman in his life. And she's right."

"She is?"

"Of course she is. Does the Führer take long walks with her to clear his head?"

I shook my head.

"Does he sit with her, side by side, and read his books with her?"

Another shake.

"Who is it, that when the stress of his war gets too much, he comes to, to unwind? To recuperate so he can go back stronger and stronger?"

"Me."

"So what if she invites Leni? So what? You just sit there and smile and know that it is you he is coming back to."

"No."

"No?"

"No. I won't just sit and take it." I looked her in the eyes. "I won't. You're right. I'm the most important woman in his life. It's about time that they all know that. That they all know I'm not just his mistress – I'm somebody."

"No, Eva, this isn't what I meant. Just smile and wear your dresses and get your hair done and enjoy the holidays he gives us. When the war is over, if he makes you his wife, then you can gloat over everyone else."

"That's all I want," I said to myself more than my sisters. The fire in my stomach was burning and I could feel its bile on my tongue. "And I'll never get it with her here. Never."

"So wait until…"

"No. I won't wait. I'm not waiting anymore. Angela has to go. I'm going to make him make her leave."

"Eva, don't be ridiculous. Please, sit down. Don't start something that will only end in disaster. Don't embarrass yourself any more."

"Any more? You think I'm embarrassing myself by being here? By letting him sneak me about like some silly girl? That I should be embarrassed because he says nothing to defend me when they laugh."

"He doesn't know about that, Effie," Gretl said.

"Well he will. I'm going to get rid of her."

"How, Eva? How are you possible going to do that?"

I stopped. How? How could I make him eject his sister from the closest thing he had to a home? How could I make him choose me over her, to rise me so much higher than anyone else had ever been?"

"The key. She has a key that she polishes in front of me every chance she gets. Magda mentioned it. Magda wants to know what's behind the door it opens."

"Magda? No, Eva. No, this is dangerous. If Magda has said she wants you to find out then it could only mean your end, not Angela's. They'll be working together."

"Gretl, what do you think?"

Gretl's head pivoted from sister to sister, deciding between which of us to choose and which of us to upset.

"I want to know what's behind the door."

Gretl ran back into my rooms with hair faced red and puffy.

"You've only gone for a walk," I said. "Why are you so out of breath?"

"I ran back. I've found it. I've found where the door is."

"So you've shown everyone in the Berghof what a terrible spy you are. Fabulous."

"Hush, Eva. Where is it?"

"Thank you, Ilse. It's on the second floor. Tucked away at the end of the corridor."

"The broom cupboard?" I asked.

"Broom? What? No. It's not a broom cupboard, Eva."

"It is. Wait. Gretl, why were you running?"

I wanted time to halt. The inexorable dripping of sand to pause indefinitely. My bones crackled with pain. My ribs thundered with the surge of fear that flooded my body. I was a thunderstorm then. A catastrophic cloud of approaching destruction. All she had to say were the words and I knew I would tear the Berghof apart.

"I saw Herr Hitler going in with her."

It had been a week. One whole week that Gretl and Ilse and I had all been trailing Angela, silently, invisibly, trying to see which door she would pull out her key for. I'd taken only the night watches because her eyes didn't do so well in poor lights and Hitler insisted that the corridors be only illuminated with lamps and not great chandeliers. We'd been patient. We'd been careful. It had seemed like a game. Like we were three sisters only, girls so very young, playing at a game of spies.

There was an orchard that our parents took us too when we were young. Far out into the Bavarian hills, its enormity was eclipsed only by its vibrancy. Thick brown trunks dug themselves deep into the soft, rich soil. I would trip over protruding roots as many times as I remembered they were there and jumped over them. Ilse laughed a lot. I got annoyed even more

that she would laugh but it made it only sweeter when she would miss a

slight raise in the ground and tumble over herself. Only Gretl never fell.

We'd each take turns to count to fourteen. The other girls, the

sisters not chosen to count, would then run out and hide. It was no simple

game of hide and seek. Hide and seek relied on the premise that no one

knows where you are hiding. Each of us knew where the others were

hiding. There wasn't a great deal of choice. We'd each hide behind a tree

and the other sister would have to guess which one. You could climb the

tree, which we only rarely did because it meant if you were seen, you were

caught. No. Hiding behind the trunk and slithering around its

circumference when you heard your sister's footsteps was infinitely more

fun. I'd watch as Ilse ran around a trunk she was convinced I'd concealed

myself behind and laugh as she tried to trick me by doubling back on

myself. All it took was a slight breath of wind to rustle a fallen leaf and she

would be hurtling around the apple tree for minutes on end, convinced I

was just out of sight.

"You know he knows about it." Ilse tried to calm me. "You know

he does. He knows everything."

"What could it be, Ilse? What could he be hiding from me?"

"It could be something political. Papers, maybe?"

"No. He keeps all of those in his office and doesn't try to hide them when I come in. He doesn't lock them away and give the key to her."

"Effie, please. We know where the room is now. Let's just stay calm and think what we will do now, yes?"

"You really think Magda knows what's behind that door? That she's only asked me to find out for her so that it can ruin me?"

Ilse nodded.

The floor fell away from beneath my feet. I tumbled through open air, only brief interludes of white, wisps of clouds breaking up the androgyny of dark, dark sky. My eyes watered as the air whipped them mercilessly. I tried to pull my arms in close around my chest but found it impossible because of the wind resistance. Or maybe it was just me? Maybe I didn't want to console myself. I certainly wasn't reaching for a parachute pull. I knew I didn't have one. I'd fallen from my room in the Berghof, not a plane. But still, wouldn't someone who wanted to stay alive have scrambled for one anyway? Wouldn't someone that had a family to go home to have tried to save themselves?

"He's lost to me," I said.

"Lost? No, Eva. No he's not. Why have you said this?" Ilse couldn't understand.

I hadn't fallen from the plane, I'd been pushed. The image of Geli, the faintest memory of her had sent me tumbling like a bomb on London.

"Leave me."

"What?"

"I said get out!" The mirror shattered into a hundred thousand glittering pieces. They rained onto the floor, tinkling like death knells of a church bell.

"We'll be just outside, Effie." Gretl pulled a reluctant Ilse. "Just at the bottom of the stairs. Tell us when you're settled."

I said nothing. Could say nothing. There was only one thing on my mind, only one thing I could think that would stop me from falling any further. I didn't want to fall anymore. I couldn't fall anymore, I wasn't strong enough. A few shards of glass were long and sharp enough but I knew I didn't want them. It wasn't right. Wasn't fitting. I floated like the ghost I was along the short corridor and into my bedroom. I went straight for the right-hand side pillow case. It could have been ten years ago. Everything was so similar, yet so different at the same time. I reached my arm inside the pillow case, the softness tickling, and felt for its dull weight. My fingers felt the cool metal and clasped around it. I wasn't falling now; I was taking control and drifting. I pulled the gun free of the pillow and felt its reassuring presence in my hand.

"Eva, I'm sorry, let's…what is that? Eva show me that."

I stood perfectly still. I didn't dare breathe. I just stood and moved my eyes from the gun to my sister. She fell to the floor. Her eyes rolled back in her head.

I saw her as she'd been that horrible night in München. I was slouched over his writing desk, my hands outstretched by his pens. I'd written him a letter, a short one truthfully, but it said all I had to say. As sleepiness took hold of the brain behind my eyes, my arm had moved so ungraciously that I'd knocked over the bottle of pills and I listened to them scatter across the table, tumbling to the floor.

"Ilse. Ilse."

She'd seen me like this. She'd seen me sprawled out across the desk, my tongue licking its hard wood. The panic she must have felt would have been similar to how I felt then, in that abominable moment when I saw her falling to the ground.

"Ilse. Ilse."

"Eva, don't. Please, not again."

"You're coming 'round, Ilse. Are you ok?"

"Ok? Eva. Why do you have a gun?" She was in my arms, my knees beneath her head, her hair curved out behind her. "I can't bear to go through it again. Eva, why do you have a gun?" She reached her hand out to my neck and traced the little scar that snaked there.

"It's not pills this time. I won't mess up now, Ilse. I won't. I promise."

"The pills? I knew you weren't trying to end it then, Eva. It was me," she sat up, her cheeks smeared with tears. "I found you the first time. It was me, Eva. It was me."

"Ilse, no…"

"Seeing you there. Seeing you on the floor, bleeding. There was so much blood, Eva. There was so much of it. I panicked like I've never… there was no one to help me. You were on the floor bleeding and there was no one to help me. Your neck – oh Eva, your beautiful neck – I thought it was all gone there was so much blood! I pounded on your chest. Over and over I pounded trying to keep you alive. But there was so much blood. I've never cried like that before. I was wild, Eva. Eva, you have to leave here." She gripped my hands. "You have to leave with me now. Come with me, Eva. Come with me away this place. From him. You can't love him. At least, this isn't normal love. You can't take your life for him. No man – not even the Führer – is worth your life, Eva. Come with me and I promise I will keep you safe."

"You found me? But…" It was all too much to process. I had thought it was one of Addie's men that had found me. That had seen me lying in my own blood, Addie's gun by my hand. My family knew, of course, they'd come to me in the hospital, but I was stitched up by then.

Myself. Just wounded on the inside. A small cut on my neck. I couldn't even do that right. "Ilse, I am sorry. Honest, I am. I was just so lonely then. I'm so lonely now. They laugh at me. I can't be seen and I am so lonely. Gretl stays with me but I am so very alone. The wives all hate me. The men all disrespect me and Angela…"

"So leave. Come with me. Eva, please. Do not do this to yourself again. I can't bear it again. I can't."

Gretl had walked into the room quietly as we spoke. Without uttering a word, herself, she wrapped her arms around us both and held us with tightly. We were three sisters then. Bonded in a way that I didn't understand. Couldn't understand. We didn't always like each other, nor did we always see eye to eye, but there was a primal energy between us that could not be explained by science. A thread of sisterhood that kept us forever linked.

"You don't deserve this, Eva. You have dreams. Hopes. You shouldn't have to pretend to be a silly girl anymore. It's killing you. Can't you see it's killing you?"

"I love him," I said weakly.

"And I love you. Gretl loves you. Mother and Baba, they both love you. Don't you love us? Don't you love us enough to stay with us?"

"I love him."

"Then give me the gun, Eva. Please. Give me the gun and I won't say a word of this to anyone. I can't make you leave Eva, but I won't let you kill yourself. And I won't watch you here. I won't watch you rot away to nothing. I can't bear it, Eva. I can't. Promise me. Right now, promise me that you'll never shoot yourself."

Her grief made her eyes glisten, but the fury – the passion behind them – dulled her tears to nothing. She held her hand out, her bottom lip quivering. She didn't let me look away.

"I promise I'll never shoot myself, Ilse. I promise."

I handed the gun over to her, a pang of relief and guilt together in my soul as it left my hand. Ilse squirreled it away in her coat and held me tightly to her chest. I knew then that there was a finality to this hug. That it meant something more than a simple goodbye. It meant a farewell for a while. A leave of absence from each other that only God knew the length of. So, I gripped my sister back. She was the wise one. The serious one. The one with anxiety for us instead of just herself. But she was also the argumentative one. The one that held a grudge far longer than the other. But then, that night as I sat huddled with my sisters, my best friends in the entire world, I learned that she was also the sister that could keep a secret longer than anyone else.

The sister that had saved my life.

I tried to not let it bother me. I tried to pretend that I wasn't furious with him.

"But what about what you promised me?" I demanded of him as he sipped his tea as if nothing had happened.

"Promised you?"

"That I could be like these girls in the movies. That I could become an actress. How will I ever get to Hollywood if you go and blow it up with some stupid Japs?"

"Eva, please, come sit with me. Don't be silly."

"Silly? Silly? You think I'm silly? I'm not the one that has decided to declare war on the United States of America. I am not the silly one in this room."

His face grew pale as if I had slit his throat and hung him by his testicle from the ceiling.

"That's not your place to say. Nor is it your place to admonish me."

"It is my place to fight for what you promised me!" I said. "You give me so little, Addie. So, little. But you promised me that I could play myself in the movie of our love when this was all over." I waved my hands, meaning the war. "And now you've gone and pissed off the people that could have made that happen."

"You can do that here. Germany will have film studios that far exceed Hollywood. Leni can film it."

"Leni. Oh god, Addie. Her? You think that's what I want to hear? Leni can film it? What about the Academy Awards? You know that's my dream. You know it is and you've still went and done it anyway."

"You don't care about politics or the war. You only need to focus on yourself. I promised you and I will keep that promise. I promise."

"Don't smile at me, my Führer. Don't you dare think a grin will stop me being angry at you. Just because I don't walk around this retreat like some back alley general, a face full of boiled sweets, doesn't mean I don't care about the war. Of course I care about the war. Of course I do. It's just not all I want to talk about all the time. I've given you so much, Addie, so very much, and all you do is take." *Shut up.* "Take, take and then take some more. America, Addie? America. You're taking my dream from me. You're trying to take it and I won't let you."

"There's nothing you can do," he said. He was right. It was a slap across the face.

"Please don't take this too, Addie. Not this. Please don't do it to me." I fell to my knees and crawled towards him. "Please don't take this from me too."

"They'll help us defeat the Bolsheviks. They'll invade from Siberia, divert Stalin's attention like the Russians and French did to us all those years ago. We'll crush the Bolsheviks before the Americans can even get a man aboard a ship bound for England. We won't kill a single American, Eva, they won't hate us. You can still have your dream."

The hope raised its head in my stomach, I couldn't stop it. "Do you promise, Addie? Promise you won't take the last thing I have left?"

"The last thing?" He lifted me from the floor and sat me in his lap. I curled against his chest, letting the smell of soap and sweat combine in my nose. "You have me, Eva. Even when that dream dies, you'll still have me. I'll be the last thing in this world that you have left. I promise you that."

She closed the door with such care that I thought she would weep as she heard the lock click into the doorframe. She rested her forehead against the grained wood and mouthed a good bye with her thin lips. Then she stood silent and still for a second, pulling herself away only when a single tear fell from her eye, rolling down the length of her cheek. She wiped it away with a quick flick of her fingers before walking down the hall towards where I was hiding. I ducked my head back into the sitting room and hid behind the door. I listened to her feet plod, plod, plod past me and prayed that she wouldn't decide to come in here, like her odorous nose could smell my fear.

I crept along the hall when I was sure she was gone. With footsteps just as careful as her own, I let my hand tickle the cold brass of the handle. A shock zipped along my finger tip, reaching the bone and making it shudder. Unperturbed, I placed my hand back on the handle and gave it a twist. The mechanism inside turned, but the bolt was slid too heavily into the doorframe and wouldn't open. I dared not jiggle it too much, a strange sense that whoever might be in there may hear me.

Was that really what I thought? Truly? That he and Angela had another woman locked up behind that door? It's true that I had no concept of the extent of the Berghof and a cavern of twisting rooms could be secluded behind Angela's lock. I'd walked around the retreat often enough, admiring the windows and wondering what they peered into. Perhaps she had been watching me, the girl locked into her rooms. Perhaps she had been watching me with envy that I was able to stroll around the gardens, while she was holed up inside. How long had she been there? Could it have been since Geli?

The next thought had my knees quivering under my own body weight. Geli had been dead for ten years, give or take a few months. Ten whole years. Plenty of time for a child to have grown. I pressed my ear against the door, desperately trying to hear even the softest sound inside. Two beats passed, my heart counting for me, when I heard a floorboard creak. My nails tore at the door. Deep grooves were gouged from its wooden flesh, new stains of deep maroon from my own fingers marring the paintwork. I clenched my teeth down on my tongue as I wildly scratched at the door, determined that whoever was in there would answer for their crimes against the love me and my Führer shared. But the door held steady. An accomplice under the employ of Angela.

"Eva, she's coming bac…Effie? Oh what happened to your hands, Effie?" Gretl said as she ran along the corridor. "Effie we have to leave. Now. She's coming back."

"I need to know. I need to know what's in there."

"Not now, Effie. Not now, not like this. You're a mess. You have blood up your cheeks, splinters in your hair and, oh, look at the door. Come on." She grabbed me by the wrist and tugged me down a servant's stairwell.

I heard Angela exclaim as she noticed the bloodied door. From the gloomy light of the stone steps, I thought it sounded more like a laugh than confusion. As if she'd known what I would do, how I would react. The conclusion I would come to.

"A daughter. A son, no. Not a son, please. Not an heir."

"Not here, Effie," Gretl said as she threw her watch at a gaping maid with a mop in her hand. We were in the kitchens, though I couldn't remember leaving the stairway. The maid had just stepped inside an open door where she'd thrown out a mop bucket full of dirty water, I could see it making streams along the gravel. She caught the watch deftly and gave a quick nod in agreement. She wouldn't whisper a word of this to anyone.

We darted across the long promenade hallway and were up the simple stairs before my guard returned to his post. I knew little of their schedules and was often as surprised as not when I saw them standing there.

"Effie, no, you've gone too far this time. You're a madwoman. An utter madwoman." She pulled me into the pink tiled bathroom and sat me by my new vanity mirror. I saw myself, but didn't recognize the woman staring back at me. Tears had torn great wounds in my cheek of pure black, as if the flesh beneath was rotted and evil. Red coated my lips and chin, residue on my wrists too, as if I had feasted on muscle and bone, slurping blood as I went. My fingers bled heavily, awkward shards of wood jutting out at strange angles from beneath my nails and along the length of my fingers. But it was my eyes that made me pause most of all. They were hateful. Not black, nor green, nor brown, nor blue. Simply hateful. They weren't the eyes of a woman at all.

"What if he has a child in there, Gretl? What if he does?" *I know exactly what I'll do.*

"A child? Oh, Eva, I don't know…" She backed away a few paces, her eyes wide and scared. "Eva, you need to pull yourself together. You do." She fell to her knees, the damp cloth dripping in her hands. She squeezed it tighter, spilling more water on the floor. "You need to pull yourself together. I can't handle this. I cannot, Eva. I cannot."

Gently, careful not to startle her, I lifted her from the floor and brought the washcloth to my cheek, still clutched in her hand. I moved the damp material in small circles, scrubbing away the makeup. "Easy, see," I said to her as her face began to recover its colour. "Just wash my face. Let's start there," I said, as my mind recovered its senses. "You got me here, that's the important thing, Gretl. You got me away from the door and back into my rooms. We're safe here. We're safe."

I poured her a mug of tea and put it in her hands. She hadn't moved in a while and as the side of my palm grazed her finger, I felt how cold she was. *Ice.* I went to the fire and threw in another log, prodding the flames so that they would devour the wood more violently. Still careful not to scare her, I sat as close to her as I dared and linked my arm with hers.

"Do you really think there's someone in there?" she asked.

"I don't know," I said. "But it felt like there was. It felt like there was something living in there. Stealing him away from me. Something that Magda and Angela make well sure to keep alive."

"I don't think it is, Eva. I don't. I think you need help."

"Please don't call me Eva. I'm your Effie."

"Are you though? Are you still? This relationship has…I don't know." She leant away from me. "Changed you. Are you still my Effie? Will you be when this is all over?"

"Of course I am. Of course I will," I said, feeling as if my fingers were slipping away from the cliff's edge, only the sea and the rocks beneath to greet me. "I need you, Gretl. I need you to stay with me. To stay by my side. I can't do this without you."

"I think you need help. You need to speak to someone. Can't you talk to Dr. Brandt? Can't he help you?"

"I don't need help, Gretl. I need support. I need love. I need you."

"No. You need him. You want me."

"When did you become so thoughtful? When did your eyes begin to see so much?"

"When my sister decided to put a gun to her heart and pull the trigger."

It was like she'd done it herself. Pulled the gun from the crook of her knee and fire its barrel into my chest.

"I'm sorry."

"No." She was crying now. "I'm sorry. I should have made you go with Peter. I should have made you leave with him. If you were with him now, you wouldn't be like this. You'd be happy, Effie. I know you would be. You'd be happy. I'd be an auntie. You'd be happy and healthy and unhurt."

"I'm fine," I said, trying to calm her so she wouldn't say his name again. It had been a long while since we'd first come into my rooms, long enough that we had both showered. There was no telling who was standing outside the door now. "Please, Gretl, I'm fine."

"Look at your hands, you stupid girl. Look at them." She tugged at the rough, loose fitting bandages she'd weaved around my fingers. The flesh was raw and exposed, already swelling and red. I had had thin, white fingers before this afternoon. Now I had blood stained claws. "Look at them. These are not the hands of someone who is fine."

"I lost myself for a second. Just a second. All I need to do is find out who is behind that door and I can go back to normal. Just help me find out."

"We don't even know it's a who, Effie. We don't."

"You're right. You're right, we don't. So let's find out. You and me. Let's find out and then put this all behind us, yeah?"

She bit her lip, so I kept quiet. I knew that meant she was thinking.

"You need to promise."

"Promise what?"

"That you won't let it get this bad again. Not ever again, Effie."

I'd never seen her so vulnerable, so open, so old looking. I'd aged her. My actions, my nervousness, my anger had all aged her older than she should have ever been. She was always supposed to be a naturally young woman, even when she was older. Her childlike innocence, the uncomplicated way she flirted with life, were all gifts she'd been given so she could endure the world with an ease denied the rest of us. Yet I had taken these from her. Over and over I'd taken them with tantrums and harsh words. Over and over she'd fought me to retain them, had battered

down any sense of dread with a strength she should never have known she

had. I did that. I took so much from her it made me sick.

"Ok, I promise."

"Then let's find out what's behind the door."

"When?" I asked as she stood to her feet.

"Now. Now, Effie. We find out now, tonight, so that tomorrow

can be a new day."

"But…"

"But nothing. You know she knows it was you. She's probably with

the Führer right now telling him. The fact he's not here yet is nothing short

of astounding. It's now, Effie. Now or never." She stood over me, her hand

outstretched. "Don't you want to know?"

I heard her voice before I saw her. I'd never heard such passion from her.

If truth be told, I knew a part of her had died the day her daughter died.

Hitler had taken too much from her, as I had done to Gretl. He'd taken too

much so that all Angela had left was spite and malice – two very subdued

emotions. Yet as we walked towards his office, the soldier outside my door

assuring me that's where she would be, I heard her roar like a wounded

lioness, terrified her captor would kill her there and then.

"It's sacred, brother. A sacred space. I've given so much up for you. Too much. You gave me this one space, this one in all the world, where I could be pure. This one space that she has torn at like a wild animal. What woman tries to claw down a door? What woman do you let slither into your bed?"

"Angela…"

"Angela, nothing," she silenced the Führer, which made me miss a step. "I have one room in all your world, Adolf. Only one. I expect her to leave. I expect you to send your whore away to München, Berlin, Tobruk for all I care. Send her where you please, Adolf, but I expect her to be gone before the sun comes up."

It's tonight then. Years of cat and mouse came down to a single evening. War had fallen on Europe but the battles in the Berghof had been happening long before Poland. The mother of the girl he loved versus the woman that took her place. *I thought I'd be more scared.*

"I'm not going anywhere," I said, pushing open the already ajar door. "What's in the room, Addie? Is it…" The words caught in my throat like a porcupine's spines.

"Now she barges in here, too? Is it not enough that she humiliates you in front of your generals? Now she must humiliate you here too?"

"I've humiliated no one, Frau Hammitzsch. No one, not ever. Addie, what's behind the door?"

143

"None of your business, whore."

"I'm not speaking to you, Angela. I'm speaking to my Führer. Addie?"

"Show her, Angela."

"What?" she stuttered. "What, Adolf, no! No, I won't. I won't let her in. I won't ever let her in."

"I deserve to know."

"Deserve?" she rounded on me with a fury reserved only for the gods. With quick feet and a manly gait, she was upon me in moments. "You deserve nothing but the bullet your tried to put into your heart. The bullet that Unity shot into herself. That's what you deserve. Nothing more. You deserve to know to – doesn't she, *Addie* – about the hundred red roses you sent Mitzi only a year ago. You think he loves you, you little shop girl? You mean nothing to him. Nothing. That's why you're hidden away, locked out of sight. That's why the glamourous women of Berlin are in the newspapers when you can't even listen to the radio. You're nothing but one in a line of stupid whores. One whose time should have been over in 1938. You're his war whore, nothing more."

"I lasted longer than Geli."

The slap was as sudden as it was brutal. I stumbled in front of her before falling onto the hard wood of the floor.

"Show her, Angela," was all he said as he sat behind his large desk.

"No, Adolf, I won't…"

"Don't make me force you," the Führer said.

She lit a cigarette as she led me silently down the cavernous halls of the Berghof. She waddled as she walked, the pain in her left hip a nuisance that was exacerbated by stress. She'd told me this once, one night when we'd gotten drunk together long ago. She hated me then, too, but she was drunk and I was there. The moon invaded the halls as if it were curling in the air like smoke. My throat was tight and dry, each swallow harder than the last. As we reached the door her hand hovered by the lock, the key tightly ensconced in her grip.

"You don't deserve to go in here," was all she said as she twisted the key and pushed open the heavy door.

It stunk of incense and the thick aroma of overly scented candles. Musty, like a window hadn't been opened inside for quite some time. The room was heavy with her. It smothered me as I stepped over the threshold. I had seen her before, of course, in the papers of my youth. Little Geli, the sweet, innocent girl that liked the opera and dreamt of Germany. It had made me sick with jealousy to see her then. And, to my shame, it had been her picture, cut out and carefully hidden beneath my modest jewel box, that I had looked at as I had fired off the bullet I'd hoped would end my life.

She was the spectre at my back, always and forever, the girl I modelled myself after but could never fathom enough compassion to mourn. She was weak. A pathetic girl from pathetic stock and, if truth be told, the only reason I didn't accidentally allow myself to become pregnant with my Führer's child – for fear it would be anything like the weak little Geli.

Her picture hung from the wall on the left of the door. As large and as intricate as the grand portrait of Frederick the Great. She hung, an angel in moonlight, watching me. The moonlight didn't invade here, but instead it prayed in this shine to the dead Raubal, prayed and honoured her memory as if she were a saint and I nothing more than a common harlot. Angela had fallen to her knees the minute she'd opened the bloody door, I turned to look at her shudder under her own grief as if by opening the door to me, she'd let the spirit of Geli leave this place and move on.

Good riddance.

It was sickening. I couldn't see the rest of the room for gawking at the portrait. She was smiling. Her fat little cheeks shiny and beautiful, round and full of vigour. I, who starved myself at every meal to keep trim and lithe could only snarl at the podgy little thing that grinned at her own buffoonery. And oh, how she smiled! With rows of pretty white teeth, her lips full but just a shade too thin to be looked at as wanton, she was a model girl. Pigtails of platted hair fell down her enormous face. She was the epitome of innocence and purity, or so she looked in the picture. This is how they remembered her. Smiling. Her hair clean of blood. Her face not yet shattered by a bullet. They would sit – Addie and Angela – and stare at her, I guessed. Each of them basking in their own nostalgia and each other's pain at what they'd lost and created together.

"He killed her," I said.

"No, no, no, no."

"Stop wailing, you stupid beast. He killed her and you know it."

"She was sick. She was ill."

"She was trapped. A caged girl and you sold her."

"No. No. No," Angela wailed louder. "It was you. You killed her. He loved her. He loved her until you. She loved him and then she found your letter." She clutched at the door handle, only half able to pull herself from the floor. Her teeth were yellow and rotten, her voice a ghastly howl of grief.

"My letter?" I smiled as I turned to Angela, who looked up at me only to see the moon sparkle off my teeth. "My letter killed your girl?"

"She found it" She could barely speak, the anguish choking her like chains around her neck. "She told me. She found it and she couldn't bear to lose him."

"She was his niece. You are his sister. You let him fuck her. You let her be touched by a man who should have loved her with purity, not lust."

She stopped crying. Her fingers fell from the door handle, throwing her body to the ground like a mother casting off her son. She tucked her knees into her stomach and rocked back and forth.

"You killed her. And he killed her with whatever monstrous appetites he had then. You know the ones I mean, don't you, Frau Hammitzsch?"

She said nothing.

"Do you remember what you said to me, that first night I came up here to the Berghof? Do you remember what you said as I sipped my wine and the sun fell down across the mountains? You said that you'd have me thrown off this mountain, one way or the other. You remember, don't you? You promised me that he'd either abandon me or you'd kill me to keep him single and alone, so that you could both come here in peace and miss little Geli together."

"He comes here all the time. He does." Anger animated her, spite invigorating her words. "He comes here and he cries. He misses her. He *loves* her. How could he ever love you when she was so perfect?"

"Oh, I have no doubt he visits this pathetic little shrine. I have no doubts at all he cries over his lost niece. But it's me he sticks his cock into. It's me that takes him in my mouth and pleasures him until he moans. It's me he walks with along the mountain trails. And it's me he watches American movies with before he takes his nap. Not Geli. Not your precious little bitch. Me. You're done, Angela. You know that, don't you? You and Magda and whoever else parades around here – my home – acting like I mean nothing. You're done. This is my domain now. This is my castle. You're done." She tried to clutch at my ankle as I walked from the room. I kicked her off, my heel making contact with her nose. The crunch was sickening but I didn't stop. As I walked away from Geli's room I imagined Angela's blood pooling at the bottom of the door, drop for drop what I left in the deep grooves I'd gouged out.

I knew he wouldn't come to me. And nor did I want him too. I needed to be alone, to let the feelings of revulsion and shame mix inside myself, each one vying for dominance. Gretl had made herself scarce and I appreciated that. I appreciated her wit at knowing that this was not a time for sisterly comfort – that would come – this was between me and my Führer. Us alone.

Did he think of her while he was inside me? While we walked from the Berghof up to that monstrosity they called the Eagle's Nest? Did he imagine it was her hand he was holding? That it was her singing songs to him? I wretched, green bile splashing onto the toilet seat. I wiped my mouth with my bare arm and huddled against the wall. It was over. How could it be anything other than over? He loved another. And I loved only him. I still had the gun, somewhere. She'd hidden it, but wasn't so brave that she'd take it from my rooms. I could find it if I thought like Ilse. I

could find the gun and then my heart wouldn't ache anymore. My soul

wouldn't scream as it was torn apart, strip by strip. I could finally close my

eyes and give into the darkness. Let it take me and swaddle me in its

nothingness, keeping me safe from the desperation that would come from

no longer being with him.

And yet – I didn't want to die.

It felt strange to think it, absurd even. *I don't want to die*. What a

peculiar thought? What an utterly ridiculous thing to think. Want. To. I.

Don't. Die. It didn't make sense. I'd only tried to kill myself once. Just that

one time with the gun. The sleeping pills had been something more

dastardly, a ploy to force his hand. I hadn't taken enough to die, not really.

It was a ploy. But the first time, I had truly wanted to no longer exist. I had

genuinely wanted to no longer be Eva, but an angel somewhere in heaven.

Not this time though. No. *I don't want to die*. Fuck little Geli Raubal. Fuck

her little shrine in my home. And fuck her mother scurrying round at my

skirt hem, causing trouble like a poisonous mouse. If she wasn't with him, if

I could pry them apart, I knew the last relic of Geli would die too. She

wasn't stronger than me. Not in life, nor in death. She had no special claim

to his heart. She was nothing but a dead girl he felt guilty about. A guilt that

Angela kept alive and fresh at every opportunity.

It clicked then, as I rested my head against the cool porcelain. I wasn't battling Geli's ghost; I was battling her mother. Magda had been nothing but a red herring. A feign to keep me from focusing on the true enemy. She hated me, Frau Goebbels, but she knew she had no power over me. She was First Lady of the Reich when Hitler was in public, when my Führer needed a mistress of ceremonies. But I, yes I, was always Queen of the Berg. I just didn't see it before.

I stood up and looked into the vanity mirror. Tangles of dirty blonde hair jutted out like a dead spider's legs. My makeup was terrible, simply awful and not fit for public consumption. My dress was stained in vomit and my fingers were crooked and scaled with dried blood. My eyes still retained their hate, that blackness that had taken over. I was a monster.

Good. He's scared of monsters.

Again there was no guard at my door. I ran across the Berg, not caring who I scared or startled, unperturbed by Dr. Morell's horrified gasp and subsequent proclamation that I stop embarrassing myself at once. I saw Herta, sitting by an open fire in the sitting room. She was reading and looked up with her spectacles half way down her nose when I galloped past. She may have called my name, she may not have, I didn't really hear.

The mania that had swept me from one side of the Berg to the other dissipated into pure calm as I reached his office door. I didn't knock. I simply pushed on the wood and let the door swing open.

151

She was there, of course. Her face as wild as my own, her make up as dastardly as my own – though, it must be said, she wore far too little for me to have known she wore it at all until this point – and she was no longer crying. No longer rocking back and forth weeping for her dead daughter. She had come for the same reason I had. She wanted to know that this was her home above all else.

"My Führer," I said. An uncharacteristic brandy was sat by his trembling hand. It was so pale that I knew he'd had to have watered it down. His cheeks were covered in a day's worth of stubble. His eyes bloodshot and his sleeves rolled up around his biceps. His head was low on the desk, as if the weight of war was a chain around his neck. "What have you done?"

"Done?" He was thrown by my question.

"To me. To us."

"I've done nothing," he stuttered, his tongue catching on his lip.

"Oh but you have, my Führer. You've hurt me most grievously."

"Adolf, please, send her away. She knows now. She knows where your heart lies now. She doesn't need to be here anymore. You no longer have to pretend."

"Is that what you've been doing, my Führer? Pretending all these years? You've played some cruel games, I know." His cheeks burned red.

"But was it all pretense? Are you the actor? Not me? Have you played the role of the lover for ten years and not meant a single word?"

"Send her away, Adolf. Send her far away. Send her to Poland, to the camps. Any camp, Adolf. She knows too much. She's a wicked woman, not like our Geli, she cannot be trusted. Send her away."

"To the camps, my Führer? What camps are these?"

"Do it, Adolf. Do it, please, for me."

"Do you still love her?" I asked, a thunderbolt across the room.

"I…"

"Of course you do, Adolf. Of course you do."

"Do you? If you do, then I will leave at once. I won't ever be a consolation prize. I haven't fought for ten years to simply have second place. I am no one's silver medal, my Führer. Not even yours."

He said nothing. Could say nothing. His eyes switched from my own to Angela's over and over. I knew she'd be pleading. I could hear the way her dry lips smacked off one another as she moved them fervently in a silent prayer to him. I kept my face stony, unmoving. I wouldn't trick him. He could either choose me, or have me banished. I almost cracked then, at the thought of him sending me away. The bravado of the bathroom was dried up, used up, depleted beyond salvation. The terror grew like a burgeoning storm in my gut, a potent swirling of a petulant desire to destroy. *He could send me away. Oh God, what if he sends me away? Where will I go? What will I do?*

"She can't stay here anymore, Addie," I made his mind up for him. "This nonsense ends tonight. Do you hear me? I may not be your wife, but I have been a loving woman since the moment I met you. I won't let you do this to me. To us. She cannot stay here, Addie."

"I am his sister!" Angela slammed her hand down on his desk, spilling a pot of pencils that rolled onto the floor. Tick. Tick. Tick.

"Half," I smiled, knowing that would be the last time I ever corrected her. "Geli can't stay here anymore, Addie. She has to go. You have to let her go."

1942

July, *The Italian Riviera*

"Mother, please just enjoy the sunshine. Please."

"He might choke."

"Choke? Chance would be a fine thing." Her hand came swiftly down on the back of my head.

"He's your father, don't speak about him like that."

"Sorry, Mother. Gretl, would you get us some more cigarettes from inside?"

"No, Gretl," my mother snapped. "Tell her highness over there to get them herself. It's your holiday too."

Gretl shrugged, trying – and failing – to hide the smug grin on her face.

"Fine. Fine." I stood up, enjoying the feeling of my muscles being stretched. "Would anyone else like anything?" They all shook their heads.

Inside was cool and pleasant. The sun was very hot for that time of year, and bright too. It took my eyes a moment to readjust to the shade inside. I waited by the curtains as slowly the room came into view. The cigarettes were tucked in a drawer in the bathroom. Why my mother insisted that that's where they should be, I didn't know. I lit one up while watching myself in the mirror, proud at the growing tan that coloured my skin.

"I need to pee," Gretl said with her skirt halfway down her thighs as she walked in.

"It's lovely here, isn't it?"

"Beautiful," she said, mid-flatulence. "Though, I do prefer the Berghof."

"Slut," I laughed.

"True." She wiped. "But I do like the mountain. There's something about here. I don't know."

"What? Tell me, Gretl?"

"Something just doesn't feel safe. Ignore me. What would I know?"

"How are things at the Berghof, darling?" Mother asked as I came back out into the sun holding Gretl's hand.

"Better," I said. "Better, but..."

"But?"

"Still strange. They hate me. That won't ever change. But now they hide their enmity behind smiles. It's unnerving. They used to not look at me at all, or when they did, they'd laugh. Now they just follow me silently, large grins on their face."

"Except Magda," Gretl said.

"Oh yes, except for her."

"She still laughs?" My mother couldn't believe it.

"Not quite. It's like she sees me as a different person now. One that shouldn't be laughed at."

"You got the Führer's sister thrown out, cast down from the Berghof. Of course she sees you in a new light. You're an equal now. She's finally realized it."

It didn't seem worth correcting my mother with a spiteful, 'half.'

"Enough talk of the Berghof. We're on holiday. Let's enjoy ourselves. Mussolini has sent over a cask of very fine wine." We all looked to my slumbering father as I said it. "And he has invited us down to some medieval town if we wish."

"He'll be there?" Gretl breathed.

"No, of course not. There's a war on. But he said they'll make fine hosts of us."

"He knows who you are?" my mother asked.

"Enough. He knows enough, has done for some time I feel. Remember the deerskin coat he sent? He calls me a 'fine German actress' but he knows more. Surely."

"That's a wondrous thing, Eva. To have a leader of Europe know your name."

"Mother, she's been stooping with the Führer for years now. A European leader already knew her name."

"I don't appreciate that smut mouth, Gretl. I don't. Don't forget I'm your mother. Have some respect."

"Sorry."

"As you should be. So, Eva, is he any closer to marriage? Tell me how your plans have gone?"

"Plans?"

"Don't act coy with me, darling. I raised you. Tell me, is he any closer?"

"You want me to marry him?"

"I want you to be happy." She shifted uncomfortably in her seat. "And I want God to be happy. You're living in sin. A marriage would go a long way to solving that."

"They don't even share a bed, mother," Gretl laughed.

"A minute ago they were stooping and now they don't share a bed?" My mother laughed too. "I shouldn't have to hear such things."

"I've just got rid of Angela. He's...uneasy now. And the war. It's...I don't know, Mother. I don't have any plans."

"Mhmm, well, keep comforting yourself with that. But I know you Eva. I know you better than you know yourself and you won't be happy until there's a ring on your finger."

"Of course I won't be. Of course not. But I need to wait until the war is over. How many times must I tell you? How many? I don't need to keep being reminded of my failure."

"Peace, darling. Be at peace. I didn't mean to upset you." She saddled over from her chair to my own and pushed me up with her rear so we could share it. She placed her arm around me and held me close. So close that I could smell the spearmint on her breath. "I know you've told me you have to wait until the war is over. I know that, sweetheart. But every time I see you, I feel like you've lost another piece of yourself. You're harder. Less you. I worry about the strain of the unknown on you. On how much more you can tolerate. You're a young girl, Eva. A beautiful and talented young woman. You could have your pick of the men. A nice soldier. A business man." Gretl and I made eye contact briefly. "Anyone you want. You could have a simpler life."

"An ordinary life?"

"Exactly," she said as if I agreed with her.

"I love him though, Mother. I do. I truly do. And he loves me. It's just this war. Once it's all over he can marry me. He *will* marry me. I promise, Mother. I promise I will become Eva Hitler before long. Just you wait and see."

"Promise you'll invite me?" Tears glistened in her eyes.

"Invite you? Mother, why would you think I would have to promise that? Of course I'll invite you. Come here. Of course I'll invite you."

"Someone said something about wine?" Baba said as his eyes opened and he wiped the drool from his face.

Days passed in a blur of sightseeing and sun lounging. Dinners were made by fabulous Italian chefs and gifts of gorgeous gloves and expensive diamonds were left in stores around the towns we visited, my Führer making sure I had an excellent time. We were sitting on the roof of the hotel, converted into a humble garden for the duration of our stay, when my father sat by my side and, for once, didn't wobble.

"Thank you for this trip, Eva," he said, while looking out across the water.

"It's no problem."

"Yes. So. How is life at the Berghof?"

"Mother already asked me this."

"Now I am too. Don't get smart, young lady."

"Sorry, Baba." It had been so long since he had admonished me that I felt a strong swell of my girlhood rise up in my chest. "It's tough now."

"But…"

"Angela, yes. I have physical control, but not emotional. I no longer need to worry about being tossed out of the Berg, but that doesn't mean he loves me anymore."

"I hear he's – and I don't want to upset you. God alone knows how much trouble I'd get into for repeating it – but I hear he's not very well."

"Not well? His tremor?"

"More than that."

"Oh. Dr. Morell."

"Yes."

"He treats him like a pin cushion. I call him the Führer's seamstress. Every meal he seems to be injecting another cocktail of goodness knows what into my Führer's veins. Every meal."

"What about Dr. Brandt?"

"He's my chosen favourite, yes. But he only comes to the Berg when the Morells aren't in residence, so he has to spend all his time with my Führer convincing him that Dr. Morell is a madman. Then, when Morell comes back, he does the same for Brandt. Over and over they go. Covering and retreating along the same ground. All the while..."

"...the Führer gets sicker."

"Not sicker, per se. But weaker. More...I don't want to talk about this."

I didn't. Not for a second. He'd lured me in with his fatherly words and I had lowered my guard to him. I shouldn't have spoken to a drunk about Addie's health. Not for a second. Those weeks after Angela left were cold and hard. His mind left him for a moment. Sometimes two. We would be walking, or reading or watching a film and he would launch himself forward and begin a tirade against the evil his family placed upon him. The brutality of his father. The weakness of Geli. The trickiness of Angela. Only his mother was left a saint in his head and I worried, as he ranted, that he could see her there, in the room with us as he yelled. He retreated into his own head, buried his feelings under maps and charts of Russia and America. He'd move little metal men along maps with large, broad strokes and his generals would have to pull them back. Where he'd moved them a hundred miles, they'd move them back ninety nine, each time having to re-explain the situation on the ground. I watched him. Quietly from the window, I'd watch him and his generals argue and I'd shudder at what they'd do to him when they'd had enough.

"I don't know enough about it."

"But you don't like what Morell is doing?"

"I don't trust it."

"Trust your gut, Eva. Trust what you can see. Is he getting better?"

"No."

"Then it's not working. Morell isn't working."

"And what am I supposed to do? I've given him another option. He prefers Morell."

"You got rid of Angela."

"That was a trick. A dirty trick heaped with luck. We both know it."

"Maybe. Maybe not. Are the men nice to you?"

"What men?"

"Himmler? Speer? Göring?"

"Yes, Baba. As nice as they can be. They used to laugh, sometimes. I think they think I'm a little girl. But they like me well enough. It's easy to send the Führer to me when they grow tired of his talks. It's not their fault, not really. All they do is hear him speak."

"And they treat you with respect?" he asked, seriously.

"Of course. Addie often makes them bring me letters. Like they're little postmen. I don't think they like that well enough. Though, maybe some of them do. They like to be trusted. Even when he's not himself he's still the Führer."

"Eva," my mother called from downstairs. "Eva, come down here please."

"You come up, Mother. You come here. I'm not ready to come in yet."

"Eva, there's a man here who would like to speak with you."

I dashed across the roof and hurtled down the stairs expecting to see a man in a German uniform with a letter addressed to me. *Maybe he's planned a day out for us all! Or even a few days out on a boat! Imagine he'd sent a great warship for us all to sail on!*

"Fraulein Braun?" the man said severely as my eyes, again, adjusted to coming in doors.

He wasn't smiling and I doubt he'd smiled in years. He was older, his head spattered with threads of grey wire coiling amongst the black brick of his hair. He had a large scar descending from his left green eye. It trailed like a tree trunk down beneath his chin where it disappeared around his jawline.

"Who are you?"

"Fraulein Braun?" he asked again.

"Tell me who you are. Who are you?"

"I am Captain Hershetz of the Einsatzgruppen division in Greece. Are you Fraulein Braun?"

"I am. You're one of Himmler's men, aren't you? Or did Heydrich send you?" I reached behind myself to the small set of drawers that were only a pace or so at my back. My fingers scrabbled for the pair of scissors I had left there the previous evening when I had trimmed Gretl's fringe.

"I was sent here by the Führer himself."

"My Führer?" The world fell away as the words left my mouth.

"No. He's not injured, is he? He's ok? Tell me," I brought the scissors around and gripped them in my sweaty hands. I pointed them towards Hershetz as the clicking of ten gun barrels rattled around the room. Hershetz didn't even flinch.

"There will be no need for that. Put them down, Fraulein."

"Do as he says, Effie."

"No. Not until you tell me."

"The Führer is fine. He is well. He just wants you to come home. At once."

"Home?" I didn't understand.

"You must be mistaken, lad," my father said as he came down the stairs. "We have another week of our holiday left."

"Not anymore, Herr Braun. The Führer asks that you come back to Germany at once."

"But, why…"

"Fritz, no. Of course, Captain Hershetz. We will pack at once," my mother cut through us all and said with authority. "Pack your things, girls. These nice men are here to escort as home."

"The war?" I couldn't believe it.

The train zipped through valleys of beautiful countryside. Sprawling green fields lay draped like velvet over soft rolling curves of the woman that was Italy beneath. The red cushion of the train seat was comfortable but still I couldn't find any ease. Soldiers marched up and down the aisle of the train over and over. Their boots clunked against the wooden floor of the carriage and I shivered at the thought of them marching into my home and stealing me away.

"How can this happen, Effie? How? What does it mean?"

"I don't know. He never told me this."

"What does the letter say?"

"Just that I have to come home. We have to return to Germany because of the war."

"But…our holiday."

"Excuse me, Fraulein Braun, may I sit with you?" Hershetz pointed to the empty seat in front of me. I nodded yes. "I'm sorry we scared you like that. We needed you out of the country at once. There was no time to delay."

"Were we in danger? Real danger?" Gretl asked.

"There's no way to tell for sure, Fraulein. But the British are mobilizing in Africa. We can't take any chances."

"Surely Mussolini can keep his country safe? Surely, we would have been quite secure, Captain?"

"We couldn't guarantee it, Frau Braun. Plus, the Italians are a long way from their cousins, the Romans."

"Is this the only letter I was to be given, Captain?"

"Yes, Fraulein. Should there be more?"

"It just…it just doesn't give a lot of information. That's all."

I should have considered myself lucky. I knew I should. There, in black and white, was a declaration of his love for me. A tender, if solemn, poem just after the words that bade me to follow the Captain out of harm's way.

"You've been very quiet, Captain," I said after we had crossed over into the German border. "For a long time."

"This isn't what I thought I'd be doing today. Sorry if I have seemed off with you. Please take no offence." I smiled at the way he squirmed a little in his reassurance that his silence was not my fault.

"Where have you been, Captain? In the war. Where have you been?"

"All over, Fraulein."

"Please, call me Eva."

"Eva." He smiled, or at least, the corners of his mouth curled a little in what I took to be a smile. But could equally have been nothing more than a muscle spasm. "I've been from Paris all the way to the borders of Russia. From Athens to Oslo."

"All over, indeed. Tell me: what's it like now? Europe. I haven't seen much, not like you anyway. But I've seen a few places. What are they like now?"

"You wouldn't want to know."

"I would. That's why I'm asking." He studied me as if he could smell the ulterior motive in the room with him. As if my forehead was glowing green with desire, a sign in the dark of what lay beneath my hair.

"I don't think the Führer would want you to know."

"He wouldn't?" I was genuinely shocked. He could see it. He laughed. "Why not?"

"Very violent. Very brutal."

"It can't be brutal *everywhere*. Surely?"

"Do you know what the Einsatzgruppen is, Eva? What we are designed to do?"

I shook my head. "You're soldiers, aren't you? You fight. Conquer. All that jazz."

"All that jazz," he rolled his eyes. "We aren't the Wehrmacht."

"Neither is the Navy or the Luftwaffe but they all do the same thing. Just with different machines."

"That's a very odd way to put it."

"I prefer unique, Captain." I shot him a smile from beneath my eyelashes.

"No. We don't conquer. We clean up."

I looked to my sister, Gretl, who was curled up on my mother's lap. There were perfectly lovely beds only a carriage further up but since I had refused to leave, refused to sleep, they had stayed with me to show solidarity. Though they couldn't refute sleep as I could. My father had scarpered off to the sleeping carriage as soon as he'd heard of it.

"Oh. I see."

"You do?" He raised his eyebrow above the unscarred eye.

"Yes." He looked too manly to be carrying a broom or pushing a wheelbarrow. Not that those activities were not manly, but this man had the look of a killer – not a cleaner. "You locked us in when we got on board. Why did you do that?"

"There are a great many horrors out there. We must keep you safe."

"You must? Horrors? In the Reich?"

"Everywhere, Eva. There are horrors everywhere in this new world. Even some in this carriage."

"You definitely smiled that time, Captain."

"I did no such thing." He scowled at me.

"You did. Indeed, you did. I saw you."

"Please, call me Hershetz."

July, *The Berghof*

"I don't like that we had to come home early, Effie. I don't. I was enjoying the freedom to walk around unjudged. We become too accustomed to the boredom here. We forget what it's like to be young and carefree. It's such a serious place to be."

"It's home, Gretl. Be more grateful. You're part of a modern day court. Not since the Tsars of Russia has there been a court as concentrated or as beautiful as this one."

"How would you know? Do they talk of such things in your magazines?" I threw a pillow at her, which she ducked from just in time. "Lousy shot. But it is terrible, isn't it, Effie? That we had to come home early."

I hated to agree with her. It felt disrespectful, like my Führer's concern meant nothing to me. But in my heart I felt it was all much ado about nothing. It was Italy for the good Lord's sake. How much danger could we have been in?

"It doesn't matter now. Herta and Annie said they would both come down to the lake with us tomorrow," I said.

"Annie's here? But I just saw Dr. Morell at dinner. Why would she come here knowing that he and that toad of a wife of his would be here?"

"She wanted to see us. Both of us. She's missed us."

"Oh la di da, the Braun sisters, missed? Haven't we risen in the world, Effie. Haven't we just?"

"That's cheered you up. But, please, don't mention anything about Dr. Morell tomorrow. It will only upset her. You know what he says about her husband."

"I know what you say about him," she said.

"Dr. Brandt?"

"Morell. The Führer does take a great deal more medicines when he's around."

"He can get sick like the rest of us. He's still a man. Nothing more, nothing less."

"Yes, we can all get sick. But we don't need an injection of potion to go for a poop now do we?"

"Gretl!"

"Oh come on. You know it's true."

"I don't like to think of my lover's toilet habits, thank you."

"What if Morell keeps him sick?"

The hand mirror fell from my fingers. It bounced on the bed. Once. Twice.

"What did you say?"

"I don't know. What did I say? Poop?" she laughed.

"No. About Morell?"

"Oh no. What have I said now? Ignore me, Effie. You know I talk nonsense sometimes."

As I brushed my teeth, I let the thought wallow in my skull. It festered, a rotting skin of scum that gathered on the top of my consciousness. I felt as if I had been given a peek into Pandora's box and had to keep silent about what I saw. Even if I had told Pandora, I knew she wouldn't believe me. Any girl would wish to have the box as she did. She'd think I was lying so that she wouldn't open it. So I could steal the mystery inside.

I was on the death train again. The single track beneath its wheel clack, clack, clacked along as moon light tried to pry its way through the ill-hammered slats. They weren't loose, I couldn't pry them open, but gaps lingered between them so they looked like the bars of a prison cell. The baby was crying again. Always crying. It drew blood inside my chest, each wail a scratch of a knife down my throat and into my stomach. Each wail made me more and more furious. We all wanted to cry. I didn't know the people I was herded in with, but I could feel their misery, their despondency on me like a cloak. The baby wailed again and I lifted my hand to my cheek and drew my nails down the soft flesh. Each time the baby cried I did it over and over again until blood was dripping down each finger. A man with a horribly crusty beard loomed out of the tight darkness.

He had no teeth which I could see because of how he was grinning. His eyes were pale blue but there was no clear definition where his irises ended and the white of his eyes began.

"So humpty," he said.

"Excuse me?"

He nodded to my fingers.

"Throw dumplings."

"I don't understand."

I tried to back away but the carriage was too tightly packed. A faceless knee jarred into my back and kept me close to the wild looking man.

"So hungry!" he said as he lurched forward and lapped his sore-ridden tongue up and down the blood on my fingers.

The baby wailed again.

"Stop it, Blondi. Stop it." I woke to see his stupid mutt in my room. Its tail wagging, adorably cute face grinning at me like it could make me love it with a stupid smile. "Go away, you ugly dog. Get out of here. Where are Stasi and Negus? Stasi! Negus!"

"Gretl has taken them out for a walk. Blondi, here." The dog immediately turned and ran towards her master, sitting at his feet obediently. "Good morning."

"Yes. Good morning. You're up early."

"I haven't slept yet. My meetings ran late. Himmler wants…let's not talk about that. What were you dreaming about?"

"Dreaming about? Nothing? Why?"

"You're sweating. And you were mumbling."

The old man's face peered out of the darkness, but quickly subsided as the fading dream pulled him back to whatever hell he'd came from.

"I don't remember. Is that breakfast? For me?"

"Unless you want to give it to the dog? Would you like that, girl? Would you like a delicious home cooked breakfast?"

"Don't speak to it like that."

"You talk to Stasi and Negus like that," he answered back as he rubbed his dog's ears.

"Yes, but…it's different."

"I'm baaacckk. Oh. My Führer," Gretl gave a little curtsey. "What an honour."

"You're cheeky, Gretl. You're the cheeky Braun girl."

"And Eva is the beautiful one," she said back easily, as if she were a true courtier and not a dimwitted girl looking for a smile.

"Get Blondi out. Not while Stasi and Negus are here."

"Oh, Eva, she's only a dog."

"Yes, but look." I pointed to Stasi who was trying to scramble under the bed away from the larger dog. "She has to go."

"Blondi. Out!" he said and at once, of course, the dog left.

"Happy?"

"Immeasurably so."

"Would you walk with me? After your breakfast?"

"We're going to the lake, Führer," Gretl said cheerfully.

"Oh," his face drooped. "Very well then."

"No. Of course I'll come for a walk. Of course I will."

"No. If you've made plans it's fine. Find me after, ok? After you've been to the lake, come and find me."

"Is everything ok, my Führer?" I swung my legs from the bed as he rubbed the crook of his arm.

"Yes, yes. Just find me after," he said as he left.

"Why did you say that?" I said to her after he'd left.

"Because we are, Effie."

"But he wanted to spend the day with me."

"To be truthful, I did think he would come along."

"To the lake? You know he won't show his body to anyone."

"He could keep his jacket on."

"Oh yes, so he could. While soldiers are diving into the water with their six packs out, old daddy Führer can sit on the banks, sweating, and trying not to feel like a sore thumb."

"I never said he had to hurt his thumb," she protested.

"Out, Gretl. Just get out and leave me with my dogs."

"How was Italy?" Annie asked as we stepped out of the long black Mercedes that had driven us to the lake.

"Oh now you ask. I've just spent from the Berg to here listening to you prattle on and now you want to hear how my holiday was?"

"What creamed in her crackers?" Annie laughed to Gretl as they took the towels from the driver unloading them from the car's boot.

"I stopped her having a walk with the Führer."

"A walk? Oh, Eva, you really need to cheer up. Tell me, please, how was Italy?"

"Fine. Until it wasn't."

"Yes, I heard about this," she said as she clasped my hand and we walked over the soft grass barefoot towards the lake's shore. "It must have been dreadfully frightening. And you had to come by train, I hear. He was scared to let you fly?"

"Enough, Annie," Herta interjected. "Stop fishing for gossip like some bored housewife."

176

"But I am. That's exactly it. I am a bored housewife. Why do you think I voluntarily came all the way up this mountain just to sit and have dinner with that quack and his toad wife?"

"That's what I called her!" Gretl said.

"She's not a toad. Don't be cruel," Herta said.

"Oh, Herta. Lighten up. You know she said you wear no make-up," Annie laughed.

"I *don't* wear make-up. And neither should any of you. It's un-Aryan."

"Un-Aryan schmaryan. Cheer up, Herta. It's a beautiful day and we're at the lake. What could be more exciting?"

"We're at war, Annie. Eva has just had to be smuggled over the German border on a train because the Luftwaffe can't keep the skies safe. Don't you understand this? We're at war."

"Don't, Herta. Stop it. You're making it sound all the more terrible than it was. We just had to come home early, that's all. And I like the train."

"You've just tasted your first consequence of the war, Eva. It's understandable you don't want to face it."

"How about who's having the first taste of wine?" Annie laughed as she pulled out a smuggled bottle from the large pocket inside her grey coat.

"It's not even noon yet," Herta said, the scandal plain across her face.

"You won't believe this, but..." Gretl pulled another bottle of wine from the picnic basket hung on her arm.

"So we have two thieves in our midst." Herta jostled me with her elbow, her face falling as she felt the hard glass curve of the bottle I had hidden in the bag slung over my back.

"It was a wonderful day, my Führer," I said as I sucked on the hard sweetie Gretl had drunkenly pushed into my mouth on the car journey back up the winding mountain road.

"Sshhh, he'll never know," they'd all laughed as we reached the gatehouse, each feigning somber faces to the soldiers on duty.

The smell of mint was strong, but even I couldn't doubt that it was plain I had been drinking.

"Excessively," he said with a smile, reading my thoughts. "You drank excessively today."

"My holiday was cut short. I was commiserating."

"I'm sorry about that." His face dropped. "Very, Eva."

"Hush. Hush." I pulled him and his seat out from the desk and parked myself on his lap. "Hush, hush, hush. No need to apologize." I placed my finger on his lips, his moustache tickling its tip. "I'm glad you were here to meet me. One day we will go together in grandeur. Celebrate our victory with our allies."

"Eva, get down." He shifted in his seat.

"No. No, I don't want to." I wiggled too.

"I have things to do, Eva. I can't spend any more time here."

"Can you not?" I wiggled again, feeling him growing beneath me. I rubbed my legs together, using the friction to stem the swell of feeling in my most intimate place. A feeling of hunger, unparalleled desire, and yet a sweet tingling of a promise to come. "I'm sure you have time, my Führer."

"Don't," he breathed as I nuzzled my nose into his neck.

"My Führer," I said again. "Aren't you angry?"

"Angry?" he whispered.

"I'm drunk. So drunk, my Führer. Haven't I been bad. *Naughty.*"

"Naughty girl." His eyes were shut, his mouth hung open. The smell was awful but his neck was clean and fresh. He'd showered today.

"Mhhmmm, my Führer. Very naughty. Do it." I jutted my rear out a little, sticking it out from the rest of my body.

"No. I have to work."

"I'll never learn if you don't…"

The smack was painful and sharp. The sound of his hand on my skirt ricocheted around the room like a gun shot. Another one came just as quickly as I gasped out in excitement.

"My Führer." The slap came down on my face this time, knocking me clean off his lap.

"Drunken girl," he said, his eyes black as he looked down on me. He stood up, his member jutting out of his uniform at an odd angle. Solid. "Drunken whore. Wiggling on my lap like a slut?"

I nodded as I cradled my cheek. My hand was cool against the hot skin, my skirt high above my knee.

"Stand up."

"Yes, my Führer." I did as he commanded.

"Stay there," he said while I stumbled onto my knees, losing my balance just a fraction. "Kiss it."

"Kiss what?" I looked up at him and licked the corner of my mouth.

"Whore," he shouted as he jabbed his trouser covered erection into my face. It banged into my top lip before sliding away down my cheek. The feel of cloth being pushed so roughly along my still stinging skin was electrifying and my fingers ached to explore the well of feelings that were bubbling beneath my skirt. But I didn't dare touch it. I knew I had to ask for permission. And it was his time in that moment. Not mine. "Smell it," he commanded. I huffed in the scent of his trousers as drool dripped from my mouth. I left large black stains on his crotch that earned me another slap. "Lick it," he said as he put his hands on the back of my head and grated his erection all over my face. "You want it? Tell me you want it."

"Please," I gasped, not realizing I hadn't been able to breath until he asked me to talk. "Please give me it."

"You call that begging?" he spat. It trickled down my cheek. Again, the urge to touch myself was powerful.

"Please, my Führer. Let me taste you. Let me lick you, sir. Please, my Führer. I'm yours. I need you. Please."

"Good girl," he said. "Undo my trousers. Slowly."

I bit my lip as I pulled on the zipper. The smell of sweat and testosterone poured out of his crotch like a murderous cloud of gas. I inhaled it in, desperate for more but knowing nothing would smell as strong as that first dose.

"Take it all," he said as it sprung into view for just a second before he rammed it down my throat all at once.

"He's too rough with you. It's not normal," Herta said as I told her about it the next morning at breakfast.

"It is normal. It's consensual and it is good for both of us."

"You nearly throwing up is good for both of you?"

"Yes."

"Please stop trying to pretend to yourself. It's not normal. He won't marry a woman that lets him treat her like that."

"Oh, that's what Ilse said. Stop it. I don't want to talk about this with you anymore. Just eat your porridge, you boring old fool."

"You can't speak to people like this, Eva. I'm your friend. But I'm not your maid."

"Eva," a high pitched, nasally voice demanded.

"Excuse me?"

"Sorry. My apologies. *Fraulein* Braun. Oh I miss the good old days when Angela was here."

"What do you want, Frau Morell?"

"Please, call me Hannelore."

"Hanni," I said to annoy her.

"If you prefer. My husband would like a word."

I almost spat about my croissant.

"About what?"

"That's none of my business." She looked me up and down as if I was a silly girl begging for money. "He asks that you meet him at once."

"I'm having breakfast."

"Of course, when you're done. God forbid the fabled Eva misses out on a slice of toast. Oh, Magda." She turned away from Herta and I completely. "Save me a seat by Emmy. Oh, that dress. Spectacular. How are the children?"

"What could he want?" Herta turned to me immediately. "He hates you."

"Thanks, Herta."

"I'm not here to coddle you. I'm here to look out for you. This means trouble, Eva. Watch yourself with him. He's a dangerous man with an unprecedented hold on the Führer."

"Illuminating." I crunched into the crescent shape of my croissant. "What a truly enlightening thing to say."

"Men don't marry sarcastic women either, Eva."

His office was set up in the West halls of the Berghof. Initially, they'd been next to the Führer's office but Morell found the light there in the morning to be displeasing, or so Gretl told me one of the secretaries had mentioned. His door was painted white, the handle a boring taupe compared to the extravagant gold and brass of every other door handle. It had been fitted poorly, I could tell, because it rattled as I twisted it, as if it hadn't been screwed in correctly.

"Fraulein Braun. May I call you Eva?"

"No," I said. "Why do you want me?"

"Want you?" He raised an eyebrow.

He was a repugnant looking man. His hairline stretched far back on his head and was covered, poorly, with a stretch of thin, greasy looking hair. His eyes were slight but magnified behind his thick-rimmed spectacles. Each one was adorned with a drooping of putrid looking flesh that hung like testicles beneath his eyes. His lips were always moist because he kept flicking his tongue over them like a pervert surveying a drunk girl in a bar. He had fat fingers too that he splayed out grandly, inviting me to take a seat in front of him.

"I'd rather stand," I said.

"Suit yourself. I need your help, Fraulein."

"Oh," I said while staring out of the window.

"The Führer is being a little...*reluctant* with some of my latest suggestions. Prescriptions, really. I could use your influence to aid his decision."

"You've been his personal physician for many years. Surely he'll take you at your word?"

"Apparently not. Please, take a seat, Fraulein. You're making me uncomfortable."

"What is your new prescription, Doctor?" I said, without moving an inch towards the seat his meaty hand was pointing towards.

"Just a vitamin injection. Nothing too dissimilar to what he takes now."

"What you give him," I corrected. "If it's just vitamins, why would he be concerned?"

"Exactly, Fraulein. Exactly. Tell him so. Tell exactly that and this will all go away. Are you sure you wouldn't like to take a seat? You're making me very anxious."

"What's different about these vitamins? What's so different that you have to ask to change the prescription at all? Surely you could have changed it and he'd never have been the wiser for it?"

"I'd never lie to the Führer. On my honour, I would not. To even suggest such a thing… He'll notice the difference. It's to wake him up in the mornings. Properly."

"He's been getting up fine. He made me breakfast just yesterday."

"That's because he didn't sleep. His sleeping pattern is incorrect and it's having a negative impact on his life. Haven't you notice his tremors growing?"

I had. But I'd be loathed to admit it to him.

"What does Dr. Brandt think?"

"The day I run my diagnosis by that charlatan," Morell roared before catching himself and quieting himself down. "No. No need for *Dr.* Brandt. Your influence and my expertise should be enough."

"Is it true?" I said, enjoying the feeling of anticipation over what was to come.

"Is what true, Fraulein?"

"That you're part Jewish?"

His face began to swell with blood. It turned a shade of puce rapidly, before falling over into outright plum. He gasped like a fish with only two breaths left before slamming his clenched fist down on his desk. *There we are. There's the man I knew you were.*

"You're a venereal doctor, aren't you? At least, that's where your specialty lies? That's a Jewish disease, is it not? Is that why you made it your specialty? To treat your family? A sister, perhaps? I'll not ask the Führer to take anything he's not comfortable with, Dr. Morell. Not a thing. Perhaps, since he is not listening to you, I should have Dr. Brandt come up anyway? Make a house call for my Führer. My Führer does love it when Brandt comes to visit. Perhaps he can diagnose what's wrong with my Führer. If anything.

"Good bye, *Dr.* Morell," I said as I sauntered from his office, not bothering to close the door behind me.

"You said what? Oh no, Eva. Oh no. He's not a man to be trifled with. He's *mean.*"

"You don't have to whisper here, Gretl. You have nothing to fear of him."

"But still...to insinuate *that.*"

"Oh, Eva, you are my favourite. He'll be blustering about that for days. Weeks even. I can't wait to tell Karl. Oh, how he'll laugh," Annie said.

"Why does the Führer listen to him so much, Eva?" Gretl asked.

"Because of Speer," Annie said quickly. "And Hoffman."

"Hoffman?" I asked.

"Oh, that's right. You used to work for him. Yes. It was he who introduced Morell to the Führer. He helped with a stomach problem or some other such thing. Got lucky and got it right. Then he helped Speer. I don't know what happened there but that's how he climbed so high. I don't think Himmler likes him much, though. Nor Goebbels."

"Who told you that?" I snapped at her.

"I am allowed other friends, Eva. Magda and Emmy aren't that bad when you get to know them."

I didn't bother to respond. Though a sharp smack would have made me feel infinitely better.

"You could ask Margarete. She'd know, I'm sure," Herta said as she fiddled with the puzzle pieces in front of her.

"You have other friends too?" I shot at her.

"Certainly not. But Margarete isn't like the other wives. She's nice. Like Albert. They're different to the usual families that haunt here."

"I thought she was only being polite when she spoke to me?"

"She may well have been. Just because she's not chums with the other wives doesn't mean she's your best friend either. Go and ask her what Morell did for Herr Speer. At least it will give us time to finish this puzzle in peace."

I didn't say that it was only she who was fiddling with it. Instead I got up and went to ask the guards if they knew where Frau Speer was.

I found her in the garden, playing with her children, which was a rare sight in and of itself. Most wives on the Berg preferred the care of nursemaids and nannies to mind their young ones. But Margarete looked as content as could be as she threw a small ball for Albert Junior and his siblings to chase.

"Oh, Fraulein Braun," she said as she covered her eyes against the sun. "We were just leaving if you'd like to have this spot."

"This spot? No, Margarete, I wanted to talk to you."

Frau Speer grew pale at the thought of it. I watched as she patted her face before fiddling with her ring finger.

"Of course. Though…"

"Though what?"

"Are we *supposed* to talk to you?"

"Magda isn't here," I said to her wrinkled face. She pursed her lips and her brow fell as if she didn't understand what I had just said to her. "So, I'm sure we'll be fine."

Albert Junior came running back with the ball, trailed by his pack of siblings, like a mother duck with her chicks. He looked from me to his mother before selecting to drop the ball in my lap. I felt Margarete flinch as if he'd thrown the ball at her face with might of ten men.

"You'd like me to throw it for you?" He nodded. "Well you better get your feet ready, because I'm going to throw it very far." I threw the ball so it landed a few feet further away than his mother had just thrown it. I knew this would keep them on my side and mothers love nothing more than people who are good with their children.

"How may I help you, Fraulein Braun?" she asked as she kept her eyes trained firmly on her children, who'd begun kicking the ball amongst one another.

"I want to ask you about your husband." She flinched again. A thought troubled me. I wondered if she was a painfully shy woman or a straight laced one? I wondered if she was so conservative that she couldn't bear to talk with a mistress, feeling it beneath her. It wasn't appropriate to ask, and so I didn't.

"About his promotion?"

"What promotion?"

"To Minister of Armaments and Munitions. In February. No?"

"Ah." I rubbed my hands on my knees, embarrassed I'd been caught out. That would have been a perfect – and more appropriate opening gambit – to talk with her. Wives loved when their husbands were congratulated. "Yes. Of course. Congratulations." She saw through my lie. "Also, I hear he was treated by Dr. Morell some years ago. You probably don't remember, but…"

"I remember. He was awful, terrible in fact."

"Really?"

"Should I be telling you this?"

"Should you not be?"

"He's he Führer's physician, it's not appropriate."

"Oh, but it is. Tell me. Please."

"There's nothing much to tell. He gave Albert a superficial exam for a digestive complaint he had. Prescribed some medicines and then that was that."

"Did they work? The medicines?"

"Probably not. He never took them – Albert. He got a second opinion from Professor von Bergman at the University of Berlin. He said it was just stress and overwork. To take it easier for a few days. So, he did. The symptoms cleared."

"But the Führer thinks it was Morell's doing?"

"I didn't tell you this to cause trouble," she warned. "You're the Führer's... *something*. And you're not a bad woman. You deserve respect. I've shown you it by telling you about my husband. Please don't make me regret that."

"I won't. Of course I won't. I wouldn't. I just wanted to know."

"Good. I don't need any hassle."

"Hassle? Who would hassle you?"

She said nothing.

"You're safe up here, Frau Speer. Very safe. Your husband is in high regard. You have beautiful children. What could you possibly have to fear?"

She let her eyes settle into my own. With careful poise, she pursed her lips and inclined her head a fraction. She listened to her children run and sing and shout the way mothers always do, but I was the focus of her attention. I blinked, pretending to have something in my eye and when I finally dared to peep back up at her, I found her eyes still boring into me.

"Is there anything else I can help you with, Fraulein?"

"No. No. Thank you, though. I appreciate your help."

It was only a few hours later, as I lay in a bay window along the long promenade that looked out onto the winding road that he would either come up or leave in the next few hours. I didn't know if he was in the

Berghof or whether he was down in Berchtesgaden. Either way I wanted to be here to see him come or go. I had sent Gretl with Herta to scout the town under the pretense of buying me some chocolate from my favourite chocolatier. Really, I was concerned I would fall asleep and miss him. My bladder rumbled in protest. The strain of being so full creating a pressure on my lower abdomen. I crossed my legs, rubbing my knees together as I squeezed my eyes closed and hoped the feeling would pass, at least for a while. I was too scared to go to the bathroom. That I could control.

"Fraulein Braun," a timid voice asked.

I opened my eyes expecting to see a secretary or a servant coming to ask me for something ridiculous. Magda had a habit of sending them to me and bidding them to ask me to do some work. It was a dangerous game she played. Addie himself wanted me anonymous and the more people she sent to me in her cruel little jape, the more began to question why a secretary – as they all thought I was – did such little work.

"Oh. Frau Speer," I said, seeing the older but still beautiful face smiling down on me. "Is everything ok?"

Images of S.S. guards coming pounding down the promenade flooded my head. Albert Speer was high in the Führer's favour, I knew, but surely not so high that I could be apprehended on the word of his wife?

"I have an apology to make."

"You do?" I couldn't stop my eyes from scanning both left and right, sure I could hear the pounding of military boots on the hardwood floors, each one a step closer to my incarceration on the death train.

"May I sit?" she indicated the pillowed seat I had my legs on. I moved them, careful not to jostle my bladder too much and nodded a yes. "You're very different, you know."

"From when?"

"When you first came here, to the Berghof, the 'Grand Hotel' as you call it."

"How do you know I call it that?"

"Annie told me."

"I didn't realise you spoke about me."

"I don't think there's a person that knows who you are that doesn't talk about you at some stage or another. I hope you don't mind me saying, but you're very extraordinary for an ordinary girl."

"Maybe I'm not ordinary," I said defensively.

"Maybe." She shrugged. "But you are very different. You came to the mountain a girl. Very shy. Very callous. Very changeable. Your conniptions were legendary. But here you sit, a graceful woman in a fine dress, a Berlin designer if I'm not mistaken?"

"You're not."

"I spoke to my husband, after you left us in the garden. He said I should be kinder to you. He has a lot of affection for you. He says your position is quite impossible, and that just because all I see is your smile, your whims being executed, doesn't mean that's how it is behind closed doors."

I said nothing, trying desperately not to piss myself in front of her.

"So I'm sorry. I shouldn't have treated you so coldly. I'm a mother," she shrugged, as if that gave her a carte blanche to do as she pleased. "Perhaps you'll understand one day."

"I only wanted to know about Morell," I said as she stood to leave.

"I know. But I'm married to a man who travels far and wide. A powerful man. A young man. I'm a woman. Forgive me that, won't you?"

I didn't have a chance to say a word as she walked slowly along the wide promenade. Her walk was so assured, so confident for a woman that shrunk away from Magda's stare as if Frau Goebbels were a Gorgon from Greek mythology and not a mere woman with a witch for a husband. Her heels clacked along the floor, a welcome sound instead of leather boots. The smell of her perfume lingered in the air, like the trail of a scarf on a windy day.

Bormann passed her, as he moved from a room on one side of the corridor, to one on the other. She stopped when she saw him, and moved her hand to her face as if she could smell manure from the fields outside.

He saw her actions and smiled. He saw me, too, and gave a curt nod. He was an irresistible force for the Führer. A powerful man that 'got things done,' as Addie would tell me. But I was his immovable object. The mountain to his gale force blow. I was an immovable object. I had to be. There was no time to pee. No time to sleep. I couldn't leave the window, not if it meant missing him. Not if it meant days of wondering if he was here or not. Not if it meant humiliating myself by asking Gretl to run to Magda…

Bormann was still there, I realized. If he was there, Addie would be too.

But still, I couldn't trust myself enough to leave the window. Couldn't trust myself enough not to make sure. If he left, he'd have to pass this window. If he was gone…

I wouldn't think about that.

I'm an immovable object.

September, *The Berghof*

I watched him as he ate his stewed fruits. He'd only eaten a little soup, the first thing past his lips all day, and he would only swirl the pears and plums around his china bowl. His arm was jittering. I could see it from the corner of my eye. Bormann had got up to attend some business a few minutes before and it was only Addie and I sitting at the Führer's table. I felt like a spectacle. A woman on display. There was no one in the room that didn't know who I was, of course. Even Traudl Junge, who had come in for only a moment with hurried words of Stalin's Brad, whatever that may be, didn't shoot me a sneer as she usually would. I felt like a Queen. Queen of the Mountain. Undisputed mistress of the Grand Hotel. But Addie's hand kept jittering and so I couldn't enjoy it.

He'd slept so little the night before. Although we parted to separate beds, I could see him toss and turn all night. His eyes would reflect the moonlight back at me as he faced me and I would scrunch my eyes shut quickly, hoping he hadn't noticed I was watching him. That was why we sat alone though, so I should have been thankful. His privacy was paramount, he used it to conceal his defects from the world. From the Nazi Court he held around him. Magda, Gerta and Hanni all sat at a table by the window, aggrieved their usual spots around Hitler's side had been denied to them. More than once a look of hatred was shot at me from their little trench. But I hadn't enough energy to care. His hand was still jittering. And, what was worse, the jitter was travelling past his elbow, crawling along his bicep and infecting his shoulder.

"More tea, my Führer?" I winked as he looked up from his fruits, surprised anyone had said a word loud enough for him to hear.

"No, Fraulein. You finished your meal." He nodded towards my empty plate that had been vacant for so long that the sauce from the beef had begun to develop a skin. "You should leave."

"No."

"No?"

"When you go, I go." I gripped his shaking hand. "When you go," I looked into his pale blue eyes, "I go."

I didn't know if it was the intensity of how I had said the words, or whether it was because he was aware we were being stared at, but he shook my hand off at once and stood up from the table. In three great strides he was by a side door that lead out onto a galley conservatory that he liked to read in sometimes. His footsteps took him well beyond the comfortable chairs and pleasant stained glass. He slammed a door shut that shook the dining room.

Everyone left rose to their feet as soon as the slammed door faded into a light reverberation around the room. Pitying glances were shared between them all, while smug smiles were hidden behind ring-clad hands. I was Queen. Queen of the Mountain. Mistress of the Grand Hotel. But with Addie storming away from me, I didn't know how long that could last.

"I'm worried about him," I whispered to Gretl in the dark. I had taken to my own apartments atop the simple stairs, even though I desperately wanted to be by his side. "He's changing. He's getting…worse."

"Worse?" she whispered back.

We were alone. Completely hidden from the outside world, but still, we didn't dare say our fears above a whisper. Even in the safety of my own bed. It was treason. Or could be, at any rate. To say such things about the Führer. The Superman of Germany.

"He doesn't sleep."

"He never slept well at night."

"This is different, Gretl. This is much, much…"

"…Worse."

"Exactly. What should I do? What can I do for him?"

"What does Morell think?"

"Morell? I wouldn't ask him. Dirty old fool."

"I guess so. Have you spoke to Dr. Brandt?"

"You think he needs a doctor? Really?"

"I don't know, Effie. I don't."

"We're ruined if he turns against me." My lips barely moved as I said the words.

"Effie, no. No. Don't think like that. He loves you. He loves you."

"Does he? Truly? Madly? Does he? Because sometimes I can't tell."

"You're still here, aren't you? Still in the Berghof. Still the woman that banished Angela. He must love you."

"Loved," I corrected. "That means only that he loved me then. What about now?"

"It's the war," Gretl said. "It's taking a toll."

"The war? The Generals fight that. He just gives his orders."

"I heard the secretaries talking a few days ago. They said something about a new law that attacks Germans. Germans like you and I."

"Germans? No. He wouldn't. He's doing all this for us. For Germany."

"Wait, Effie. It's only if they help the Jews."

"The Jews?" My heart sank.

"Anyone caught helping an escaped Jew from the Warsaw Ghetto will be punished."

I said nothing.

"Effie, you don't think…"

"Don't say it."

"But, Effie…"

"No, Gretl."

"If it does happen, you have to help her. You have to, Effie."

"Stop it, Gretl. We aren't talking about this."

"She's your sister, Effie. Just like me."

I'd never heard her sound so small. So, innocent. Her voice became childlike then, as the reality of her position became more and more clear with every time I avoided promising to support Ilse if she was caught under the new law. Gretl, pure and licit Gretl, understood then what would happen if I were to make a choice. I guess it was the same conclusion my mother and father had made long ago, that first afternoon they'd seen me descend from the Führer's motorcar, my face abuzz with happiness. It was the same conclusion that snaked down Ilse's throat from that first evening she'd found me covered in blood, a bullet lodged in my neck. And now Gretl, darling Gretl, had finally come to understand too.

"He's not worth everything, Eva," she said. "No one is worth everything. If he makes you give up every little part of you then he's not worth it."

"Stop it, Gretl," I warned.

"We're your family. We'll always be your family. We'll always love you, no matter what. Muma. Baba. Ilse. Me. We'll always love you.

You. Love. Ilse. Me. Baba. Always. We'll. Muma. I tried to lock them out my head. The words. The feelings. The people. The bonds between us all, as fine as a spider's web but as strong as steel. The guilt each of them would have brought into me if I had let them in would have been all consuming. Terrible and all consuming. I couldn't. Not for a second. I'd made my choice. I'd made it when I had placed that revolver by my heart and whispered his name as I'd pulled the trigger. I'd made my choice then and I wouldn't change it now.

"Ilse wouldn't break the law," I said, more for myself than Gretl.

"I hope you're right, Effie. I do," she was crying. "I really, really do."

"Shhhh," I pulled her closer to me, wrapping my arms around her as if it would be the last time. As if, by talking about it, we had brought Ilse to the Berghof, ourselves, the blood of escaped Jews on her hand. Caught red-handed. I knew I'd let them pull the trigger on her, as easily as I had done it to myself. And I knew that Gretl would never again let me hold her if I was responsible for her sister – our sister's – execution.

I sat alone. I sent Stasi and Negus away with Gretl, who promised to look after them all afternoon. Herta, poignant and fearful Herta, could only be kept indoors, away from me, by threat of poisonous words in the Führer's ear. As I sat in the grass, running my hands through its damp blades, I saw her face recoil as if my breath smelled of faeces and my nose had fallen off revealing a cavern of maggots rotting inside my head. If I'd had more patience, just a fraction more gratitude for her caring of my wellbeing, I'd have been able to sneak away without hurting her. But there was a canker beneath the shadow of my heart, a little bud of something dark and black that made me lash out like a snake, biting deep with my fangs.

The trees swayed in uneasy concert beneath me. The slope of the hill I was perched on declined at a steady rate, allowing the thick roots of the trees to plunge deep, holding themselves still on the hill face. Wind rippled their green canopies and I imagined an auditorium filled with adoring fans, all gazing up at me – Eva Braun – sat on stage before them.

In my mind's eye, I wore a gown of expensive red. Cut from silk that rippled as I walked, hemmed with sparkling rubies and laced with gold thread along the straps, I had just walked in from the warm California air, a thousand glittering bulbs all flashing greedily to ensnare my image. Magda and Emmy and the other wives wouldn't be here, they'd be far away, still in Europe – my husband's Europe – but they would see the photos, I knew. They'd see the photographs of me in the silk red dress hemmed with rubies and laced with gold. I'd make sure of it.

They laughed at the jewellery I wore. They sniggered behind jeweled hands with large engagement rings and golden wedding bands that clattered against sapphire or pearl earrings. I wore only cheap chains and fake silver, all on his word. I had a treasure chest of jewels. A pirate's trunk filled with diamonds and glittering emeralds. I wore a chain of delicate gold links. A ring with a beautiful black pearl set amongst glittering fragments of diamonds. And his most affectionate platinum watch ticked by

202

methodically, putting the simpler, plain green bracelet I wore around my wrist – always – to shame.

I had to hide these treasures. Had to hide everything but the clothes on my back. Clothes, he said, were perfunctory, but jewels were pride. So, as they laughed and sniggered, thinking me a pauper at the court of a prince, I could pore over my haul, my booty of wealth, and know that I was a woman with a fortune in the world.

The trees rippled again, the wind chilling my arms and drying out my lips. *This must be how he feels. As he stands at a rally, the crowd hanging on his every word, he must feel like a God-King on Earth. The most Beloved and powerful man in existence.* I knew I would feel that way one day too. I had too. *I simply must.*

I ran through my acceptance speech in my head. I thanked Germany first, knowing that my new life was in service to my old country first and foremost. That's how he'd want it. I would be the First Lady of the Reich, not just Queen of the Mountain. I knew I wouldn't like it. Not really. But the gentle fear of failure would be an easy price to pay for the gallantry success I would surely endure. I thanked him next, and I'd call him 'my Addie.' The war would be over, Germany would be triumphant and finally, *finally*, it would be my time to shine. My time to show the world the Führer as the man Himmler desperately tried to separate him from. The man he tried to distance himself from. All the pictures I've taken will be worth even more than the vast sums Hoffman paid for them. They'd become propaganda gold. Jewels to Himmler's eyes. A valuable resource that Addie

had allowed only me to possess. He'd reinvent the Führer as a man as well

as a myth, and the steady pile of evidence I had taken to that effect would

become more prized than oil. And in every frame, most of them anyway,

would be a beautiful blonde, just at the fringes of the shot, who had

injected herself into his history. Who had been there since before the world

knew who she was.

I saw the gold statuette being brought out to me by a smiling

American woman. Her gown was fine, but nowhere near as magnificent as

mine. I kissed her cheek as she put the hefty weight into my hand. I knew I

should have received this before I started my speech but I simply

rearranged the order of things in my head. I felt its significance rest in my

hands, its cool body steal the heat from my fingertips and I looked down

onto the audience of trees and thanked myself, the me sitting on the hill in

1942, for having the strength to continue on, to stay true to herself when

the people around her thought she was nothing but a shell. To me. *The most*

underrated woman in history.

That's where Gretl was wrong, I knew. She saw me as a vacant,

vacuous vessel that the Führer could drink or fill whenever he chose to.

That I was so hopelessly in love that there was nothing left in me apart

from the greedy desire to be with him. The pathetic despair of no longer

being by his side. And that was true. That was most of me. That was mostly what I had left. Except from one black canker in my heart. That one black canker would never, could never be his. That one black canker was the only part of me he couldn't take, that no one could take.

Ambition.

1943

February, *The Berghof*

It was very still. We waited in my rooms, Gretl and I, careful not to be the first people he saw when he came back. My body ached to hold him, to grip him in my arms and not let him go. But I knew that the defeat had been too great, the humiliation too profound, the pain unbearable, he'd want no one but himself. I knew that. But still, I wanted to go to him.

"Is it really bad?" Gretl asked as she sat with her legs folded over on another in a chair by the window. "Could we not…" she let sentence trail off as she so often did, hoping someone else would finish it.

"It's bad, Gretl. Magda warned me he was coming back today. Magda. That's how bad it is."

"She might like you now."

"Of course she doesn't like me. She likes only herself, and loves only the party. She's scared. She knows he'll need me."

"So why aren't we waiting by the door for him to come back?"

How could I have explained it to her without betraying his confidence?

"Because he needs to be alone right now. He needs to be by himself."

"Where is Stalingrad, Effie?"

"In Russia."

"And was it really, quite so important?"

"It must have been, mustn't it?! I'm sorry. I shouldn't have raised my voice. I'm sure it's not *very* important. It's only one defeat. One in how many victories? It can't be that important."

"Will you go to him later tonight?"

"Maybe. Maybe tomorrow morning. Definitely before tomorrow afternoon."

The sun set along the Obersalzburg Valley as I tread along the stone terrace to where he was standing. He was alone, which I was thankful for. He had a glass of wine in his hand. I froze when I saw it, my blood clotting into icebergs in my veins. I spluttered on a trail of saliva that I tried to breathe in in my absentmindedness. He turned when he heard me, his eyes cold and hard.

"Addie?"

"Go away, Eva. Not tonight."

"I know, Addie. I know, but..."

"I said go away, Eva. Leave me."

"Ok. Ok. I will. I only came to bring you this," I placed the book Gertraud had sent me from Münich on the table where the open bottle of wine sat breathing. "You know where I am when you're ready."

And I walked away, even though every inch of my being begged me to reconsider and throw myself at his feet, begging to be allowed to stay near him.

I lay in the bathtub for hours. I watched the moon walk across the sky, the diamonds sharp points of brilliance all around it. A few winter clouds drifted by like travelers, lost on their way back home.

I hadn't felt scared in a long time. Now, I felt fear. The irrational fear that the world would slip away from underneath me. The irrational fear that I would wake up on the death train with a hungry old man licking my cut fingers. The irrational fear that maybe, after all these years, he would just toss me aside and never look back. He loved me. *He loves me.* I knew it. I knew it in the core of who I was. I knew it in my black canker. It's why I stayed. Or maybe I would have anyway, even if he hated me. Even if he told me I was nothing but a silly whore, maybe I'd have stayed then too.

But I knew he loved me. I didn't have to worry about that. I didn't have to worry that he didn't love me. *He loves me.* But I felt fear as I lay in the empty bathtub. I felt it grip at my muscles and peer at my bones. I didn't know why I felt it. Nor why it was so potent. But I did and it was. The air tasted different. As if something was rotting over Germany. As if it were being burned alive. Its flesh blistering and cracking. Its ligaments frying in its own blood. As if he'd just been stabbed in the heart and all we could do now was wait and let him bleed to death around us.

The door opened. The hinges creaked. Gretl complained often that I should get them fixed, get them oiled, but I liked that they squeaked. It reminded me of Herr Hoffman's shop and the little bell that would ding whenever a customer opened the front door. I said nothing as Gretl came towards me. I could feel her hovering in the doorway, her shadow cast against the wall in the corridor, pushed out by the lunar light that filled my bath tub with something more powerful than water. Something that would drown me all the same.

"Tschapperl?" he said, his voice cracking. *He mustn't have spoken for a long time.* "Are you ok, Tschapperl?"

I didn't turn towards him. I didn't move my body, only my arm, which I unfurled from my stomach and moved my hand to tap on the space beside me. He hesitated. For a second, he wasn't going to come in with me.

And then I heard him huff as he untied his boots and hung his oversized uniform onto the chair by my vanity mirror.

"You're so cold," he said as his warm body gripped my own. *We fit so perfectly together. Two pieces of the same puzzle. My body fits wholly into the curves of his own. Two halves. One whole.* "You're so cold. Are you ok?"

"Are you?" I never once took my eyes from the night sky.

"I am now. Right now. Only in this moment. For right now, I am ok."

"It's bad, isn't it?" The fear caught in my throat. The hairs all over my body stood on end as if they could summon a suit of armour to protect me.

"Not right now," he said. He kissed my neck. His breath was mild. "Not right now."

"I won't leave." His grip tightened around my body. His forearm pushed against my lungs. His forehead dug into the back of my neck. I could feel the scratch of his moustache at the summit of my arm. "I won't. Not ever. Not even if things get really bad."

My back grew damp. Either from the sweat or something else, I didn't know.

"Not ever, Addie. You and me. You and me. Always, always. You and me."

"It doesn't have to be," he whispered so low I barely dared to breathe in case I mistook his words for my own sound. "You could find another."

"Don't talk like that," my voice cracked on the last note. "Never, Addie. Not ever."

"The war is only taking more and more of me. Eva. Please. There's almost nothing left to give you."

"I don't need much."

"You'll get nothing."

"I won't," I said as panic seized my lungs and twisted them this way and that. "You'll walk with me. You like to walk with me, don't you, Addie? And I can sit by your side – quietly, of course – while you read. Every night you sit with me. You drink your tea while I sip wine in my dressing gown. You'll come back here. You have to. I keep you sane. Rested. You won't be gone from our Grand Hotel forever, Addie."

"Eva, I mean it. You should find a lover. Find someone that can warm you in the lonely winters to come. And maybe, maybe if you still have an ounce of feeling left for me, some warmth you can spare, we may see what happens after the war."

"Adolf, that's enough. I mean it. Enough of this…of this…*nonsense*." I couldn't turn from the moon. I watched it watch me. I watched the stars all sparkle impassively, each one of them listening to my soul mate bid me to fuck someone else. "Only you. Only ever you."

"Ok," he said as his voice became thick with sleep. "Ok. I'll say no more. You and me. You and me. Always, always. You and me."

"He said that? Truly?"

I nodded as my cheeks burned with shame. My eyes were rung red and puffed out like I had been stung by wasps all morning. Herta stood behind me as I sipped my tea as best I could, watching myself in the mirror. Trying my best to cover up the morning's agony.

"You can't. He won't allow it."

"I don't want to, Herta. I don't. And he would allow, he practically goaded me into doing it."

"Men say things, Eva. Selfless heroic things. Men always play at chivalry in the dark. They fancy themselves as Knights of the Round Table, though most don't take it as far as Himmler." She watched my reflection to see if I would smile at her joke. I didn't. "He'd kill you both."

"He'd never hurt me. Physically. I meant physically. Wipe that look off your face."

"He hurts you sexually," she said unabashed.

"That's just games. And how dare you throw something I told you in confidence back in my face?"

212

"Just don't, Eva. Not even to get back at him."

The thought hadn't even crossed my mind until she placed it there. In a rush, newspaper clippings, radio gossip and the rumour mill of the Berg all hounded the foxes in my mind. Actress after princess after politician's daughter after common working girls. Leni Riefenstahl. He had a plethora of women all dangled before me for ten years. Each one beautiful. Each one maddeningly ridiculous in comparison to myself. Unity Mitford. All of them a great torture to me, a torture he knew he was inflicting.

"I wouldn't. Not ever."

"You wouldn't what?" Gretl said as she stuck her ahead around the bathroom door.

"You know fine well what."

"Oh, become a whore in deed as well as name," she laughed and it brought a little smile to my face to see how shocked Herta was at her brazenness.

"You Braun sisters." She shook her head and tutted.

"Effie, I have news."

"News?"

"Yes. News."

"What news?"

"What news indeed."

"Gretl will you just tell me and stop with this buffoonery!"

"Cheese and sauerkraut you're moody. Annie told me that Magda told her that you've to come and meet her to talk."

"Magda wants to speak to me?"

"Yes, Effie. She does."

"About what?"

"Well how would I know? What part of that chain lent a link to the name 'Gretl'? She wants to speak to you."

"Do you think it's very important?" I grinned as Gretl's foot tapped with impatience. She wanted to know what Magda wanted as much as I did.

"Tell her to come to me. At the lake."

"But, Eva, we aren't at the lake."

"I know that Herta. But we soon will be."

"It's too cold, Eva. Why would we want to go to the lake in this weather?" Herta countered.

"The mountain, then. We'll go further up to the slopes."

"The snow isn't set enough for skiing. Why would we need to go anywhere?"

"Because she's not summoning me like some skivvy girl. She wants me, she can come to me."

"You'd cut your nose off to spite your face, wouldn't you? Gretl, if your sister insists on playing games, tell Frau Goebbels to meet her at the *Kehlsteinhaus*. It's a much shorter drive away."

"The Eagle's Nest?" I didn't understand. "But it will be freezing. The heating needs to be on for at least two days for it to be comfortable."

"Says the woman about to sit by a freezing lake for the sake of precedence and ceremony. Yes, Gretl, go. *Kehlsteinhaus*. It'll be cold, but as long as you don't shiver, Eva, it will seem like a power move. The Ice Queen. Plus, it is a great gift given to your lover. She'd do well to remember who she's dealing with."

"Now whose spiteful?" I smirked at her.

"Not spiteful, no. I'm just sick of them laughing at my hair," she said sadly. "Let's get you presentable. Didn't your mother collect a new Trench coat from Paris that you ordered? That should keep the chill out."

The drive to *Kehlsteinhaus* was steep and treacherous. More than once I convinced myself that the wheels were slipping out from underneath us and we would be cast down to our deaths because of my vanity. It was petty, I knew. Petty and mean. She probably didn't even try to summon me, in the confusion and her hurry, Gretl probably just phrased the words incorrectly. As we approached the grand building, I felt like a stupid little girl who broke her new hand mirror only a few hours after waving it in the faces of all the girls on the playground.

"It's freezing," I said as we stepped inside. The servants shot me a look of contempt that said 'you don't say?' far better than any words could express. Herta's face, too, looked on the cusp of uttering 'I told you so.'

"They'll be here soon," she said instead, more wisely.

When Magda and her ladies arrived, a courtlier visage of what it was to be an upper echelon Nazi woman than I could ever have hoped to achieve, only Margarete Himmler shuddered at the cold. A small luncheon of sandwiches, tea, water, cakes and biscuits sat on a wide circular table that overlooked the mighty valley below with a glass window that stretched the entire length of the wall. I sat with my back to the view, choosing to reflect the majesty that was behind me in my magnanimous grin.

"Frau Goebbels," I said. "Ladies. Sit, please." Gretl and Herta flanked either side of me, Annie on Gretl's other side, creating a buffer between our two groups. "We're like ladies of the round table," I smirked at Frau Himmler who hid her face behind her hands, a fresh bruise up crawling up her wrist. "How can I help you, Magda?"

"I would like to organize a party," she said without a pause, as if this was all entirely normal to her. As if she hadn't been the most powerful woman in the Reich until last year. Quickly, like many women before me, I realized that my power depended on the favour of a man – an unsatisfactory state of affairs.

"You want to discuss a party? With me?" Herta coughed as I stumbled over my words. "Why couldn't you just organize it yourself?"

Goebbels blushed.

"I thought it best to ask first."

How the words didn't choke her I would never know. Emmy all but gagged in her chair.

"What is the occasion?" I said as high handedly as I could.

"A few Einsatzgrupen men from Poland will be attending the Berghof. Their work is…*bloody* and I thought it only right to organize something for them."

The enormity of how childish I had been in dragging her and the other wives up here tumbled around my ears like falling artillery fire. An opportunity for peace, for mutual cooperation had existed that afternoon and I'd destroyed it with that charade. For all her shame at being summoned here like a common girl, Magda would be ill-likely to forget what I had made her do. I knew that because I would have been exactly the same.

"Yes. Yes, let's do it. I shall have Frau Schönmann contact some of her artist friends in Vienna. We will have a grand ball, formal and in the style of the Kaiser." My mind fell over itself rapidly, excelling in its area of comfort. "We shall have a new mural painted, depicting their heroism and we shall invite the generals that can be spared. A pageant of war and beauty."

"As you wish, Fraulein Braun." Magda stood and looked as if she would curtsey in reverence, but a disgusted look from Emmy kept her back rigid and reminded her that she was still vying for second place, if not first.

"They didn't touch a single sandwich," Gretl complained as she gathered up the plates.

"It was a twenty-minute conversation, why would they?"

"Oh, Herta, could you just not please? Don't make this worse than it is."

"You humiliated them. For what? Hmm?"

"She showed them the extent of her influence," Annie corrected.

"You think this was a good idea?"

"Of course not," she shrugged. "But it happened and here we are. Let's look at the positives. They now – firmly – know who's in charge. And, what's more, we now know they know. Let's leave it at that."

"Gretl, will you get in touch with Marion for me? She'll need to contact her friends in Vienna at once if we're to have a mural. A mural? What was I thinking?"

"Grandeur," Herta said as she busied herself loading plates atop one another. "It's a rather good idea. Be proud of it."

"March. It will be easy. What month are we in now? We have time? Don't we?"

No one uttered the word February for fear I would hurl myself through the long glass window.

It came covered in brown paper. Three men and a strong, working woman hauled it from the back of an army green truck. I clapped as I saw its immense size. Squealed as a corner of the paper came loose and I saw the wonderful blacks and blues that swirled in cannon fire. Herta stood impassively at my side, Gretl nattering to Marion, whose eyes were focused on the masterpiece being unloaded.

"I told you it would be completed on time," she said as she walked down the stone steps towards her accomplishment. "Vienna is punctual if nothing else."

"The party is this evening. The men have already arrived and have had to be housed in one of the other houses on the compound. We're an inch away from riot if we don't hurry," I said back as another truck pulled up the driveway, the tinkling of champagne bottles clacking against one another filling the air.

"You're beautiful," Gretl smiled as I stepped from my dressing room into the dull amber light of the bedroom. "Those buttons!" I wore a green dress, styled after a WW1 trench coat, that wrapped itself around my body.

Golden buttons emblazoned with the swastika glittered down its length.

"But only that bracelet? It's so cheap, Effie. Is that how you want the

soldiers to first see you? First impressions mean a lot."

"The soldiers won't know who I am, Gretl. And if I swan about in

sapphires and emeralds they'll ask questions and then where will we be?

Besides, this is my favourite. My very, uttermost favourite."

"Oh, Eva," Marion gushed as she and Annie spilled in through the

door. Annie wore gold, with a glittering shawl. Annie wore royal blue, a

sailor's cap tastefully applied to her hair. "You're a picture. A true picture.

Give me your camera. Now, please. We must take a picture. You," she

shouted to the guard by the main door to my apartments. "Take our photo,

will you?"

Dutifully, he came through and snapped two shots. I insisted on

the second, mindful that he was inexperienced and could have easily cut out

my shoes or hair.

"The room is swarming with men, Eva. All soldiers. Manly soldiers.

The testosterone!"

"You're a married woman," Herta said.

"A woman all the same."

'Oh, Marion, that many! The caliber of beauty to look at has grown

stale recently, like a cake left out the sun. Are there really so many soldiers?"

"Wanton sluts," Herta said sternly, only the mischievous twinkle in her eye belying her joke. "Have some decorum."

"Is that make up on your face?" I said like a soldier hurling a grenade into enemy lines. I smiled at myself in the mirror as I waited for the bomb to go off.

"Oh my, she is!"

"Herta Schneider! You hussy. Rouge! Lipstick. And…" Gretl took a deep sniff of Herta's cleavage. "Perfume!"

A servant brought in a platter of champagne glasses, resting them on the table by the day-old flowers.

"Cheers to a wonderful night, ladies," I tried to say through the fits of giggles that wracked my body at how red Herta's face had grown. "And to the wasted rouge on Herta's face, whose cheeks are so red that she didn't need any make up at all!"

We laughed then as if it was the only thing we could do. The only thing we should do. Tears poured from my eyes. I gripped my sister, my best friend in this world, and held her tight, lest I fell onto the floor and crease my dress. Music played on the record player, old songs from long ago. I didn't even care, not in that moment, that I couldn't have the wireless on and listen to the most current music. I was happy. Utterly, blissfully happy, then. Queen of the Mountain. Lady of the Grand Hotel. True love of the world's most powerful man. And befriended by women that didn't judge me, nor berate me, for being nothing more than who I was.

And then it all went to hell and I knew it would never come back. It's ruined. A cloth of gold, torn, and not a seamstress in the world whose fingers were not broken.

I see him first, but it is Gretl's shriek of delight that draws his attention. We two, both Braun sisters, watch as his blonde hair is shucked from his face by the sheer force of his head alone. His teeth are white, bared in a smile that curves delicately at the corners of his lips. He's clean shaven, only a few stray hairs loiter beyond his sideburns. But it is his eyes – it's always the eyes – that have us both gawking like school children. They're the clearest blue I had ever seen. Clearer than the water that glistened on the Italian Riviera.

I knew it. I knew it with all my soul. My knees began to quiver and a violent rush of emotion flooded my most intimate area. The closer he walked towards us, swimming through the rising tide of people in the room, the more I wanted to grasp him and throw myself onto the rocks.

"Herr Soldier." Gretl stuck her hand out before he was within reach and captured his attention. Just. Like. That.

"Fraulein Gown. How beautiful you look," he said in a thick Bavarian accent.

"You're from around here." Gretl batted her eyelids in a motion I could never hope to mimic.

"Not for a long while," he said honestly, his chin hung low in modesty.

"Where have you been?" she asked, like a wondrous girl standing on the dock asking where a sailor had just returned from.

"Poland. Belgium. France. Battling the devils in the East."

"Oh no," I said, cracking the tension between my sister and this handsome soldier.

"This is my sister, Eva," Gretl turned and introduced me. She gripped my arm tight, I could feel how nervous she was. *Gretl is never nervous.*

"How do you do, Fraulein?" He took my hand and laid a gentle, whisper of a kiss on the skin above my fingers.

"Very well," I gasped in pleasure.

"Ah, Flegelein," Traudl Junge said as she bundled herself over from the tables laden with wine and champagne. She was a simple looking girl. But beneath her mask of ignorance lay a fierce wit that burned all day and all night long, a fire that couldn't be smothered.

"Flegelein?" Gretl asked to commandeer the conversation back to herself.

"A loutish brat," Traudl said too loudly. "Aren't you, Flegel?"

"I'm anything but the sort," he winked at her, a move that nearly knocked the drink from her hand. "You're embarrassing me in front of these beautiful women."

She looked at us then as if she hadn't noticed us before. On meeting my eyes, the mirth in her own died away and she gave a curt nod to her friend before bowing her head a fraction, before turning away from me. Fegelein noticed the deference and his attention was mine.

I burned.

"Eva, yes?"

I nodded. Gretl still clutching my arm.

"What a lucky father to have two daughters as beautiful as you both."

"My father?" Gretl said.

"Surely your mother must be equally as radiant, a woman of fine Aryan stock. Only an angel could have given birth to two beauties such as yourselves and rarely do angels fall in love with men."

"Our mother is very pretty, yes," Gretl said coyly as she sipped her champagne.

"See," he stood a little back from us and opened his arms out wide. "I told you so. Am I very clever or am I clever very?" A few soldiers behind him all raised their glasses and gave a cheer at the sound of his voice.

"He's popular," Gretl whispered into my ear. "Popular and handsome. Oh, Effie, what a find! I will marry him. I shall. I shall become Frau Lout!"

The thought curdled in my stomach.

"Eva," the hateful voice of Christa Schroeder came through the heavy noise of music and growing enjoyment. "The Führer bids me to tell you goodbye."

"What?" I spun on my heel, knocking the glass from Herta's hand. "But I haven't unveiled the mural? Is he in his office? I will make him stay."

"He's gone, Fraulein," her severe face said without a care either way. "He left ten minutes ago."

"He can't have left. He wouldn't have. We're past all that. He never said goodbye. Surely. I will see him." I made towards the door, my voice an octave above the din of the party, drawing the attention of the people standing around me. "His office."

"Eva, no. He's gone. He doesn't want to attend a party. You know he wouldn't. This is his space. And you have…he's gone, Eva."

"He wouldn't have left," I said like a mother discovering her eldest boy is missing. "He wouldn't have left without telling me. Maybe in the past, but… you're still here."

The weight on my chest relaxed a modicum.

"He wouldn't leave without you."

I saw the hem of her travel coat, the thick leather gloves on her hand, as I said it.

"I'm leaving now. I was to wait behind to tell you. Goodbye, Fraulein Braun."

And she turned, her hat askew on her head and walked away from me. The spectators in my immediate vicinity turned back to their partners, to their drinks, and resumed their idle chit chat. Chit chat only made possible by my efforts. Enjoying the wine I had procured. Dancing to music I had arranged. All to my own error, it seemed.

"Effie, stay," Gretl tried to grab me as I left the huge hall.

I stormed down the straight corridors, not knowing where I was going. I walked right up to the front door, passed the window seat I had all but pissed my pants in, and let my hand hover over the handle. I could have opened it, but that would have made it all so real. He'd be gone if I opened it. He was gone even if I didn't. I ran back along the corridor, my eyes filled with bitter, bitter tears. Two patrol men rounded a corner. They were deep in conversation, muttering words about how they couldn't get the night off to see the new arrivals. I threw myself into a room and clammed the door shut behind me. I rested my back against the wood and tried to steady my breathing. I was floundering. My ship getting ever closer to the rocks and now he was gone there was no light to guide me through them safely.

Leaning against a wall, sat the mural. Still covered in its brown paper, folds of red curtain sat in a pile by its side. I had planned a great reveal. Soldiers would bring the mural in and hang it from pre-hammered hooks in the wall of the great hall. The curtains would be fixed over it, generating a buzz of 'what could it be?' as the guests swarmed towards it. He would have taken his stand in the front row and I would have climbed onto a small podium that stood me a little over the height of everyone else in the room. I had a short speech prepared. Nothing fancy, nothing over the top; just a simple paragraph about the glory of the Reich, about the links between first, second and third. I knew he'd like that. Would have. And then, with a flourish, my only indulgence of the evening, I'd pull the velvet rope and the curtains would part like grinning lips. The crowd would gasp. Applause and cheers would ring out across the hall. Marion would well up at the sight of her accomplishment and none of that would matter. Because I'd look at him and see him beaming, not at the picture, but at me. He'd be smiling so passionately that – and this was where I let my fantasy run wild – I'd jump down from the podium, right into his arms, and he'd hold me tight, swaying, before letting his lips find mine and kissing me in front of his court, the Nazi court. The most powerful court in the world.

But he left instead.

The room was cold.

Dark.

Unforgiving.

Is this hell?

A hammer sat on a chair by the mural. Nails were scattered on the

floor. Carelessly. I felt the smooth wood in my hand. The weight of its

metal head similar to the gun hidden upstairs.

He's left. He left me. Again. He'll always leave. Always.

I gripped the hammer's handle tighter. I rubbed my other hand

across my face, not caring that I was smearing my makeup. I was sick of the

Berghof. Sick of the women. Sick of the monotony. Sick of him. Most of all

I was sick of him. My Führer. The man I would follow into the very heart

of the Bolshevik Army if he asked me to. The man who wouldn't say

goodbye to me. I struck once. Then twice. Over and over. Over and over. I

was crying and wailing at the same time. Angry tears. Fury-filled wails. I was

a woman possessed. The brown paper mixed with the deep blue swirls, the

orange scratches and the emerald green brush strokes of the mural. The

hammer got caught and I had to pull it free, its disobedience infuriating me

all the more. My wrist grew tired but I didn't stop. Over and over. And then

the mural was gone. But my anger wasn't.

The glass of the lamps shattered into thousands of shiny shards.

The walls fell away under my onslaught, huge craters left were once there

had been wallpaper. The tables. The chairs. The windows. The cabinets.

Nothing was safe. I spun, hammer in hand, and nearly hit him in the head. His beautiful, handsome head.

"Shhh, stop it. Shhh." He grabbed my wrist, his strong fingers squeezing the soft flesh tight. "Let it go."

As the hammer fell to the floor, it pulled with it my righteous anger. The evening air bustled in through the smashed windows. My stomach fell away. My muscles ached and my head felt heavy.

"I love him," I wept into his uniform. "With everything I have I love him."

"I know. I know." He stroked my hair, like he was consoling a child.

"I've given up my entire life for him," I said without thinking, without the careful consideration I knew too keep about me. He'd done something this time, taken a step too far. He'd cracked whatever veneer I had built around myself and decade's worth of bile and hatred were pouring from me like a lanced boil. "My family. Friends. I only have Gretl. He knows this. He knows this and still he just leaves me. I have nothing. No one except him. He let his sister torment me. He let Magda laugh at me. He doesn't let anyone speak to me, know of me. I'm not allowed to visit their homes. I'm not allowed any connection – any real connection – but him. He hides me in the shadows, like an ugly daughter or a psychotic woman. He only lets me go to Münich or Berlin with him. I'm a secret. A hidden

229

lover. I'm not even allowed to listen to the radio." I laughed. "How ridiculous is that?" I couldn't stop. "I love a man that doesn't let me listen to the radio." I pushed Fegelein away and gripped my knees to hold me steady. "The radio. The radio."

"He doesn't treat you well," the soldier said.

"Excuse me?" I stood to my full height, the laughter dying on my lips.

"You shouldn't let him treat you like that. You're beautiful."

"How dare you?" I itched to pick up the hammer again. "I shouldn't have said any of this to you. Pretend you didn't hear it. I'm just drunk. Drunk and stupid. It's been a hard few days. The hardest. No one knows how hard it is," I said. Having opened up made it hard to stop. "But I shouldn't have told you any of this. You shouldn't know this. Don't tell anyone."

"You deserve better."

"And who are you? Who do you think you are? Saying such a thing to me? You don't know me."

"I could see you were in pain the moment I laid eyes on you."

"Don't. Don't you dare do this to me. Do you know who I am?"

"Eva Braun."

"And so you know who I'm in love with. Who my lover is."

"He doesn't deserve you. Not if he treats you like this."

"I'll tell him you said so," I threatened.

"Do," he shrugged. "You should be treated like a queen. Respected like one. You're beautiful. And funny."

"Funny? You don't know me. How would you know if I were funny or not?"

"I have friends up here. Friends that served with me in Poland. They noticed you. I asked about you."

"Me?" I said, flattered despite myself. An instinct somewhere deep within me told me to stop. Stop talking and leave before it went any further.

"Yes. The moment I saw you in the garden at lunch time today. I asked about you."

"Today? I never even noticed you."

"Beautiful woman rarely notice men like me," he said to his boots.

"Eva? Eva? Oh…" Herta walked into the room, Gretl at her back. "What happened here?"

"Effie?" Gretl ran past Fegelein and pulled me into a hug. "Are you ok? What happened?" I watched her turn her head to Fegelein, her face already dark with anger. "Did he…"

"No," I said quickly, pulling her off me. "No. He found me here. He calmed me down." Her face brightened as if it had never been any other way.

"Thank you for helping my sister, Herr Lout," she said as she touched his shoulder. "I owe you for your kindness."

"Enough, Gretl. Thank you, sir," Herta said. "You can go back to the party now."

"Thank you," I said since he didn't move. Only at my gentle smile did he retreat from the room, Herta's glare following him out before meeting my own eyes.

"Gretl, you can go back to the party too."

"Effie?" she looked at me innocently, her heart torn by her worry and her desire.

"Go. I'll be fine."

She needed no more encouragement as she ran from the room. I knew she would be hoping to catch up with him.

"No."

"What?"

"Eva, please." Herta gripped my hand.

"What?" I asked again.

"Don't play dumb, it doesn't suit you. This is dangerous, Eva. I saw the way you looked at him. The way he looked at you. Don't do it. Don't even think about it for a second. You're in a house full of people that want to see you disgraced, torn down, to even think of such a thing would be to invite them to your execution. Please, Eva."

"I don't know what you're talking about, Herta. I love my Führer. You know that."

"But you love you more."

I could say nothing. My tongue too heavy to move.

"And you love to feel wanted. Desirable. Don't do it. Please, Eva. I mean it. Don't do it."

"I never even thought about it," I lied. "He could never be Addie. No man in the world could. I wouldn't risk him for anything. Especially not some soldier in a uniform. Besides," I sighed, "Gretl likes him. I wouldn't do anything that would hurt her."

"Eva, please. Just stay away from him."

July, *The Berghof*

He sent me a letter. Göring delivered it to me personally, without much grace. His wife wasn't in residence at the Berghof, but his demeanor was equally as hostile.

"Mussolini has fallen," he said, curtly, before realizing to whom he was speaking. He nodded before departing the sun terrace and disappearing into the darkness of the Berghof.

"He shouldn't have told you that," Herta said as she adjusted the parasol to better cover her legs.

"Why?"

"It's none of our business. We don't need to know."

"I want to know," Gretl said. "Anything to distract me from my agony."

"You've known him for two days, you silly girl," Herta said. "You are *not* in love."

"Oh but I am. I am, truly. I love him. He's all I think about. All day, all night. I dream of him. I love him. I do."

"I'm going inside," I said as I stood up and followed Göring's footsteps. I prayed that they thought I was just eager to read my letter, that they couldn't see the jealousy stamped across my face as if trodden on under the boot of a Bolshevik soldier.

I sat by the window of a small study that stood sentry at the top of the stairs leading to the lower levels. I locked the door from the inside and moved the heavy office chair towards the clear glass. It looked out onto the kitchen's herb garden. Sprouts of green and sprigs of deep yellow sat in organized rows, overlooked by plant pots filled with purples and pinks. The envelope was smooth beneath my fingers, the seal on the back unbroken. I placed it to my nose and inhaled, hoping that a trace of his smell still lingered. I was disappointed. All I could smell was paper.

Dearest Tschapperl,

I grow weary of the East, the relentless howl of savage winds and the bitter cold and sweltering heat of this barbarian climate. My generals fuss, the stuntedness of their own minds astounding even to me. They have no soul. No heart. No dream grand enough for the future. One set back — the only set back — and they quiver like women without bread. I feel their gluttony as if I were a pie and they hungry children. They are only happy if the pie is full, if their dinners are bountiful. Once a slice has been taken, two, three, they grow hungrier and hungrier as if they hadn't eaten at all. They are children. Petty children. I have delivered them to the gates of Moscow, of Leningrad, and all the ask is 'why not Siberia?'. It is their job, too. Their job is to help in this war; not belittle my achievements. I am so very sick of them. Of their ingratitude. And that's what it is, Tschapperl. They are ungrateful. Ungrateful swines. They watch me as I come in for meetings, for conferences, for councils. They watch me with their sad, tired eyes — wholly defeated — and they complain about weather and supplies and material and vision. Vision? My vision is flawless. A few of them cooperate, so do not fear my darling, I am not entirely surrounded by enemies, by imbeciles. There are great men here, too, German men, that strengthen their backs at the prospect of more work. I miss you.

The words were there. Plain in his scrawl. Free of scribble or smudging. Plainly it said it so, 'I miss you.' I had never felt happiness like it.

And the way you smile at me. The way you laugh when someone drones on and on and you can see my eyes falter, my attention being thrown away. I imagine your face when they lecture me. When they talk to me of tactics and strategy — all excuses for their own laziness — I see your silly smile behind their heads, keeping my spirits high, my morale at its summit. Were it not so dangerous, were I not so busy, perhaps I would invite you here. You'd enjoy this new German countryside. There are a great many hills, so I'm told. Wild forests to be explored. Grand rivers that only men should swim in, yet you would anyway. You're a daredevil, Eva. My only anchor in the world. Without you I would have given up long ago. Without you I would never have gotten this far. Without you there would be no war.

I dream of you and I in Linz,

Your Führer.

I held the letter to my heart. I hoped the words would leave the page and tattoo themselves there, never to be forgotten or taken back. Never to be burned as if they had never been.

The reprieve was instant. I saw then the folly of what I had done and cursed myself for causing him such stress. I wasn't sure which part of 'war' I didn't understand, of why I thought it such a trivial concern compared to myself. He was scared, I could see it in his letter. And instead of keeping his world quiet and controlled, I had opened it to revelry and chaos. How many times did I have to hear him turn to me, his face already drooping from the nap that was clawing him down into its clutches, and say 'this is perfect, just this. Us two, alone.' I'd been swayed by Magda, bowled over by her willingness to rely on me.

I am a fool.

Linz. That was the goal. When the war was over, when his plans were completed, we could retire there. Speer had already come to me – begrudgingly if the harder tone to his usually kind words was any indication – and asked for my advice.

"The Führer insists you must decide on the garden," he'd said.

His stomach couldn't handle the mantle of power, I knew. For all the myth around him, the veil of supremacy that cloaked him, he was a simple man at heart. He loved his animals, my animals. He loved to read children's books and drink mild teas with plain biscuits. He wasn't built for war, for politics, for power – though God alone knew the talent he possessed for it. A secret part of me, buried beneath the anxiety and fear, hoped that once the war was over, Germania in its middle stages of construction, he would name an heir. Once he named an heir, once he chose his successor, he'd already have one foot out of the chancellery and placed in Linz.

October, *The Berghof*

"They fell from the sky like angels," Gretl told me hurriedly as we walked to lunch. "Angels, Effie. They descended from the sky and swooped him free of the Campo Imperatore."

"How?"

"On gliders. Gliders of all things! What a world we live in, Effie. Where men can become angels and rescue heroes from our enemies. What an absolute age to be German."

I kept my mouth closed and hid the smile on the corners of my lips. I knew all about the Duce's rescue, had known since the night it occurred. Addie himself had told me over the phone one evening as I sipped crisp white wine and played with my toes, listening to his voice boom down the line.

"Are you not amazed?" she asked.

"Of course I am. Of course. How could I not be?"

"You don't seem very amazed," her eyes scrunched, forming little wrinkles at their corners.

"Sorry." I stopped walking and threw out a pair of jazz hands and danced a little with a huge grin on my face. "Better?"

"Silly," she laughed.

And then he was there. I noticed him first. He stood in uniform against the wall. A lazy smile played across his face. I burned red. He'd seen my dance. Seen me make a fool of myself. I made to turn and walk away but Gretl held onto my elbow tightly and whispered into my ear.

"He's here. Effie, he's come back to me."

"Hello, Braun sisters," he called along the hall as he stood up straight. Both of us saw the walking stick in his left hand at the same time. The same noise of confusion and worry left our lips as we made towards him.

"Are you ok?" I asked at the same time Gretl said, "What happened?"

"Yes, yes, I'm fine, no need to worry, Brauns. I had a little mishap against the Bolsheviks. Nothing too serious."

"You're using a walking stick," I said, highlighting the severity.

He smiled like a little boy caught stealing, perfectly assured he wouldn't get into trouble.

"It helps on hard days."

"You're back," Gretl said.

"Permanently, it seems."

"Permanently?" My breath quickened.

"Yes. I'm to be Grupenführer. I'm Himmler's new liaison officer with Hitler."

"My Führer?" the thought of them being so close together made me dizzy with fear.

"Yes, apologies. Liaison officer with the Führer."

"Would you like to come to lunch?" Gretl shot across our conversation. "There is carrot soup today."

"Carrot, you say? I do enjoy a good carrot. If it's ok with your sister?"

Gretl beseeched me with her eyes, a silent beg on her lips.

"Of course, Herr Grupenführer, you may come to lunch with us."

I regretted my decision as soon as we stepped through the door. Like wary cattle, all eyes fell on me and the handsome S.S. man at my side. Gretl chatted nervously about the skiing trip we'd taken over the summer, the weeks we'd spent in Münich, too. I took my place by the window table always kept back for my friends and a waiter immediately came over to take our order.

"Wine," I said hurriedly, drawing odd looks from both my sister and her crush. "Please, I mean."

"White or red, madame?"

"French?" Fegelein said.

The waiter nodded a curt yes.

"Speak when you're spoken too." His handsome face grew dark.

"Herr Lout, you…"

"I said speak, dog," he interrupted Gretl's reprimand.

"Of course, sir. Yes, I am French."

Fegelein spit on the waiter's trouser leg. It clumped above the knees before trickling down the black material. Slightly green tree sap.

A few tables around us noticed, but no one said a word. As soon as their eyes had seen what had happened, they turned back to their food and their company and got on with their afternoon.

"And anything for you, sir?" the waiter asked without a glance towards his dripping knee.

"I'll have wine, the same as Fraulein Braun. She will too," he nodded towards Gretl who hated white wine and preferred a warmer red. "Animals. How we put up with them for so long I'll never know."

"So you're sure you're not in any pain?" Gretl moved the conversation on as if it had never been.

When lunch was over, Gretl left to phone our mother, her excitement brimming over like a boiling pot left unattended. He'd been courteous, charming, even flirty with her the entire meal. She'd taken it as he intended, I knew, as only a sister can, that he liked her. That she had a chance.

"Do you love her?" I asked, hoping I kept the jealousy from my words. The smile he shot at me was enough to confirm that I hadn't.

"Love is a strong word. I'm a romantic man, but I don't fall in love that easily."

"Does any man?"

"Some pretend to," he shrugged as if it were nothing more than a pastime, and not the mine field it was. "I certainly like her. But I like another a little better."

"Don't." My words were ice, stalactites falling from the sky.

"You worry too much," he said, laughing. "Never fear, Fraulein Braun, your honour is safe with me."

"My honour is not yours to safeguard," I said back.

"We'll see."

"You're very arrogant."

"I know what I know."

"And what is it that you think you know?"

"How I feel. What you feel."

"You said you didn't fall in love after only two meetings?"

"I lied. I'm a liar."

"You noticed her first," I said, petulantly.

"A gift, to her. When I noticed you, she paled away."

"She's a wonderful woman. With a fantastic heart."

"Second place." He shrugged again.

"Please don't talk like this." He sensed my weakness. The cracking of my resolve. I hadn't thought of myself as fragile, not in a long while. But there, before his eyes, I knew just how delicate I was. "Don't."

"Effie," Gretl yelled as she barged in on Fegelein and I, our foreheads almost touching. "He's back. The Führer's back."

I snatched myself away from the handsome soldier like he was a scorpion, rampant in the desert.

He sat with his feet in slippers. A mug of warm tea was on the table by his side and I was curled in on the other. My dressing gown was freshly washed and he would steal sniffs of it when he thought I wasn't looking. The movie was American – forbidden – but when you're with the person that makes the rules, you can break them. I sipped my wine as the credits began to reel across the screen.

"You'll be a beautiful star," he said wistfully as he stood from me and shuffled towards the projector.

"My Führer. You're too kind," I stuttered.

"You think I don't think of these things?" he laughed, a wheeze running through each breath. "How the world will envy me when you take the stage. I knew it from the first moment I saw you, organizing those shelves up that ladder."

"You remember that?"

"Why wouldn't I?" he said with genuine shock across his face.

"No, no, it's just that…sometimes I wonder."

"You wonder?"

"Never mind."

"No, Eva," he said, his voice strict, his eyes hard. "I do mind."

"Sometimes I wonder if you love me at all," I said as small as I could.

He said nothing.

I closed my eyes and waited for the slap, for the rant, for the anything that would show his displeasure in all its glory. Instead his hand rested on my cheek, turning my chin towards him.

"Stand with me?" he said as I opened my eyes.

I didn't reply, I didn't have to, I followed his hand upwards and stood awkwardly before him. It was like being back at school and having the smallest breasts while getting changed. I felt judged.

His chin was warm and soft as he placed it on my shoulder. His hair was coarse, I thought about buying him new shampoo. Something to soften his head. His uniform was rough. Unwashed, I believed. A putrid smell of days-old body odour clung to it. But it wasn't strong enough to overpower him. The smell of him. The heady aroma of power.

His arms were bands of iron, holding me tight against his body. I rested my hands on his shoulders, linking them around his neck. He swayed, taking me with him. We rocked gently, lulling like a summer sea. We stood for moments which turned to minutes.

"Are you ok?" I whispered.

"Just hold me," he said as he gripped me tighter.

I felt it then, the potency of the vacuum within him. His careful reservedness was a front for the unending hunger in his soul. In his heart. A gulf that drained all feeling and emotion from him, creating only primal desire to battle the destitution. An inherent will to sow against the famine.

"She loved me," he said as he continued to rock side to side with me in his arms.

Geli?

"Before she died. After, I hope. She loved me. She loves me. And she's gone. She'd have been so proud. She'd have been so proud of me, Eva. Why can't she see me? Why couldn't she stay?"

"Who?" The word scratched at my dry throat, making it sound hoarse.

"Muma. My Muma. I was only a boy. A boy. And she left. Me. She left me," he said through garbled tears and the thick flesh of my shoulder. "Those years after he died were our best. But she left. Why couldn't she hold on for longer?"

"I don't know," I admitted, honestly. "But you need to be strong now, ok? You need to be strong, for Germany."

"But my Muma," he wept even more. We were no longer swaying. His weight was pressed against my body, his legs quivering against my knees. It was like holding up a distressed woman who had just found out her son had been killed in the war. It was unmasculine. Un-Führerlike. He was my love, my one true love, and so I tried my best not to wretch.

"She's gone. But she's watching over you, Addie. She is. You can see her?"

"I can?" he said as he pulled his head back from my shoulder. A trail of snot left his left nostril, a tentacle clinging to my dress. His eyes were glassy, like he'd been drugged on his own grief. Drool trailed from his bottom lip, numbed in agony, I supposed.

"Of course you can. Shall I show you where the dead are?"

He nodded as he rubbed his eye like a sleepy toddler.

"See there," I took him to the window and spoke as I threw open the curtains and the window. I stuck my long arm out into the cool air and pointed towards the glittering veil of stars. "That's where the dead are. Close your eyes," he did so at once, "and when you open them, the brightest star you see is your mother watching you."

He was a child on Christmas morning. He opened his eyes and the delight fought against the grief to make them sparkle. Over and over he closed his eyes and opened them again until he'd chosen a star he was happy with.

"Muma," he said as he leant his torso from the window, like he could slither free unharmed and then fly high into the sky to be with his mother.

"It's bed time now."

"Bed?" he said, the shadows beneath his eyes more pronounced under the pale moonlight.

"Yes. It's bed time. But we're going to do something special," I said, quickly. "Would you like to have a sleepover?"

He nodded, barely able to keep his eyes open.

"Let's sleep here, on the couch. Would you like that?"

He nodded again and allowed me to lead him to the couch. He was asleep before his head had touched the cushion. I undid my dressing gown, the thin material over my breasts making my nipples go hard. It was cold. I hadn't yet shut the window. And I watched him sleep. Knowing he was entirely at my mercy. For this evening, anyway. I lay my dressing gown down on top of him and tucked it into the folds of his flabby body. I gave him a quick kiss on the forehead. "Sweet dreams, my Führer." And I meant it.

I hoped that he would have dreams of his mother in Linz. That he would remember the picnics they'd shared in the warm spring sun. How they'd hidden indoors during the summer heat and read as many books as they could stomach. Racing against one another and talking about what they'd read over apple slices and fresh bread. How they'd flown kites along the streets in the blustering, leaf-filled winds of Autumn. But most of all, I hoped he dreamt of how they'd snuggled together in those few Christmases between his father's passing and his mother joining Alois, thankful for each other if nothing else.

I couldn't sleep. Not because there was nowhere comfortable for me to do so, but because I couldn't. My eyes were held open with the same grief that had robbed my Addie's of their mystery. I was losing him. Slowly, relentlessly, he was losing ground to the monsters in his head – the demons that demanded his soul. He was being pushed ever further backwards and he simply didn't have the strength to rally back anymore. The shadows of his mind were touching on his sanity for the first time.

I watched the sun rise through tired eyes. Everything felt simple at dawn. It was a new day. A new day to be conquered, as if the night had never been. He stirred as I yawned.

"Did you not sleep?" he asked, rubbing his eyes, which had regained semblance of himself again.

"Not well," I shrugged.

"Why are we here? Why didn't we go to sleep in my room?"

He doesn't remember. Not any of it.

"Do you not remember last night?"

"WOULD I BE ASKING IF I DID?!" He threw last night's tea cup at me. It shattered by my feet, missing only because of his poor aim.

I said nothing.

"Where is Blondi?" he asked after he'd steadied his breathing.

That bitch?

"In the garden, I presume. Taken for a walk." I held my knees tight to my chest.

"She'd better not have been. Or the person who had won't enjoy what happens," he said while he stalked from the room.

"You must know what Morell is giving him? How could you treat him otherwise?" I slammed my hand down on Karl Brandt's desk.

"Please, Eva, sit down. Don't be like this. Let's talk like adults."

He'd been a handsome man when he was younger, I was told. His features still retained some of that youthful charm, but his face was, overall, too plain for my liking. Smooth patches of skin stretched from eye to mouth like untouched farms in the French countryside. There was no character there. He was slim. Wore a well-fitted suit and smiled politely most of the time. He was as simple and boring as any man could be while still being called a 'man.'

"You have to know what he administers to him. You must. How could you give him anything yourself if you did not?" I said, throwing the entire weight of my medical knowledge at him in that one sentence.

"I don't, largely." He shrugged.

I shrugged, too, in sarcasm. Over and over. I shrugged while looking from side to side.

"Don't act like a child, Eva," he said, sternly.

"Could you ask him then?"

"Morell? That quack? No. I wouldn't lower myself to it."

"I don't care if you think he's a London clown, I am telling you to ask him."

"Fraulein, I think you overreach yourself."

"Overreach. You think I overreach myself." I listened as my voice rose like a quivering storm. The night's tiredness and my own desperation creating a vortex of cruelty that spun free of my gullet. "You'll do as I ask. You'll do as I tell you to. Or I'll get rid of you. You and your wife. I'll send you back to Berlin in an instant, disgraced and never able to work again."

"You couldn't."

"Oh, I couldn't?"

"Otherwise you'd have gotten rid of Morell long ago," he said with a self-satisfied smile that made me wish my nails were claws and I could scratch his eyes out.

"Morell doesn't depend on me for Hitler's favour. You do," I said, much quieter than I had been before. Menacing. "And don't forget it again, Doctor. I want to know what's going into my Führer's body. And then I want you to give me something to counteract it."

"This is dangerous, Fraulein. Too dangerous. If he's being poisoned, we can't rely on an antidote."

"Poisoned?" I collapsed into the chair he had offered when I first stormed in. "If only it were as simple as poison. We've been friends for a long time. Your wife is dear to me," the fight was sucked from my body into the seat's cushions. "Please. Just try and find out."

"Fraulein, what happened? Why the urgency?"

I was going to tell him. For a second, I thought I would spill the entire night out onto his table as if it were a simple jigsaw I was just too stupid to fit together. But I clamped my mouth shut, shook my head and sighed.

"Just find out, please?"

"I'll try," he relented. "I promise I'll try. But Morell is very secretive about his practices, he doesn't like them to be examined. And the Führer allows him his privacy."

"I just need to know."

His buttons were polished and gleaming. He stood by Gretl's side and ran his fingers up and down her arms languidly. He smiled at something she said, parting his lips to a crisp white sea beneath. I could smell the mint even from the other side of the room. I knew he'd smell of mint.

His eyes found mine. At once, they grew darker. Gretl didn't notice, or, at least, she didn't act like she did. She continued with her story as his fierce look pulled me towards him, dragging me closer to danger.

"Hi," I breathed at him.

"Effie? I thought you were down by the lake today?"

"Hello," he smiled back, enjoying me wriggling on his hook while my sister floundered by my side.

"Effie?"

"Yes. Um, yes. I was. But now I'm not. The Führer's gone."

"Gone?"

"Yes. Um, he just left an hour or so ago, I think."

"Are you ok, Effie?" She turned from Fegelein as if he wasn't even there, her hands tight on my elbows. "Sit down. Come on, sit down."

"No. I'm fine. I am. It's the war. He has to go. I understand." Not once did my eyes leave his.

"He's gone?" Fegelein asked, a flair of lust widening his nostrils. "Without me?"

"He likes to do that. He likes to make people play catch up."

"Excuse me, ladies." And then he was gone.

"You're taking this awfully well. Usually you're crying, at least."

"It's happened so often. I don't know, I feel…anaesthetized."

"Hundredth time's the charm," she smiled. "He loves you, you know?"

My stomach clenched. My bowels rippled like her words were stones thrown into a pond.

"He does?"

"Of course, he does. He just doesn't know how to express it. He runs away. Probably because he's scared of his feelings."

It took a few seconds for me to realise that she wasn't talking about Fegelein.

"You're right." I smiled back at her and linked my arms through hers. "What would I do without you? You're the only one that keeps me sane."

"He probably thinks the same about you. Oh, Herr Lout, you're back."

"He's left. Without me. He's just *gone*. I'm his liaison officer, how could he leave without me?"

"By driving?" Gretl laughed at her own joke. Fegelein's face creased demonically, his cheeks razor sharp at the sound of her laughter.

His fists clenched and relaxed before took hold of himself. Gretl didn't notice. But I did. I felt my cunt clench each time his hands did.

"Funny," he said unamused. "I'm going to get in touch with Himmler, see what I should do. Fuck."

"Leave him." I grabbed Gretl's arm, keeping her from following him. "He needs time to be alone. To adjust. He's used to being in charge. Now he's got to learn like the rest of us."

I found him outside smoking.

"Did you get ahold of him?" I asked.

"Who?"

"Himmler."

"Oh, him? Yes. He told me to wait. Just wait. He said I must have angered him, somehow. Or someone did, anyway. This is what he does when he's angry?"

Again, my stomach clenched with fear, seizing at the prospect that he was so powerful he knew my thoughts, could use them as treason against myself.

"Not always angry. The war takes a lot from him."

"From him? He's never seen the war. The Wolf's Lair? Here? This isn't war. This is peacetime. You drink champagne like we are surrounded by wineries. Eat like we live on a farm. That's not war. Not for most of us."

"You're not one of them anymore," I said, hoping it would help, though I was sure he was exaggerating the suffering.

"Maybe. Maybe not. Perhaps I want to be."

"You want to be on the front?"

"I want to have a gun in my hand and the enemy in my sights." He flexed his muscled arms at the thought.

"Surely you're glad you're not being shot at anymore. Now you know you won't die by a bullet to the head?"

"Not all our enemies have guns," he grinned, his mouth tearing up the sides of his face like a horror clown without its face painted.

"You must surely be grateful you aren't in the midst of battle."

"You don't know," he whistled seductively. "How powerful it feels to fight. How raw it is to kill another man. You don't know the energy that crackles between brother and brother on the grass while we move like a pack on the hunt. Ready to kill. It's like no other feeling in the world." I was breathless. He was so close to me I could smell the cigarette smoke on his breath. I backed up, my shoulders hitting the cool glass. He stepped forward too. "Well, maybe just one other." He whistled again. And I came in my panties, shuddering against the glass. He looked shocked for a moment before realizing what he'd done to me. He grinned again, softer this time, and put his lips to my ear so that I could feel the heat of his body on my lobes. "Dirty slut," he whispered. And I came again.

December, *The Berghof*

They were playing in the snow. He balled a clump of fresh white in his hands and threw it – lightly – at her body. She ducked, as he knew she would, instead of dodging out the way. It splattered into a puff of broken flakes as she laughed.

"You don't need to sit with me," he said as he mulled over a pile of papers on his desk. "Go out and enjoy the snow."

"I'm fine here," I said sharply.

He raised his head from his work and stared at me. "Something the matter?"

The matter? The matter? Is something the matter?

I couldn't tell him, though the words rose like a snake in my throat. I wanted to yell at him, to scream how unfair it was that my heart was shackled to his. I wanted to roar about the luckiness of my sister, how she was free to be young and happy while I had to spend Christmas after Christmas alone. I wanted to heckle him as the limp-dicked old man that he was, and how I hated him as fiercely as I adored the ground he walked on. But worst of all, I wanted to throw myself to my knees and beg his forgiveness for allowing another into my heart.

For two months, he had courted my sister relentlessly, all the while teasing me with secret smiles and inside jokes. He'd brushed my hand with his own, knowing that it sent sparks through my body. He would hold her hand and rub her thumb with his own, waiting for me to notice so that he could smile in victory. I had to listen over and over about how he fucked her senseless, how she had bitten her own lip so hard it had swollen because he'd taken her out in the garden. My only respite was when he left for a few days, a week maybe, but then all Gretl would do was mope and that was no fun at all. She'd sit coiled and anxious, waiting for his phone call. But I couldn't tell Addie any of this. So instead I shook my head and picked up my book.

"You shouldn't read that homosexual's work."

"Where he puts his dick doesn't change the beauty of his words."

"Eva. Don't speak like that. Not to me."

My cheeks flamed but I refused to apologise.

"Could you get…get…"

"Addie?" I looked up from my book to see him clutching his chest. Sweat covered his forehead with a sickening sheen. His cheeks looked grey with tinges of green along the bone. I leapt from my chair, scattering the book across the floor. The world stopped. It melted away. All that was left was him, him tumbling to the floor and a shrill, primal scream from somewhere far away.

"Effie?" Gretl was banging her hands against the window. "Effie!"

Like cannon fire I heard the glass shatter and the sound of heavy boots hit the floor. Christina threw open the office door and her mouth fell open. I watched her and wondered if it had been her that had screamed.

"Get help. Morell," Fegelein commanded her. She spun on her high heel and ran along the corridor, her footsteps ringing like bullets.

"Pressure," he muttered to himself as he began to push up and down, up and down on the Führer's chest.

"No. No, you're not doing it hard enough," I pushed him away, catching him off balance and sprawling him across the floor towards my book. I took over where he had left off and prayed to God in my head that he would be ok.

He has to be. He has to be ok.

"You saved his life," Morell congratulated me.

I slapped him so hard that he stumbled from me, five finger shaped welts growing dark across his cheek.

"What have you done to him?"

"Excuse me?" he blustered.

"With your poisons and potions. You're a dabbler in black arts, Doctor. You're killing the Führer."

"It was my *potions*," he hissed, "that just saved the Führer." He brought his hand to his cheek and massaged the tender flesh. "If you ever strike me again, I'll…"

I slapped him again.

"You'll what?"

"I won't tolerate this. I will tell the Führer, I'll tell him."

"Go ahead. Go and tell the Führer. Nothing will happen. Nothing can happen to me. Not here. So run and tell him that a woman hit you and now you're sad."

He looked at me from a furrowed brow, his options dwindling as quickly as the pain in his cheek.

"I don't know why you're so coddled with the idea that I am trying to kill him," he said plainly. "Perhaps it is just womanly rot. I didn't believe Speer when he told me of how dull you keep the conversation around you, not until right now. This is not a learned court. A vibrant court of the arts and creativity. It's a gossipy court. One of frivolous scandals and childish backstabbing. Because of you. You and the shadows you see dancing on the walls." The room grew colder with each of his words. Like he'd conjured a devil from hell through word craft.

"He likes to be the cleverest person in the room," I said, barely above a whisper, though I felt triumphant in my heart. "And so I keep his world dumb, so that he may shine. But all that will be for naught if he dies.

If you kill him, Morell, then we are both of us finished. Our sway, our power, our positions in the world are held by the whim of Hitler alone. Even you are not arrogant enough to deny that."

He thought on it for a moment, his piggy eyes inspecting the filth beneath his finger nails. He licked his lips like a fat, lecherous child before rubbing his chin.

"He needs what I give him." Morell shrugged.

"Please don't do this. It wasn't a heart attack this afternoon, it was a reaction to one of your prescriptions. Just cut back on what you give him," I said, knowing full well that Addie wouldn't allow himself to go cold turkey. "Or give him a placebo to wake him up in the morning. The energy your injections give him is unnatural. Ungodly. It's what caused his seizure today."

"It was?" Morell smiled. "And which part of your education informed you of this?"

"A fool could see it."

"But I am no fool, Fraulein Braun. Nor am I a sister that can be so easily discarded."

Half.

"So don't dare come in here and demand anything of me, you foolish whore."

"Or you'll what?"

"I'm not threatening you, child. Simply insulting you. I will do nothing to you. There's no need. You'll get just enough rope to hang yourself in the end. Women like you always do."

"Goodbye, Dr. Morell."

"Cheerio, Fraulein. I have to get the Führer's medicine ready for after dinner."

"You don't need to take so much," I tried to reason with him as he changed into his night clothes. His pale, saggy buttocks looked as if they had something crawling from them with the black tuft of hair protruding from the crack. "Brandt says…"

"I know what Brandt says. And it wasn't a seizure. Or a heart attack. My body is just wracked with exhaustion, anxiety. I need *more* medicine and Morell – the fool – should have seen it."

"More?" I couldn't believe it.

"Yes, darling. More. To keep my heart calm. To keep my brain running. You have such a gifted life you couldn't possibly understand."

"You think I don't understand worry? Anxiety? You don't think that I wonder each day you're gone if you're dead? If a stray bomb has found you? If a traitor's knife has disappeared into your throat?"

"My poor Tschapperl," he said as he climbed into bed, placing his cold hands on my warm stomach. "You need not worry about me."

"I don't?" I smiled as I moved closer to him beneath the sheets, my most intimate place already wakening in expectation. I panted, just a little, in his ear as I spoke.

"No, no. I am quite safe. They can't catch me, I'm the gingerbread man," he laughed as he bit my neck, gripping harder with his teeth as I gasped.

"Oh, my Führer," I let my hands travel down the soft folds of his body, my fingers running over moles and patches of hair. I felt the waistband of his pajama trousers and he gripped my wrists. I felt my panties begin to sodden with anticipation.

"Don't," he said.

"Yes, sir," I growled back as I rolled onto my back and let him pin my arms above my head. "Yes, sir. Three bags full, sir."

"No. Not tonight."

"But…"

"I said not tonight." He threw my hands back at me and rolled free of the bed.

"Addie, what's going on?"

"Nothing's going on!" he shouted. "Nothing. I'm an old man. Of course nothing's going on. You lie there like a wanton whore and I can do nothing. Nothing."

"My Führer, please."

"DON'T CALL ME THAT!" He picked the lamp from the bed side table and hurled it to the floor. It shattered, stealing away the rooms light with it. I listened to the pieces scatter across the floor as the room was thrown into darkness. "My name is Adolf."

"Adolf," I said formally. "What's wrong? Is it the other day? Your…" I didn't know what to call it without angering him further. I pulled the bed sheets around my exposed breasts and tried to breathe. If I was calm, I could calm him, I knew. And I had to calm him. I had to. If he wanted to kill me, there'd be no one able to stop him. *Except me.*

"There's nothing wrong. Nothing wrong with me. I'm an old man. It's you. There's something wrong with you. Why are you here, hmm? Eva? Why are you here? With me?"

"Because I love you," I said. "All my heart. All my soul. I love you."

"All your heart?" he repeated, turning my blood to North Sea water.

"I love you."

"Why? Why would a beautiful woman like you stay with a man who treats you this way?"

"What way? You don't treat me poorly," I said to the moonlit demon that stalked the bottom of my bed. More boogeyman than gingerbread.

"Oh, I do. And you know it. Slipping away without saying goodbye, not telling you when I'll be back, banning the other wives from inviting you to their homes. I treat you poorly. And yet, you stay. Like a whipped bitch you stay with me."

"A whipped bitch? Is that what you think I am, Addie? Some beaten dog that knows no better? Don't flatter yourself, not for a moment. I am not so desperate as to stay with my captor for no other reason than staying's sake. I love you, you arrogant man. I love you and that's all I know. All I know in this poisoned world is that no amount of parties or walking can dispel, is that I love you. That I am history by your side. I pray only for this war to be over so that you can return to me. So that we can be together. When this war is over you'll step back from politics, I know it. You'll step back and we can be together. But don't take me for some beaten woman, some silent mistress in the corner, fearful of her lover's hand. Because I am not, Addie. And if you want to get violent, to get angry, then go ahead, but at the very least you'll get a black eye in return. Do you understand?"

I was heaving like a winded beast. My eyes were dry from not blinking. I had to watch him. Like a cat mindful of a passing dog. My lips were dry too, stuck to one another so that each word was physically painful to say.

"You don't deserve this." He sank into the bottom of the bed, resting his head in his hands.

"I don't, no. But you're under a great deal of stress, so I will endure it for now. One day you'll be the old Addie I knew again."

"What if I'm not?" He looked at me with shining eyes, emotion trembling in his voice.

"Then you're not. I'm not the same Eva anymore, I suppose. But we still fit. Two pieces of the same puzzle."

"I wish you'd find someone else."

"Enough of that." I tried to put my hand on his shoulder but he shrugged me off.

"No, I do. A young man that could make you happy. Keep you *satisfied*."

Though the room was dark, the light finally clicked on in my head.

He can't get hard.

His outburst made sense now.

"You want me to find a younger man?" I smiled, leaning back on the pillows. "You want me to love him?"

He gulped and said nothing.

"A man with a hairy chest, perhaps? One that glistens with sweat after a run through the woods?" I parted my legs, the moon creating a silver trail from ankle to groin. Like lace stockings. "Big muscles? Thick, hairy arms that quiver as his muscles move beneath the taut skin. A man that knows how to shoot a gun. That delights in shooting it in fact." I closed my eyes and tickled the tip of my nipple with my finger. I brought my finger to my lips and gave it a lick, before putting it back to my nipple. I sighed. "He has strong legs," I said, seeing Fegelein's in my mind's eye. "I can see them because he'd just pulled off his running shorts. Oh, Addie, they're so hairy!" I paused, not daring to open my eyes. I was embarrassed. But equally as turned on. I could hear his steadying breathing and took that as all the encouragement I needed to continue on.

"He's smiling at me." I let my finger trace down my chest towards my stomach, painfully slowly. "He can see the lust in my face. He knows I want him, Addie. His stomach is flat and strong. The air is filled with the smell of his sweat, of his manly odour that only the strongest, most alpha males possess. He's calling me a naughty slut." I paused again, fearful I was pushing this too far. "Says that I should know better than to stare at men. He's only in his underpants but now…oh, Addie, he's taking them off and I can't look away. His pubic hair is so thick and golden. Two large balls nestled in his fur. But his cock, Addie. Oh it's too big for me. It's so big, Addie." Fegelien stood naked before me. He tugged on his dick, even though it was solid like only a young man could be. I had described only what Gretl had told me. About his body, the length and girth of his appendage. "He's telling me to bend over and…"

The feeling was underwhelming, far smaller than what I could see in my imagination, but still, I had been circling myself so delicately that the roughness of him entering me sent me over the edge and I had to bite my lip from crying out the wrong name. He rutted like a virgin on top of me for a few seconds before the gentle warmth of his seed spread out inside me. I hated Gretl in that moment. I hated the way she told me Fegelein's essence dripped from her before he'd even pulled out. How he could continue to penetrate even after he'd came so that her own orgasm could continue. Addie froze, his muscles locking around his bones as he emptied himself inside me. My orgasm had been weak, nowhere near powerful enough to satisfy me after the fantasy I had constructed right in front of him. But as he slid out of me, rolling onto his back silently, I thanked God for giving me a tool to keep him interested in me, however shameful it may be.

He disappeared the next day as I knew he would. He hadn't said a word to me since he'd bid me to find a younger man. He was emasculated, I knew. Broken by his own perversion. It stung to find him gone from the bed, his car vanished from the driveway, but I was happy we'd had sex before he left. It always made me feel more secure, like our connection was stitched each time we did it. Which was sparingly now.

I couldn't get the image of a naked Fegelein from my head. I had

dreamed about him. About the harsh spanking he would deliver on my

exposed buttocks before he entered me. I was permanently aroused. I had

caught myself, more than once, staring at the subtle bulges of the

servicemen and soldiers that milled about the Berghof. And though my

heart was reserved, my cunt was a greedy whore with low standards and less

loyalty.

I masturbated twice before I got up. Always finishing with an

image of my Führer on top of me as if that cleansed away the sins of the

fantasies that had preceded him.

The shower was warm but I wanted it hot. I wanted it to sting and

scald my skin as the shame sunk in like rot along my flesh. I didn't want to

be a slut. To think like one. I wanted him, only him, but Fegelein held a

sway over me that allowed more than just his lust into my soul. I wanted to

be married, to be true to only Addie. Each fantasy, each time I touched

myself was another step away from that dream. I promised myself there and

then that I would never think so disgustingly of myself again.

I'm a lady. Ladies do not think like this.

I shut the water off.

I stood dripping, the air growing colder as it curled around my legs,

my arms. The steam wisped free of the shower and pooled across the tiled

floor. I was crying. I gripped my body in shame as I wept at how low I had sunk. Touching myself in front of him. Talking about another man inside of me. I wretched. Hot bile spilled from my mouth. I wretched again but this time my feet slipped on the wet tiles and tumbled to the floor. My knees hit the shower floor first and pain rocketed up my body. So I cried about that, too. What were a few more tears? That's where she found me.

"Eva?" Gretl said as she grabbed my shoulder. "Effie, what's wrong?"

"I can't bear it anymore. I can't. Oh, Gretl." I gripped her in return as if she were a rock that was all that kept me from sinking. "What have I done? What have I done? I can't do this anymore. Gretl, I just can't do this anymore."

"I know. I know." She hugged me closely to her, uncaring that she was getting wet. "I know, Effie. Just get through today. Promise? Just get through today and everything will be ok."

"How? How?" I wailed as she held me.

"I don't know." I heard her crying too, so far was she from her comfort zone. "I don't know."

I sat by the window overlooking the steep decline towards the Berteschgaden. It was covered in snow. Pristine as the morning guard hadn't made their rounds yet, the last snowfall had stolen the steps of the evening patrol. I was in loose-fitting pajamas that hid my body beneath curves of silk. The Berg was quiet. Addie was gone. The wives had retreated

to their homes on the compound, taking a few private moments before

Christmas came upon us all again. It was peaceful. Oddly so. Like the

minutes before you fell asleep.

I felt sick. A pain grew roots in my stomach that didn't hurt

necessarily, but constantly ached. It reminded me of those days after I had

first swallowed those tablets. How I had burned a patch of stomach so

badly that it pained me for weeks. I'd wanted those tablets then. And the

gun. Both of them together. Morell was right. The wives were right. Even

Addie was right when he called me a whore. It was sickening how much it

hurt. How deeply it sent my heart into shock. I didn't want to be whore. I

didn't want to feel so wantonly about another man, to degrade myself for

his pleasure. I didn't want to be an object that Addie could watch be soiled

by another man. How could I become a mother? Looking my children in

the eyes when I knew what I had done to myself. To be allowed done to

me.

Is this how she felt? That little girl in the Münich apartment? Did she get to

this understanding far quicker than I? Is that why she took the gun and placed it at her

temple?

Will I again?

The sun began to rise. It spilled diamonds across the world, or

uncovered them at the very least. The sky was pink, and I thought back to that summer all those years ago in which I thought the sun had pierced its own heart on the mountains just to be near to me. My arrogance astounded me now. The years had been hard on me.

I heard a car pull up outside the house as the servants began their daily chores. I ran past them all, unperturbed by my casual attire, towards the front door. A secret part of me prayed it was him, returned to me. But as I wrenched open the door, I was disappointed and elated all at once.

"Ilse? Muma?"

"Eva," my mother wept as she ran across the gravel. Ilse was more reserved, but still she pulled me in tight to her.

"I haven't seen you in so long."

"Months," my mother said, though I knew she'd know to the day how long it had been.

"Ilse, you look well."

"I look tired," she admitted with a smile. "We set out at four this morning."

"Why are you here?" I stepped back from them both. "I never invited you."

Suddenly I felt like I was at the centre of a plot, watched on all sides by spies.

"No one can come here unless I invite them."

"We're here to see you, sweetie." My mother hooked her arm into my own.

"No. Has something happened? Is it..."

"No one has died," Ilse said. "Or, at least, no one that would bother you or your lover."

"What do you mean by that?"

"Ilse, please. Not just now. Let us get inside. Have some breakfast. Keep all that unpleasantness for another time."

We both let it go, neither one of us wanting to upset my mother.

Of course it was Gretl. I'd known the moment I saw them, but when she confirmed it I had to sit down.

"Why wouldn't you tell me?" I said, a piece of me annoyed that she'd gone behind my back, exercising power in her own right.

"Because you'd have told me no. And as long as the guards think you invited them up then they'd get in. If you told them no, well..." She shrugged.

"But I don't need them here."

"You were weeping in the shower. Talking about guns and pills. Wailing. You need help."

"And God forbid you have to tarnish your happiness with Fegelein to do so."

272

Her mouth opened at the unwarranted mention of his name.

"If you think I wouldn't ram a butter knife in that man's eye to keep you happy then you're more stupid than I am. I love you, Effie. More than I could ever love him. And yes, I like being happy with him. But that doesn't mean you don't come first. You always come first, Effie."

I turned my face from her, ashamed at my own disloyalty to her.

"Besides. You haven't seen Ilse in too long. We're all sisters. All of us, together. You shouldn't take that so lightly."

"I don't."

"You do," Ilse said as she walked into my room without knocking. "Muma's downstairs talking to Magda."

"Oh is she? I can barely get a 'hiya, how you doing,' but Muma gets a full conversation?"

"Don't be bitter. Be better. Gretl says…"

"Gretl says a lot of nonsense."

"Where is it?" she asked, not needing to elaborate further.

"Where you left it."

"Really?"

"Really, yes. I haven't touched it." Which was the truth, she didn't need to know it was because I was scared I would see it and want to use it. Either on me or someone else.

"Good. What's happened?"

I gave her the same look I'd always given her. The same look I used to fire at her whenever I didn't want Gretl to hear.

"Could you go and make sure Muma is ok?"

"Me?" Gretl asked. "She's only downstairs, of course she's ok."

"Yes, but we don't want her talking Magda's ear off do we? Go and sit her down for breakfast and I'll finish combing her majesty's hair."

"Fine." Gretl made for the door. "But do be quick, I've told Fegelein you're here and he would so love to meet you both."

I winced at the mention of his name. At the realization I had lost him. There was no way, absolutely none, that I could have him introduced to my mother as my sister's boyfriend and then take him away. Not that I wanted to, but the option would have been nice.

"So, you like this Herr Lout?"

"Like him? What? No. Of course I don't, I'm with the Führer."

The reflection of her face fell. I could see her tongue pulsing as a hundred different insults jammed in her mouth.

"You stupid bitch," she said.

"Excuse me?"

"You stupid bitch. A man? All this is over a man? Again, Eva? Are you serious? How can you be so pig-eyed stupid?"

"What do you mean?" I stammered.

"I asked if you like him. Only if you like him *for Gretl*. It's plastered all over your face how you feel. Jesus Christ, Eva. You can't do this. You can't mess with him like this. Not the Führer. You don't know what he's done. Eva, he'll kill you if he finds out. How far has it gone?"

"Done? What has he done?"

"How far, Eva?"

"No far. I mean, not far, nowhere. It's not gone anywhere."

"Does he know?"

"Know what?"

"Don't act with me. Does he know you want him?"

I nodded.

"Oh fuck. Can he be trusted?"

"Trusted, Ilse, what's going on?"

"It doesn't matter. All that matters is that he won't tell anyone that the Führer's girlfriend wants to fuck him."

"Don't be so crude, Ilse. I'm still mistress of this Grand Hotel. And you'd do well to respect that," I stood and shook her from my skirts.

"You'll be Mistress of the Camp if you're not careful," she said from the floor.

The image of the train leading to nowhere shot across my mind.

"What does that mean?"

"Does he like you back?"

275

"Yes," I admitted.

"You can't. You can't take this any further. It has to end. All of it. It has to."

"It's not as simple as that. How I feel, it's..."

"Immaterial. Magda will have you reported in a moment. Her husband, too. All the wives. Gretl tells me how they watch you. How they treat you now. These are not women that easily bow. These are vipers waiting to strike! Vultures willing to strip you of everything. If they even suspected something like this!"

"I didn't ask you here. I didn't want you here. And now you're shouting at me? Warning me? What kind of sister are you?"

"What kind of sister are you, Eva?" she said calmly as she stood.

"She loves him. Gretl loves him. More than anything apart from you. She loves him. How could you do this to her when she's sacrificed so much for you?"

"Nothing's happened."

"Yet."

"Do you think anyone will suspect?"

"We need to act. Now. Does he like her?"

"Yes," I said reluctantly.

"How much?"

"Very much."

"Ok. They need to get married."

"What?" It was like a physical blow to the head.

"She and him have to get married. And soon. No one – not even Magda – would ever suggest you would stoop so low as to fall in love with your sister's husband."

"You've not even been here four hours and already you're organizing the man I love to get married to my little sister."

"You love him?"

"No. Yes. Maybe. I don't know."

"Good. Never know. You can never know. If you don't, they won't. Will he do it?"

"Marry her?"

"Oh, God, don't play dumb now. Yes. Do you think he would?"

I know he would.

"Yes."

"Well I'll speak to him then."

"When?" I said, wondering how long I had left to enjoy him.

"Tomorrow. Organise a party. He can do it there. They'll be married before the summer's over. Eva, look at the mess you've made."

"I'm sorry," I said.

"I know you are. Truly." She pulled me into her arms. "I know you are. This isn't your fault. Not yet. But let her be happy. Promise me? Let her be happy. Don't take this from her as well."

And I wondered, as she whispered that into my hair, whether her plan hadn't already been in her mind. Whether the thought of Gretl's marriage wasn't already brewing in the cauldron within her to give her something else other than myself. A life beyond Eva. If it was, I knew then that Ilse was a far better sister than I.

And a far more dangerous enemy.

The room shimmered with gold and silver cloth. The walls were covered, royally, my sister remarked, but to me it looked like rotting flesh melting from a diseased skeleton. I'd smiled as I'd placed every order. Laughed with the service men – all old and glad of a young woman's smile – as they'd unloaded hurried orders from Münich. Danced on the graveled stones while the scents of fresh baked cakes from the little town of Berchtesgaden wafted through the cold air. But in my heart, I was a ruin.

"A marvelous job," Magda said as she stepped forward in a gown of flawless silver. "And quite the rushed affair as well. Kudos, little Fraulein. Kudos indeed." And she wisped away like passing steam.

"Have you seen him?" Gretl asked, her long gown held on a bangle on her wrist. I'd done her hair for her, styling it upwards and bolting in butterfly clasps into the folds.

"Not yet," I said back as my eyes had another pass of the room, hoping to see his grand height.

A group of young secretaries called Gretl to them. I nodded approval of her leave and she giggled uproariously as she ran to them.

"It's like a school dance."

"Yes, Ilse. It is."

"Herta's sick, she won't be attending."

"She told you?"

"Why would she not?"

"She's my friend."

"You were busy." Ilse shrugged easily.

"Fraulein Braun," one of Magda's children said to me as she tugged on my skirt.

"Yes…" I couldn't remember her name.

"There's someone that wants to talk with you."

"Who?"

"Over there." She pointed out towards the lit terrace.

"Who?" I asked, but already the child was gone, vanished like her mother into the crowd. "I'll be back in a moment, Ilse," I said as I snapped my fingers at a servant, casting the illusion that I was storming off on party business. I took a glass of champagne and drank it in one gulp before helping myself to another.

"Hello?" I said as I wrapped my arms around my goose bumped skin.

"Do you really want this?" he said, his face half lit in cigarette light.

Of course it's him.

"Come out of the dark?" I asked him.

"You come into the dark. Come into the shadows with me."

"She loves you," I said, trying to sober his desire.

"I know. And she loves you."

"We can't do this to her."

"Do what? We aren't doing anything."

"We could be."

"Could we be?" I saw half his smirk. "Is this what you really want?"

I was lost for words. Stunned by his complacency. He was a man, a soldier no less, and there was as much gumption in him as I would have found in a flowering bud in Spring.

"You're leaving the choice up to me? Me? What's the matter with you? Do you love her or do you not?"

"Does that matter?"

"You look like a devil. Step into the light."

"Never. I prefer the darkness."

"I'm not playing these games with you. I refuse. You're in charge of your own heart, you tell me if you should marry her or not."

"That's not what your sister says."

"Ilse?"

"Yes, her. She promises me the firing squad if I don't marry Gretl. That I'll kill you and her both if I let myself be carried away with lust. And that's all it is, so Ilse tells me, lust."

"She thinks you're a social climber," I admitted. If someone were to peer from the hall windows they would have seen me standing talking to myself, singing with shades. "That you're only interested in us to advance yourself."

"Is that what you think?" he asked, the cigarette pulled from his mouth, limply hanging by his side. "Is that what you think of me?"

"No." How could I? When I had seen how he'd looked at me.

"Run away with me."

"What?" I said, his words making no sense.

"Come with me. Now. Let's go. Give me your hand." The shadows released the soft white of his palm. "And let's run."

"We can't. We'll get caught."

281

"Is that all that's stopping you?" he said, hopeful. "That you're worried you'll get caught?"

I stepped towards him. It was my story. My place in history. I could change it if I wanted to. I could take his hand and be gone. Gretl would be heartbroken, but she'd survive. I had. This was her first love, and if that didn't hurt then you'd wasted it. I reached my hand out to his.

"Come on. Take it," he whispered in a voice deeper than his own. "Let's leave this place. Leave here and be free."

"It's cold. Winter."

"I'll keep you warm. Always. No matter what. If I have to set my arms on fire before I wrap them around you then I will. I'll always keep you warm. I promise."

My legs ached to walk to him. I felt heavy, exhausted, and I knew he had strength enough to share. All I had to do was take his hand and it would be all ok. He'd take care of me.

The room erupted into applause behind me. His eyes darted towards the glowing windows like a fox that had caught the scent of the hounds. His hand was still outstretched, the cigarette a second or two from being extinguished, and I could see his fingers shake. The jesters I had hired were hooting and laughing like demons finally freed from hell. I could see them all, the Nazi court, in their finery. Each one had their faced covered by feathers and masks and scales. Each one of them was a debutante of evil playing at witchcraft. Their delight was sorcery. Their laughs howling wolves. Wine was poured like blood and spilled down endlessly cackling mouths. The applause continued, thunderous and wonderful.

I pulled my hand back from him.

"No. Do it. Marry her."

"Fine," he said as he retreated further into the shadows and I was left alone.

"Are you awake?" I peeped my head into Herta's room and was surprised that the light was on by her bed. "I thought you'd be asleep."

"So you stuck your head around my door and hollered, 'are you awake?'" she said, smiling as she looked up from her book. "Why aren't you at the party?"

"Could I not just be coming to check on my friend?"

"You could. But you aren't. What's going on, Eva?" She patted the side of her bed after wiggling further from the middle to make a space for me to sit. Reaching over to her bedside table, she picked up her teapot and poured me a mug.

"He's going to propose to her," I said with a smile.

"Oh dear. Come sit. Come on. Tell me about it."

Her sheets were warm and soft on my arms, I lay in the crook of her elbow and held the mug of tea tightly. I didn't say anything. Instead, I tried to think of the words to show how I felt without admitting how I felt at the same time.

"Is it because he hasn't proposed to you yet?"

"Who?" I said, startled.

"Who do you think? Herr Führer. I know it must be painful for you, to see Gretl getting engaged first. But you have to be strong for her, she deserves this. She deserves to be happy."

"Do you think he'll make her happy?" I closed my eyes, afraid to hear the answer.

"Maybe. For a time, perhaps. She always struck me as a two-marriage girl anyway."

"Herta!" I said, scandalized.

"Oh pish posh, don't act offended. You know what a flirt she can be. How she can swing from idolization to procrastination in a hair wash. This will be good for her. A strapping soldier for a husband."

"You think she'll say yes?"

"You don't? Of course she'll say yes. It's in her to say yes to whatever is asked of her. Even if she didn't want it. Which she does, of course she wants this. He'll propose to you one day."

"Who?"

"What's wrong with you tonight?" she laughed as she placed her book down by her teapot. She began to cough, covering her mouth with her sleeve.

"You know what's good for a cough?"

"What?" she spluttered.

"Whisky," I said, leaping from the bed.

"Oh no, Eva, don't. Come on. I'm sick. Don't do this."

"Hush, Herta. You can have one glass. Look," I said as I opened her underwear drawer and fished through a pool of lace and cotton, my fingers spreading out for the cool touch of glass. "Here we are," I said, brandishing her private stash of whisky. "We can see where he'll propose from your window. Look." I pulled back her drawn curtain and pointed down to a heart shape wound of candles sitting in the snow. I retrieved two glasses from her bureau as she looked down.

"Oh, isn't it romantic?" she gushed, holding her hands to her chest like the women in the movies. "Not to my taste, obviously. But it is, darling. Look," she laughed as I joined her with two – perhaps fuller than they should be – glasses. She shot me a stern look as she took her glass. A cold-looking little lad shot out from the trees near the heart with a lighter in his hand. One of the candles had flickered out in a puff of winter wind and he was desperately trying to light it again before anyone saw. "We'll make sure to find him tomorrow, chuck him a penny or two for his work. He must be so cold, the angel. Do you know, Eva, if you hadn't have come in here, no one may have known what that little boy was doing tonight? He's part of your story, our story, Gretl's story and we wouldn't have noticed – no one may have."

"Someone asked him to be there," I said rationally.

"But we don't know who. It makes me wonder," she said as she took a sip, her experienced mouth not feeling the burn of alcohol as anything other than exhilarating. "How many other people affect our lives without our knowledge? How many cough and give us the cold? How many tell a joke that makes us laugh? How many die so that we can stand here?"

"Illness makes you morbid. And if someone tells you a joke, you know who made you laugh, surely?"

"Not so. Not if my darling husband simply overheard the man say it. If he hadn't, I wouldn't have laughed."

"Did your Erwin tell you a joke?"

"No. Not in a long time. The war has changed him." She shrugged.

"The war has changed us all."

"Do you mean yourself?" she asked, knowing answer well enough. "You were changed long before the war."

"What do you mean?" I let the fire burn my tongue and energise my stomach.

"You've not been the same since Herr Wolf first walked into Hoffman's shop."

"I have. I'm perfectly the same. A little wiser, maybe. More hard, of course. But still me. Still Eva."

"If you say so."

"You don't see me as Eva?"

"Of course I do. You're Eva Braun now. Only Gretl sees you as Effie any longer."

"Effie was a young girl," I said, defiantly.

"You are still a young girl."

"I'm a woman."

"You always said that too. Do you remember how I used to laugh when you told me you had an eye for the movie stars in the picture house? How I scolded you, telling you they were far too ancient for you?"

"Yes," I laughed, grateful she was lightening up. "And I told you that that was how a real man was supposed to be. Older. Stronger. More powerful."

"I should have listened to you then. I should have known the moment you said Herr Wolf's name."

"I didn't know who he was when I first saw him."

"If you say so." She shrugged. "You only worked in a shop filled with his photographs, in a city dominated by what he did and did not do."

"I was young. I didn't pay attention."

"And now you're not allowed to," her eyes never left mine as she took another sip.

The sound of cheering filled the night beyond Herta's window and drew us both from our memories. He was out in front, his confident shoulders only outmatched by his proud walk. Gretl giggled behind him, I could hear it through the window. She wore his jacket, and he was left to freeze in his crisp white shirt. Not that he looked cold. In fact, he looked scalding, filled with the boiled steam of his own desire. He led her into the centre of the heart, the trail of her foot blowing one of the candles out. The boy in the bushes looked torn, not knowing whether he should reveal himself or stay hidden. The crowd came spilling out behind the lovers, a tail of bright colours and metallic gowns. He fell to one knee, blowing out the candle at the heart's other end. All was silent for a minute, then two. Until my sister burst into tears and jutted her hand out to his own, where he slid a diamond ring onto her finger. It glinted in the moonlight, a star fallen to the Earth. I watched her look around for something, as if her happiest moment was incomplete. Snow began to fall and drunken squeals crackled through the air with delight. All at once, the guests slithered back into the warmth of the Berghof. The boy in the bushes came out only when the last guest had gone in. He looked down on the heart, and I looked down on him, and I wondered if we both thought the same thing together.

The heart looks broken.

"Cheers. Congratulations." Herta clinked her glass with mine without me saying a word. "Eva, help me into a dress and let's celebrate."

I couldn't take my eyes from the cracked heart, flaming in the snow. It was like a witch's circle, cut into the ground to summon the devil to us all. The boy was gone, his hands too cold to bother about digging the candles out. He knew, probably, that they would be there in the morning when it was warmer. Perhaps those are what he'd been promised as payment. It seemed a waste, to leave them there. Flickering with no one to see them.

"Eva, will you clasp me up?" Herta asked, her slim body already bound in green. "It's far easier to get ready when you don't bother with make-up." She smirked before seeing the tears in my eyes. Her smile vanished at once. "Are you ok? Are you not happy?"

I couldn't tell her. I couldn't bring myself to admit the hatred I felt inside me. In the shadowy space beneath my heart flickered a candle of my very own. Mine was green and unperturbed by falling snow. There was no little boy required to keep the flame going, no brother candles to stand watch with him. It stood alone. Beneath my heart. Waiting to fall and set my body alight, consuming me with its dark power.

"Of course I'm happy for them. Come, let's go celebrate."

There was only a few of us. The centermost of the innermost circle. The most fanatic, devoted. The fawning. The beloved. Music played from a record player in the corner of the room. It was a low, gentle sound that mixed favourably with the crisp drinks and formal attire we all wore. The music bound us with thread, thin gossamer that webbed between us all in that room, waiting to bring in the new year.

Magda and her husband stood with Emmy and hers. Emmy's dress had just a touch more sparkle, her rings just a fraction larger than Magda's. Gerda studiously ignored her husband, Martin, who stood looming by my Führer's side. The Bormanns were indispensable and they knew it, the second-place status an easy price to pay for security. Erna stood with Hanni, both of them conspiring by the window as midnight approached ever closer. Margarete sat slumped in a chair by the record player, her eyes sealed shut and her mouth moving along to the words of a song that wasn't playing.

"It's very somber," Gretl said to Marion.

"It's been a difficult year. For all of us," she replied.

"Doesn't Christa's dress look fabulous?" Ilse said to us all.

"A gift," I said back. "From my Führer. For the work she's done this year."

"A generous gift," Ilse observed.

"Silver lace isn't gold, is it? Do you wish you'd stayed in Vienna, Marion?"

"No. This may not be a party as such, but at least it's with the people I love. Vienna would be each of us trying to impress the other, blah." She mouthed her fingers. "At least here it's tranquil. Have you set a date yet?"

"Not quite. Effie is handling all that for me." Gretl blushed, hiding her eyes beneath her long lashes. "I wouldn't know what to do, where to start."

"He's a handsome man," Marion said, the lust plain on her words which made Gretl smile. "Exceedingly so."

"I'm a lucky woman," she said with faux modesty.

"Indeed," I said bitingly.

"And will that be easy for you?" Marion asked me.

"Easy?"

"To prepare your sister's wedding?"

"Yes, won't you be embarrassed?" Emmy said as she passed us to collect another drink. The servant by her side evidently not working fast enough. "The youngest Braun sister is the first to be married."

"I'm married," Ilse said.

"Quite," Emmy creased her face in such a way that there was no doubt by any of us that she had no idea who Ilse was. "Humbling, perhaps?" she smiled, spitefully. "Have a nice evening."

"Horrible cow," Marion said first.

"Effie, are you sure about this?"

"About what?" I said to my sister as I drank another sip of warm red wine.

"Planning my wedding. I never even thought. It didn't occur to me that it may be hard for you."

"Don't listen to her, Gretl," Ilse waved her hand dismissively. "She's just causing bother.

"Effie?"

That was my moment, my chance to back out from the hell that spanned before me, a dark horizon of blazing ships. I wanted to go and sit in Addie's lap then. I was his ship, not yet burning, and he my lighthouse, drawing me ever closer to him. But no matter how fast I sailed, the storm of war kept us apart. If I could just have his arms around me, his lips on my ears, then I know I could find the strength to back away from my sister's wedding.

"Of course I don't mind," I said while avoiding Ilse's hard stare. "I'm more than happy to do it for you. It will be an event like no other, a true Nazi wedding."

The sound of spoon on crystal tinkled like fairy chimes throughout the room. All conversations died on their words, half spoken and dripping from everyone's lips. The Führer stood from his arm chair, Bormann a growling hound by his side.

"Thank you all, my friends, for being here with me tonight. This year has brought us our heaviest reverses, as I'm sure you are all aware. The Bolshevik scum has not crumbled as we anticipated, their Red devils sprouting from the mud around our valiant men. But I will not give up. Germany will not give up. And I know, in my heart, that no one in this room will give up, not until we have succeeded in bringing about the consolidation of our Reich!" We all clapped while he sipped a watered-down glass of wine. His arm trembled, his eyes laden with dark shadows set in so deep they could have been bruises. He didn't look at me. As his eyes moved around the room, meeting the gawking stares that fell upon him, using his intensity to drive his words home, he missed my eyes completely. "1944 will make heavy demands on all Germans. We know that. More than most, we know that. But our vast war will reach a crisis this year. And we. Will. Survive. It." The room burst into yet more applause. "I have every confidence in our services, our armed men, whether in the sky, the field, or on water. The Allies will land this year, it is all but certain." A mumble ripped through the room as the rumour solidified into fact in their ears. "But the defences I have lain will surprise them far more than any landing would ever surprise us. We will throw them back into the sea. We will rebuff them from our lands, from our hard-fought soil. And for every German that dies in their folly, we will drop ten bombs on England in revenge. Attlee says that 1944 may be the 'victory year,' and he is right. It will be. A victory for Germany! A victory for our party. For our people. For our future! When we have drowned them in the channel, they will never again crawl towards our beaches. Once we have broken their armada, the Americans will melt away and leave England mistress of her own island once more. And we shall be magnanimous in victory. We shall not colonise them, as they have done so much of the world, nor will we brutalise them. We will treat them as equals, and show the world our civility! And once England has knelt, Russia will burn away in a blaze of flame and gun fire. We will scorch the ground so violently that the devil himself couldn't raise their guns from the mud.

"To 1944. Our Victory year!"

"Our Victory year!" I called back with the rest of the room. "Heil! Heil! Heil! Heil!"

"Do you really think we'll win the war this year, Effie?" Gretl asked me as the rest of the room congregated around the Führer.

"Maybe. But that's not for us to bother about, is it?"

"It isn't?" she said, her face so young and innocent that I wanted to wrap her in my arms and never let her go.

"The world is too dangerous for us. Too violent. We are the lucky ones. Don't you see? We're the lucky ones. Hidden up here, away from the war. There is no war here. There is no war for us. 1944 may be our Victory year, but it will certainly be the year you get married. That is our victory, Gretl. That is my victory."

"Effie, you're hurting me."

My hand was clasped around her wrist, my nails burying into her soft skin. Deep red welts were left behind, blood filled trenches in the Russian snow, when I released her.

"Sorry, Gretl." I turned from her, crying. "I'm just so excited for you. For us."

"Are you sure, Effie? You've been funny since I first got engaged."

"Funny? No, there's nothing funny about it."

"You don't talk to…"

"Let's go and see Addie, shall we? Let's go and see the Führer. It's almost midnight! Can you believe it? Another year gone. Another year passed and we're still here. Gretl, we're still here. I wonder where we will be next year?"

1944

February, *The Berghof*

In just a few short months, he had collapsed in on himself like a ruined shack. He walked up the gravel path dragging his left leg behind him. His cheeks were hollow, creating a sallow face that could barely command a smile let alone the hearts and minds of the Wehrmacht. I ran down the stairs, passing the S.S. man that had stood outside my door, and threw myself towards the Führer as he walked through the door. Until I stopped. Frozen, the breeze cooling my tongue, I tried not to cry.

"What's happened, my Führer?" I said as he shuffled past me, his entourage idling by the open door. "Addie, please, what's happened?"

"I'm just tired, Eva. Please, just very tired. I am going to sleep. Wake me for dinner, would you?"

I nodded and assured him that I would, of course. We all stood in silence as we listened to his hobbled footsteps approach his room.

I'd known that things were bad. His short visit to the Berghof had been hidden from his generals and senior military men. The Wolf's Lair in East Prussia had slept soundly over the new year, believing him in Berlin. Those stolen moments with me, with his family, had been a needed remedy to his growing anxiety, Morell had told me. But now I saw it as nothing more than a dirty bandage on a gouged stomach.

It was inexplicable to me. *How could this have happened so quickly?* The military men began to set themselves up in the Berghof, returning to rooms they remembered and getting their court back up and running in a new location. They walked around me like I was not there, an invisible woman – a ghost – haunting the halls of the Berghof. I needed answers, I needed to know. *Why?* Why? *How?* How? How could this be? *How can he be such a wreck?*

I had two choices, I knew. Only two people could explain this to me. And I hated both of them. They hated me in return. But I hated one less than the other.

"Frau Junge?"

"I think we are well beyond that, don't you? Traudl, please."

"Traudl, how is the Führer?"

"You should ask his doctor," she said like she didn't know. For a second, I thought I had made it all up. That my anxiety was too great, my nerves fried. *Maybe I'd dreamt it all?*

"I don't want to ask Morell," I said back, beginning to gush. "I don't trust him. And the Führer, he's become so old. So severe. Do you know what worries him? He doesn't talk to me about these things," I said shamefully. "But I suspect the situation isn't good."

I'd never admitted that to myself, or anyone else. I wasn't supposed to know, and didn't, really, not for sure. But my gut told me that Addie was a broken man because he was fighting a losing battle, one that even the Devil himself couldn't help him win.

"We're losing," she said bluntly, the force of it a hammer to my face.

"Losing? But... Addie? He's so different. Did you see his leg?"

"His leg? His leg has been lame for months. He drags it like a wounded soldier. He scuffles into meetings, his head bowed, and his arm behind his back, always trailing that leg. He's too sensitive a man for work like this," she said as she pulled a hanky from her pocket and dabbed at her eyes.

"He is," I said, finding the feeling of agreeing with her on something strange.

"He needs to rest."

"I think so, too. It was me...I..."

"I know. And he'll be unhappy about it for a while. But he'll come around. Whatever I think of you, Fraulein – and I do think so very lowly of you – he loves you. It's plain on his face. He's buoyed after he speaks with you on the phone, when he receives one of your letters. It's a brief respite in the unending storm. Thank you, I guess."

"There isn't enough letters in the world to bring him back from this, is there, Traudl?"

She shrugged. "You know the Führer better than I do."

And she walked away.

"Have some tea," I said, trying to keep my voice light and frivolous. My eyes wanted to trace the deep crevices in his cheeks, so I made them study the ambient light of the coming evening as we sat – alone – in the peaceful enclave of the Teehaus.

"I don't want any."

"I'll just pour a cup here, by your arm, in case you decide you do. You might change your mind and I would hate to have to get up again."

"But you would?" The faintest whiff of a smile caught the side of his lips.

"Of course, but I'd rather avoid that if I could."

"And why would you get back up? Even though you don't want to? Is it because I am the Führer?"

"No," I played along.

"Then why, Fraulein Braun? Why would you get back up?"

"Because I love you. I love you and that means you come first. No matter what."

The smile never grew across his lips, the payoff not quite what he was hoping for.

"How's your book?" I said in a chirpy tone that I'd only ever heard from Gretl.

"I don't know. I can't focus," he threw it across the room towards the window.

The purple cushions at his back were crushed and wrinkled. He wore his uniform but the shirt was creased and stained with spills of yellow and brown. His left hand shook terribly, and the only comfort I took from it was that he didn't try and cover it up like he did around the men of his entourage.

"Let me take your boots off," I cooed as I got to my knees. "That might help."

His laces were dirty and clumped with dirt. The knots were too tight which meant someone else had tied them for him. I fiddled with the string for a few seconds, the tips of my fingers sore and numb at the same

time, before it fell loose. I lifted his thin calf up and hauled the boot off.
Then the other. The smell was horrible but I drank it in like a thirsty whore,
knowing that when he left me I would hate myself for not doing so.

I looked up at him and he looked back down at me. Had we been
younger, had the war been going better, had a whole host of other things
that weren't coming to fruition happened then perhaps I'd have taken him
in my mouth and moaned around his manhood while he bucked it ever
deeper down my throat.

"There we are," I said as I clambered to my feet, dusting off my
knees. "Better?"

He nodded and I let out a breath I hadn't realized I'd been holding
in.

It was night outside before someone came tentatively down the
wooded path to knock on the door of the Teehaus. I waved them away
impatiently before I sat with him, forcing him to choose the couch to sit on
instead of a solitary armchair, and ran my hands up and down his arms.
He'd fallen asleep and woken a little before dozing off again. Over and
over. Drool left his mouth and I mopped it up with a handkerchief I knew
I'd never wash again. His hairs felt very fine beneath my fingers and, as the
light had grown too dim for me to read my own books, I'd taken to
studying his face.

Nose hairs pried their way free of his nostrils. Dry skin flaked around his eyebrows and hair line. His eyes lay sunken in his head, broken ships that had drowned in the mysterious blue of his eyes. I was thankful he was sleeping, if I were honest with myself. I couldn't bear the dimness of them now. How they looked, less inviting, less foreboding, and more *ordinary*. Like the eyes of a farmer or a baker. Not the majestic eyes of the Führer.

He was so peaceful in his sleep. His arm didn't shudder. His leg didn't shake. He didn't scratch at his legs or stomach, the dry skin peeling off like rotting flesh. He wrapped his arms around himself, like he'd never been hugged before. He breathed through his nose, a gentle whistling – like an autumn wind through brown leaves – languidly floated around the room. I nestled my head into his shoulder and he opened up, a blooming flower welcoming the sun. Instinctually, for his eyes were still closed, he wrapped himself around me, legs and all, and locked his muscles tight, fearful he would fly away if he didn't.

I didn't know for sure that's why he did it, of course. But I believed it. And that was all that mattered. My legs grew numb, my bladder full, but I didn't move. I couldn't move. My heart wouldn't allow it. He needed a safe place, a safe feeling against him so he could rest. I needed him to rest. The country did, too. My only regret was not having my camera nearby. A photo of this would have been worth more than a thousand trains of gold. But, I

302

had to admit to myself, that would have cheapened the mood immeasurably.

I drifted off to sleep, not ever deciding to. I tried to fight it, battling it with all the strength I had. I didn't want to miss a single moment of his tenderness. Plus, I was worried – like he'd done on so many mornings – that he might leave me to awake by myself. And find myself touched by the cold morning air.

I stood by a river. It was wide and fast flowing. I could hear thunder in the distance but it was oddly comforting, despite its violence. The water was a pale red, like it was an artist's water bowl and he was painting in thick maroon. A city stood behind me. Proud, it shone like silver under the strangely positioned sun. It wasn't directly overhead, but setting, though the light around me told me it had to be closer to noon than sunset. I watched people mill about their lives. They wore strange clothes – far from fashionable – but I didn't judge them for that.

It started to rain. Slowly at first, before increasing in volume. It spattered on the hard, paved streets and created a mist that rose a few centimetres above the ground. I heard scratching behind me. Like claws on rock. And turned. I wish I hadn't.

On the opposite bank of the river stood an army of demonic like men, with gnarled faces twisted in hatred, growing horns and with missing teeth and eyes. They howled in unison, wolves on the horizon, before fire erupted behind them. It fell in an arc over the river, engulfing the rainy city with its jaws. I couldn't hear them screaming for the sound of roaring flame and howling men. The water began to sizzle. People burst from the wall of fire, burning, melting, crisping, and threw themselves into the water. They found no respite there. The water was already so hot that all they accomplished was adding boiling to the list of pains that were torturing them.

I wanted to scream. To run. To fly away. But I knew I couldn't. There was nothing I could do. So, I watched as the city burned, as the demons howled and as the people threw themselves out of the fire and into the boiling water.

"Eva?" his voice boomed from the sky, incorporeal, but a hand all the same. "Eva?" It curled around me and lifted me high above the river. I could see them now, more clearly, the hordes of them. Half a million red devils all baying for blood. "Eva?"

"What?" I was back in the Teehaus. My hair was stuck to my neck, the air cool against my sweat lathered skin.

"It's just a dream." He gripped me tighter. I was wriggling against him, fighting to be set free but he kept firm. I tired, my muscles weak with fear. And I stopped struggling against him.

"Oh, Addie," I began to cry. I put my face to his shoulder and wept. I clutched him back.

"It was just a dream. Just a dream."

"Was it?" I asked, pulling my face back from his shoulder. "Was it?"

He walked into the room with the same confidence he always slathered over himself. He came directly to my table, his eyes alive with fire, and kissed Gretl on the cheek, his eyes never leaving my own. I shuddered at the memory of the dream and looked back down towards my jam roll.

"How's my wedding coming along then?"

"Oh wonderful, Lout. Wonderful. Eva has so many fabulous ideas. Guess where we are to be married? Guess?" She fizzed in her seat, her hair bouncing around her ears.

"Hmmmmm, Berlin?" he said as he kissed her ear.

"Better."

"Vienna?" He picked up one of her rolls and ate it.

"Salzburg," I interrupted, their endless cooing making my skin crawl. The shadowy place beneath my heart howling.

"Effie!" Gretl turned and pouted. "I was going to tell him."

"You can tell me where in Salzburg." He brought her attention back to him, raising her mood with a word.

I didn't like how easily he could play her. How simple he found manipulating her moods to suit his whims. An easy smile and a generic line about love and she looked ready to throw herself down the mountain for him.

"Mirabell Palace! Can you believe?" she squealed, drawing the attention of everyone at the tables around her. "Me. Us. The Mirabell Palace. How grand!"

"Grand? We are practically royalty to get married there." He picked her up from her chair and she wrapped her legs around him. His strong arms strained through the material of his jacket. I imagined how tight the muscles on his stomach would be clamping together, drawing the hair on his stomach closer to one another. "And I am the luckiest man in the world to do it with you." He kissed her. The room broke into scattered applause for their favourite Braun sister. Even Magda, resplendent by her husband near the window, put down her fork to clap lightly at the young couple.

"I'm feeling sick," I said to no one as I stood and left the table. I felt Magda's eyes on me as I left, her nose twitching at the scent of weakness.

"Effie, what's wrong?" Gretl crept into the bathroom with a sad look on her face. It made me want to kick her. My foot spasming.

"Nothing," I said, looking away from her, back out the window to the world beyond.

He'd asked me to leave with him. He'd put out his hand and begged me to run away. We could be anywhere by now. Africa. Ireland. Argentina.

But I had chosen an old man with failing health and a half-life of perpetual limbo instead.

"There must be something wrong. You never get in the bath without there being something wrong."

"You think you know me so well, don't you? You brush my hair and fetch my tea and you think that means that you know who I am inside. Maybe I just like the view here? Maybe I enjoy the colour pink? Maybe I just like sitting like a crazy woman in a bath, fully clothed, with no water in it. Have you ever thought about that?"

"Effie, what's wrong with you? Is it Addie?"

"NOT EVERYTHING IS ABOUT HIM!" I slammed my hand down on the side of the bath and heard my wrist click. "Now look what you've done," I said to myself, weeping.

"Effie, stop this. Come on."

"No, you stop it. Stop it. Stop it. Stop it."

"Stop what?"

"Being happy. Stop it. You're killing me. You know you are. You're killing me."

"Effie, I'm sorry…"

"Yeah, right. So you should be."

"No." She stood away from me, pulling back the arm she'd extended to comfort me. "I'm saying I'm sorry for you. But I won't stop being happy for you."

"What?"

"I've given up so much for you. So much, Eva. And I love you, I do. You have no one up here. Not really. And you've needed me. I've been happy to be there for you, I have. But I can't give up any more of myself for you. I won't. You're not being fair. You know you're not. You chose this, this life. You chose it and I stood by you. But now I have a chance. I have a chance to be happy and married. Married, Eva, me! And you want me to feel bad about that. Guilty? No. No, Eva, I won't. And shame on you for asking it of me. Shame on you for asking it of the one person in this world that loves you so much that she's carved out a hollow life just so she could stay by your side. Shame on you for making me – your sister – feel anything but happy for finding the love of a good man. I've never thought this of you before, Eva, but maybe you're not a very nice person. Maybe you're not a good soul after all." She was crying so heavily that some of her words got lost in the tears, but not once did she falter. It was like I had shot a hole in her defences and the entire thing was crumbling around her ears. "Shame on you, Eva."

"Get out," I said. "Get out."

And I was alone.

My heart was breaking, falling apart at the seams. I could feel each brick tumble from its place, the beats of it banging against its soon-to-fall brothers, echoing throughout my soul. She deserved better than me. I knew it. I knew it. But I couldn't be better. There was no more left of me to give to her. I'd promised it all to another. And that's what I was most jealous of. It fell on me like a silk shawl as I sat and wept in the empty bathtub. It caressed my skin, smoothing down my arms as it settled into place. That's what I hated most in her, most in everyone: that they weren't as bound as potently, as toxically, to Addie as I was. The war was ending. I knew it because he knew it. It was what had ruined him. The knowledge that he'd lost. He'd not admitted it to me yet, and probably not to anyone else either. But, he wasn't a stupid man. You didn't become the Führer by being a stupid man. He wouldn't stop, though. Not for a second. He'd give himself no moments to contemplate what would happen when Germany lost.

When he lost.

And so he could never have won.

And that's what I hated her for. She'd have a life after the war. I could see it. Her smiles. Her laughter. Her satisfaction. When the war was over, she'd go on. I knew I couldn't. I wouldn't. Because he wouldn't. I'd bonded myself to him in a pact of steel, far stronger than any marriage, and if he sunk – which I knew he would – I would too.

When he dies, I die.

When he dies, I die.

When he dies, I do.

My marriage vow to the Devil.

April, *The Berghof*

"Wake up, Eva. Wake up," Gretl shook my shoulders and brought me out of my dream. A siren was going off in the compound, the low drone of bombers buzzing like angry wasps overhead.

"We have to go to the bunker."

"The bunker? No. It's just some underground rooms."

"Still, we should go."

"No. No, we don't need to."

"The Führer is there."

"So? The Americans aren't here for us. They're on their way to Vienna, to Hungary. They don't care or don't know about us here. Go to sleep, Gretl. We have a long day tomorrow."

The first time the Americans and British had flown overhead in their huge aeroplanes, I had been hidden in one of the underground rooms. Like rats, we gripped each other and prayed that the bombs would spare us, vowing to leave and never return once they'd passed. And they did pass. As did the next wave. And the next. Until the only person that still hid was the Führer.

If I go, he'll only think it's more serious than it is.

That's what I told myself so that I could get back to sleep.

I wore a black dress when I got up. It hugged my body tightly, a slender figure in the oversized looking glass. I hadn't slept well since he'd been back, but still my face was relatively unlined – a joy of youth.

I sat by the window at the front door, waiting for Gretl and Herta to come down the stairs. I should have been with them, as they were getting ready, but I couldn't bring myself to do it. To sit with them. The Berghof was already so tense, so filled with anxiety that every meal time took an age and was as sombre as a funeral feast. The wives did their best to keep spirits high, but we all knew we were just circling the drain, avoiding the one topic we all wanted to talk about.

"Hello, little soldier. Are you lost?" I said to the eight-year-old boy wandering aimlessly around the halls.

"No, ma'am," he saluted, a grin taking over his face. I recognised it. It was one of pride.

"What are you doing here? So far from the front?"

"Hunting undesirables, ma'am."

"Here? In the Grand Hotel?"

"Grand Ho-...you mean the Berghof? Yes, ma'am. They get everywhere. Like muck from a chimney. They get everywhere."

311

"Well don't let me stop you, young soldier. Get back to work. The Führer might see you slacking."

His grin fell and his cheeks turned rosy. At once he pulled the magnifying glass from his pocket and ran off down the corridor, intent to find something to show his father.

"Wasn't that Magda's child?" Herta asked as she came down the grand staircase, my sister at her side.

"Yes. He's a soldier today."

"Little dreamer," she smiled. "It's a shame he doesn't see his parents more. I'm glad I raise my children myself. They know their mother."

"Yes." I smiled awkwardly. "Shall we go?"

We all got into the long stretch Mercedes and fiddled with our gloves, or our hats, in lieu of speaking to one another. We pulled down the driveway, past the checkpoints, each showing our weekly given cards from Bormann, before we hit the winding roads of the mountain side.

"So how did he die again?" Herta said in an attempt to break the tension between Gretl and I.

"An air raid," I said. "Though how the Allies could have struck Münich, I don't know."

"If they can fly over Berchtesgaden, then they can fly over Münich," she said back logically.

"He was such a funny man. Such a fantastic spirit."

"Yes," I said, trying to catch her eye. She studied something just outside the window, keeping her gaze safely away from my own.

"Driver, have you taken a wrong turn?" I said as we turned a corner and faced a fallen farmhouse. We'd only been in the car for an hour and a half.

"No, ma'am," he said solemnly. "Please," I saw his desperate eyes in the rear-view mirror, "don't be scared."

"Scared?" Gretl asked.

"Yes, ma'am. Münich may not be quite as you remember it."

"What do you mean? Driver? Tell me. What do you mean?" I said, but Herta's hand was on my elbow and her gentle squeeze told me to be quiet, that this was not his fault.

Buildings watched us as we drove by. Each hollow window was another eye, daring us to look at what we had done, what we had escaped. Scorch marks rung them in soot and black and in every window, I saw Hitler's eyes. Autocars lay abandoned in the street, littering the road like dead animals left to rot. Their windows were smashed. Some of them were beetle husks, empty of their creatures. The light that bothered to grace this dark place was grey and tainted with the gloom of smoke. It stole the world's colour, making each lane and alleyway devoid of anything other than death.

"No. No, we must tell someone. We must tell Addie," I said.

"The Führer knows, Eva, of course he knows," Herta tried to console me.

"Eva, I don't like this." Gretl moved herself closer to me, her heat a familiar anchor staving off the panic.

"It's just this street. Don't worry. A loose bomb would have caught it."

But it wasn't. As we moved further into Münich, the devastation grew worse. Buildings collapsed like melted faces, huge craters were dug into the road like welts from a belt, and glass shimmered menacingly on every corner, diamond snow waiting to cut.

"Those children?" I said to Herta. "They're playing?"

"Yes."

"But how? Why? It's dangerous, why would they be playing outside?"

"It's not fair to keep them indoors all day." She shrugged.

"But...aren't their parents worried about them? What if they were to fall? The glass is everywhere. And look, those children are playing on that pile of rubble. Stop the car, driver. Stop the car and let me out."

"Eva, no. Don't. This is their world now. This is the price they have to pay for victory. Don't interfere. Don't draw attention to yourself. To us."

"Their world? But surely this only just happened? How can they be so used to it by...oh."

The rest of the day passed in a blur of platitudes and silent grieving. We stood by the graveside and paid our respects, before getting back in the car.

"Aren't you hungry, ladies? Should I take you for lunch?"

"No, thank you, driver. No. Just take us home. Take us away from this place."

"This was our home," Gretl said, too shocked to cry. "We played here, Effie. We did. And now..."

"Shhhhh, it's ok. It's ok. Close the curtains." Herta and I pulled the curtains along the car windows shut. It made the interior dark, but that was easier to deal with than the horror beyond the glass. "We'll rebuild. When all this is over, we'll rebuild. I'll speak to Addie; he knows how much Münich means to us. We'll get it rebuilt first, ok? I promise you. Promise."

"Addie, did you know about Münich?" I said a few days later.

"What about it?" he said, not taking his eyes off his beloved dog. I spoke in low whispers, keen that Bormann and the Goebbels, who stood only a few feet away, didn't hear me discussing this.

"That it's ruined. It's been bombed, Addie," I said, hoping for a look of shock across his face.

"Everywhere's been bombed."

"No, Addie, it's a ruin. A ruin! My home. It's all gone. What's left is so terrifying that it may never be home again."

"Sit, Blondi. Sit." The dog sat diligently.

Stasi and Negus were upstairs in my rooms. They didn't like Blondi much, but it was his birthday, so I let this fight go.

"Addie, did you hear me?"

"Yes, Tschapperl," he said. "Yes. And I promise we'll bomb them back tenfold. London will slip away into the Thames. Glasgow to the Clyde."

The thought of retribution hadn't crossed my mind until that moment. All I'd hoped for was a promise of rebuilding.

"Rollover, Blondi," he said to his dog who, again, did so dutifully. Traudl Junge and Frau Schröder both clapped. The fire crackled as the dog knocked into a log nearby the fireplace and the image of me kicking her into the vibrant orange took hold of my mind. "She is the cleverest dog, don't you think?" he said to Bormann who nodded back his assent. "She hunted rabbits today. We took a walk along the mountain paths and she caught the scent. Off she went like a bolt of furry lightening." He rubbed her chops as he spoke.

"My Führer," Frau Schröder asked, "did she catch the rabbit?"

"Two," he beamed. "She caught two, the clever girl. That's what I had cooked up for her dinner. A birthday treat of her own. The two rabbits she

316

caught. Blondi, sing!" Hitler shocked the room as he began to emit a low

howl. To my surprise, the dog did too, a perfect harmony of master and

hound dumbfounding the room around them. "Good girl," he said as she

continued her solo. "Lower, Blondi – sing like Zarah Leander!" At once the

mutt gave a long, drawn out howl, more wolf like than dog like. "She really

is the cleverest dog I know."

As midnight struck and his birthday arrived, servants opened the main

doors and tray after tray of glasses and champagne were brought in. We all

took a glass and raised them in unison. I imagined it shattering in my hand,

the champagne seeping into the open wounds the glass had torn in my

flesh. I imagined them all shattering under the powerful boom of a bomb

falling on top of us all. "Happy Birthday, Mein Führer," I said, shaking the

thought from my head. The room burst into "All the best, Mein Führer!"

around us as he sipped his small glass of sweet white wine.

I didn't get to bed until three a.m., not daring to drift too far away

from him while the Berghof came out en masse to toast his birthday to him.

He slipped away at half one, but I wanted to set up a little surprise for him

in the morning.

He does so love to be spoiled.

After only a few hours of light sleeping, I got up and put on his

favourite dress. It was navy silk and spattered with sequins. I wondered, as I stared at myself in the looking glass, if they looked like bullet wounds in my body. I prayed no one would think so.

I stood by the *Geburtstagstisch* I had prepared for him the night before and was surprised by how early he came down the stairs, jubilant on his special day. Gretl stood by my side, thought she didn't hold my hand as she usually would. He looked at us dotingly as he began to unwrap his gifts. I'd deliberately put the gifts sent by the house wives and children of Germany on the table, so that the people that gathered around us could see his benevolence and the adoration afforded him. He opened a small wooden bowl. Knitted items. A statuette of a young girl that made my heart seize as I saw Geli's face on it. Homemade cakes and chocolates sat uneaten by the beautiful Spring flowers, waiting to be burned – such was his fear they were poisoned.

Bormann hovered unpleasantly at our side, but I gave him only smiles on the Führer's great day, careful not to antagonise him, knowing his power grew when the Führer left.

"A wonderful spread," a voice whispered in my ear as I stood by an open window and looked out onto the snow-covered ground. "Such a shame there aren't many Spring flowers out for you to pick."

"Why are you here?" I said back.

"Gretl would like me to know what's going on for our wedding. Usually I would brush it off as woman's nonsense." His breath smelled like bread. "But, since it's you, I thought I'd come and find out."

"You'll have a spectacular day. You'll have to do nothing. And my lover, the Führer, will be there by my side." I drew myself to my full height. "Is there anything else you'd like to know?"

"How stringently do you define 'lover?'" He smiled, then walked off. I stood furious at his brazenness, but I couldn't take my eyes from the defined curves of his rump.

6th June, *Mirabell Palace, Vienna*

A cloud lived with us those few months until the wedding. Although I tried to remain calm, to busy myself in preparations for Gretl's wedding and avoid the anxiety that plagued the footsteps of even the lowliest secretary, it was he who snatched at the corners of my mind. It was he that haunted the centre stage of my dreams. And it was he I thought about when I let my fingers dance southward.

"Stop barking," I snapped at Stasi as Fraulein Heise set to work tailoring in my dress.

"It fit only a few weeks ago, Fraulein Braun," she said, concerned. "Are you not eating?"

Something in the way she spoke, the twinkle of her eye or the curl of her pin-holding lip, told me that she highly doubted that I hadn't been eating.

"I have a lot of worries. My sister has left me to plan her wedding entirely. Food is not always an option." She couldn't hide her snort of derision. "Something to say?"

"For many people – you may not know this yourself – but for many people, food isn't always an option."

"As thin as I have become is as unkind as you have. Tell me, how many dresses have I bought from you over the years? Enough to make you a wealthy woman that's for sure."

"Eva, we're friends."

"Are we?"

"She looks beautiful," Ilse said as she walked into my apartments in the palace with my mother and father. "A vision."

"My little girl," my father said, tears in his eyes.

"And how are you, Eva?" my mother asked. It was plain on her made up face that she could smell the tension in the room.

"Done," Fraulein Heise answered for me. "The pins will hold until after the ceremony and by then I'll have your evening dress taken in."

"Two dresses," my mother exclaimed at the excess.

"Four," the dressmaker shot behind her as Stasi barked at her leaving.

"You look wonderful, dear." She kissed me on the cheek. "You make your mother proud."

"Should you not be with Gretl?" I asked them all, though the question hung in the air that shouldn't *I* have been with her.

"We came just to see how you are. We're going back to her now. Are you sure you wouldn't like to come? She's your sister, this is her wedding…"

"I planned it. I know that. And no. I want to be alone."

"Is the Führer attending?" my father asked.

"Yes. He's doing some business just now," I waved their suspicious stares away with my hand. "He'll be here just before the wedding begins. Now go, go back to her. I'll see you there."

"Such a big day," my mother said as she hugged me tightly. I let my eyes shut – just for a second – enjoying the feeling of being a little girl again, safe in my mother's arms. "You'll have one, too. I promise. You'll be married to." She pulled away and tugged at my father's sleeve.

"I'll stay with Eva," Ilse said to them both as they waited by the mahogany door frame.

My mother nodded gratefully before piling off with my father down the hallway to my sister.

"I know this is hard for you. But it's the right thing to do." The words had barely left her mouth before I slapped her.

"You *know* this is hard for me? You do, do you? You've had to plan the wedding of the man you love to your sister?" I hissed each word, a viper ready to strike again.

"Love? You think you love him? Don't be ridiculous. You don't *love* him Eva. You loved Peter. You love Hitler. You do not *love* Fegelein."

"And you'd know, would you? How would you know? You don't know me anymore, Ilse. You don't."

"I want to." She gripped my hand. "I want to Eva. Please, let me in. I'm your sister. Please. Let me in."

"I think about him." I sat on the plush cushions of a window seat that looked out along the ornate gardens before the landscape dipped away into the Salzach. The fresh blue of the river's water drew a pining for the mountain air again. "All the time. And Fegelein. I think about them both. There's no room left for anything else. No dreams. No ambition. I wander around the Grand Hotel and pine for one man then another. You think I'm pathetic, don't you?"

"Pathetic? No. I don't think that. I think you're young. Too young for all this," she gestured around the grand luxury of the palace. "Who'd have thought that one of the Braun sisters would get married in a place like this?

We're ordinary Münich girls. You'll always be an ordinary girl from Münich.
And maybe that's your downfall. That's what he loves."

"Who?"

"Does it matter which one?"

"My heart hurts. To see her walk down the aisle will kill me. I love her.
I planned all this so that she would be happy – she *should* be happy. I want
that for her more than anything else in this world. But not with him.
Anyone but him."

"She's made her choice."

"And she's chosen him over me."

It was the first time I'd said it aloud. I could hear bells ringing in my
head. The room grew fuzzy, like a bomb had gone off below and the world
above was shuddering from its might. My stomach lurched once, twice,
three time before I wretched onto the rug. Over and over.

"That's it. Get it out. Get it all out."

Over and over.

"What can I do, Ilse? What can I do?"

"You can bury it. Bury it all beneath rubble and dust. Bury your
feelings for him and be happy for her. She's your sister, much more so than
I've ever been. She's your soulmate, Eva. You're one of the lucky ones,
you've been born with your soulmate. This is your sacrifice. You've had to

make so few. This is what you have to give up in order for her to be happy. Can you do that for her?"

"I need time. To think," I said after a pause. S.S men were patrolling the gardens outside. Great anti-aircraft batteries stood like wicked metal nests at the summit of each of the tallest buildings. The bells rang again; time was slipping through my fingers so quickly. "Can you give me time to think?"

She smiled as if she'd known that's what I would ask. Sadly. She stood from me and kissed my cheek lightly. "Of course I can, Eva. The wedding is in an hour. Take time. But when you show up in that hall, he has to be buried. Do you understand? Once they're married this has to end. You can't think that way about your sister's husband. It will eat you alive inside."

"I know, Ilse. I know."

He came to me in his military finest. I hadn't sent for him, but I'd wanted him all the same. Like he could hear my thoughts, drawn to my longing, he knocked on the apartment door and strode in.

"Eva," he said quietly. The timidness on his voice, the lack of self-assurance made my head snap around from the window. "Am I ok to be here?"

"Ok? You're asking my permission?"

"Of course I am. I don't want to do anything to hurt you."

"The day you're marrying my sister, you don't want to hurt me?"

"Please, Eva, don't be like this. You know I have to."

"Have to? Is that all my sister is to you? A necessity? You don't *have* to do anything. You could be a man. You could tell her that this isn't what you want. That you can't go through with it."

"But it is what I want," he said, avoiding the pile of sick on the rug.

"Then why are you here?"

"Because I want you more." He sat close to me, his eyes on the soft curves of my breasts. "I asked you to run with me that night in the garden. And I'll ask one more time: run with me. Let's run away together. You and I. We can go to Switzerland. To Spain. Just take my hand, Eva. Take it and we can be gone."

I moved my hand to take his. It was so steady, so still. It didn't shake as he waited for what he knew I would do. He was confident. Young. Healthy. Strong. And his eyes still sparkled. He was a man through and through. I knew that if I ran with him, he'd keep me safe. No guards, no soldiers, no Bormann, or Morell, or memories of Geli. Just him. He'd keep me safe. And warm. And loved.

"I can't." I drew back, hugging my arms around myself tightly so that they weren't tempted to take his. His hand fell to his lap. He got up to leave. "Wait."

"No, Eva. I won't wait. Not anymore. You were the only one that could save me from myself. From what I'm about to do. And you've left me on my own. You've left me out to hang." The rumble of engines drew nearer in the distance and both our eyes scanned the crystal blue skies for any signs of aircraft flying over. "The Führer is here," he said. "I hope you don't regret your decision."

I fidgeted through the ceremony, Addie by my side. Gretl was a vision in white, a true German girl marrying a true German boy. Hitler beamed at the new extensions to his family and his body only trembled a little. I slid my hand into his. It was sweaty, the moisture sickeningly warm. But I held it anyway. And tried not to dream of Fegelein's. The moment came for the 'I do's,' and I found myself holding my breath. Gretl said hers first. Then it was his turn. He lifted her veil, though he wasn't supposed to do that until the kiss, and stared into my sister's eyes as if he was searching for something. His deep blue gaze swept clear of her face and met my own stare. With a deep voice, trembling lips and no degree of uncertainty he said, "I do."

And I wept.

July, *The Berghof*

The Führer held my hand as we walked the length of the Grand Hotel's halls. He spoke to me of how beautiful the winter was in the East.

"But isn't it dreadfully cold?" I said, trying to sound enthusiastic and smother the peripheral sense of dread.

"Quite, yes. It gets very cold. But always beautiful. There's a lake, near the Lair, and it freezes every winter and thaws every Spring. If I was a younger man, I'd like to go skating on it – as you do on the Königssee. Gretl sent me a picture of you last Winter on it."

"She did?"

"You didn't know?" he chuckled at my raised eyebrows. "Yes. She sent me a photograph and promised me that you missed me dearly."

"She never told me she did that. Has she sent you any photos since?"

"Not in a long time." He shrugged.

He stopped by the door to his office and flung it open wide. I followed him in, but banged against his shoulder. He stood, still, by the door. Unmoving. His eyes roved over the chair, the desk, the window, before settling on the large portrait of Frederick the Great. He said nothing as he stood, appraising. His hand trembled at his side, so I clasped it in my own. He smiled, though whether it was at me or not I didn't know. He smelled the air, as if he could suck in a decade of memories, before heaving out a sigh and shutting the door behind him.

"You miss her," he said as we moved on, my hand still in his.

"Of course."

"Is it truly so unsurmountable that you must give up?"

I shrugged.

"I hate to think of you alone here."

"I'm not alone," I said back. "You visit me."

"You need more company, Eva. You know you do. My little Tscahpperl finds it difficult enough, I know."

He'd never admitted the toll his absences took on me before. I didn't push it, though a thousand questions formed and melted away in my mind, all one after the other. The undercurrent, the deep drone of the bagpipe beneath them all however was, 'why?'

But I said nothing.

"How about your cousin? Gertraud? They young girl at the wedding. She likes you a lot."

"I haven't spoken to her, not properly, in years. She's a young woman now." I smiled with pride, knowing my own hand in it.

"Get to know her. Eva." He stopped and turned to me. I thought, for a second, he was about to say something, something vital and important – final. But instead, he reached behind me and opened the door to the drawing room that he used to retire to with his generals.

Again, he stood by the doorframe and gazed in longingly. He was a child by the cold, hard window of a sweet shop. A poor child. He knew he could never go in, the temptation to stay and never leave would be too much. And he knew he was weak, that child by the sweet shop. Innocent. He knew the temptation would be too great and so he never went in.

"I think you should," he said as he closed yet another door. "Please," he kissed the top of my forehead. "Help this old man have one less thing to worry about."

"I have Herta."

"She's a mother. You'll never be first for her. Invite your little cousin, please."

"If you think it would be best. If it gives you peace of mind then I will, my Führer."

All the erotic meaning behind the phrase had dwindled away so peacefully, so quietly, that I hadn't noticed until that moment. It used to drive him wild for lust, a beast with an erection that stayed hard for hours. Now it drew only a self-satisfied smile from his lips, that opened from beneath his neatly trimmed moustache.

We reached the grand hall where we'd held part of Gretl's wedding reception, the other half being up in The Eagle's Nest. He stood by the door and stroked the wood of its frame.

"You're saying goodbye. Aren't you?"

He didn't say anything for a moment. "I used to watch you as you danced, you know."

"When?"

329

"Always," he shrugged. "Whenever I could. It's what I think about when I'm far away from here. Your dancing. And laughing. The way you would nudge Gretl just half a step out of line and she would knock into someone. They'd be so angry but they couldn't resist her devilish smile. They never noticed yours. I did. I've hidden you away. Do you ever wonder why?"

"Why?"

"Because I can't bear to think of you becoming like them. Hard like Magda. Spiteful like Emmy. Broken like Margarete. You're something special and I've hidden you away. I'm sorry for that."

"Don't you dare."

He continued as if I had said nothing. "I thought it was best. Now? Now I'm not so sure. I've made you so miserable. So very miserable. It's the worst thing I've ever done and for that, I'm sorry."

"Stop it, Addie." But on he went, stroking the doorframe while he spoke.

"You deserved – deserve – so much more than I could ever have given you. You know it wasn't my fault, don't you?" His eyes were on me suddenly, inflamed with his passion and looking more like his own than they ever had. "Tell me you knew that? That I didn't say goodbye before I left because I couldn't bear to. I couldn't stand seeing your face so hurt. I wish I could have taken you everywhere with me. But…it's not safe. It's never been safe. I have to keep you safe, Eva. My little Tschapperl. And maybe I haven't always done that. Maybe I've hurt you more than they ever could. But you know I love you, Eva, don't you? Don't you?"

"Are you saying goodbye now?" I choked.

He smiled sadly and turned back to the grand hall.

"My car's waiting outside. Be strong, Eva. Whatever comes. Whatever happens. You'll be strong for me, won't you? You'll be strong?"

"You'll phone me, won't you?" I said, following his long strides with a run. "Phone me, Addie. I need to hear your voice."

"I'll call, Eva," he promised as he reached the front door. The wind was icy as it blew in from the July sunshine outside. "I'll call, of course. Stay strong. I'm sorry I couldn't make you a star. A wi... I'm sorry."

He shut the door as he left. I stood, dumbstruck as I heard his weight on the gravel. I threw the door open to call after him, just a second too late. He was already in the car. Already speeding away.

He never said goodbye.

I ran to the white door a woman possessed. I had never been ill, not truly, period pains at best, and the thought that a sickness had taken root in my Führer was as horrid a feeling as the night – so long ago – when my father had told me a bomb had gone off. The fragility of his life, his precious, beautiful life, was baffling.

How can a man like him be taken from us? A man as loved as he is. A man whom I love so dearly. God wouldn't take away such a man, surely? God wouldn't take his life? From me? From Germany? But if it isn't God that has stricken him like this. Then…who?

"Morell," I cried as I threw open the door.

He looked at me, his same piggy eyes gleaming when Addie's had been dulled so resolutely.

"Fraulein Braun? What can I do for you?"

It made me sick. I was ashamed to feel it, but the thought of begging this man for anything made my skin crawl. It was a deal with the Devil and I knew it.

"Please," I threw myself to my knees at his feet. He stood to tower over me, his power never more apparent than it was in that moment. "Please save him. Please."

"Save him? But the Führer is fine, Fraulein. He just needs to rest."

"Promise me?"

"Promise you what, Fraulein Braun?"

"That you'll help him. That you'll help him get better."

"My dear girl, I wonder often if you are deliberately stupid or if it is all a rouse. Stand up, don't humiliate yourself like that. Lord knows Bormann will try and do that enough for you." He helped me to my feet, his hand slick with sweat. It stuck my fingers together like tree sap. I didn't want it on my face and so let the tears fall on their own, not bothering to wipe them. "If I could have rested him faster in the East, I would have." His voice quivered on the last note. His brow was as sweaty as his hands. His eyes furtive, like a criminal pig.

"You don't know what's wrong with him, do you?"

"Of course I do," he blustered.

"Then you don't know how to heal him."

"I know that too."

"Why haven't you, then?"

"Because I am just a doctor, Fraulein. I can sedate him, I can ease his worry, his physical pain – but I can't cure him."

"Who can? Who can cure him then? Please tell me. He's gone. Do you know that? He's gone and he won't ever come back. How can I help him now that he's gone?"

"Stupid, stupid girl," Morell said as he licked his fat lips. "Are you not listening?"

1945

March, *The Führerbunker*

I don't remember deciding that enough was enough. That I wouldn't be the girl that you didn't say goodbye to. Nor do I remember when I finally understood what Morell meant. It took me all summer though, that's for sure. All summer and most of Winter.

Frau Mittlestrausse came with me to Münich. I dithered. Then remembered why I'd descended the mountain in the first place and continued on.

The ruins were physically painful. All through Germany, through fields and streets and stations and road, the destruction was insolent, offensive. I drew the curtains where I could but the darkness began to creep into my mood, silently, and I couldn't bear it for long.

I missed Gretl. But, in a small way, I was thankful she wasn't here, that I didn't have to tell her to stay behind because, maybe, just maybe, I wouldn't have. I couldn't think of that for long. I didn't want to think I could be that selfish.

Arriving at the Chancellory was familiar, though everything was so different. I knew my way around well enough to be left alone but the guards insisted that they accompany me. Their uniforms looked so new. So untouched. I lifted my hand to the youngest one's lapel and drew off a stray feather that had clutched itself to the deep green material.

"Thank you," he said. I smiled.

Going down the steps was intimidating, but I didn't let it show. They were steep and perilously thin, my heels edging closer to the lip, desperate to throw me down the stairs. The air was putrid. Clouded with fear, wound with tension. It clogged my throat, snarling deeper into my body the further I got into the bunker. If there was an opposite to Wonderland, then this was it.

"Eva," he said as he leapt from his chair. Hard looking men with grim mouths and stony faces looked at me as if I was a rabbit in a headscarf. "Oh Eva, thank God." And he hugged me, briefly, right there before their eyes.

"I told you not to come here," he said as we sat in the claustrophobic little sitting room he had set up by his office. "I forbid it."

"I couldn't stay away from you. Not now."

"I'm glad you're here, Eva, I am, but…"

"I'm not going, Adolf. Save your words. I'm not going back. Me and you." I took his hand. "Me and you. Together. This is how this ends."

"It might not end. Eva, I have a plan," he said as he launched into a diatribe of Generals, kilometres, Wenck and the Hitler Youth. The more he spoke, the more animated he became. His hands took up the tiny expanse of room with large sweeping gestures. He wiped his mouth with his hand and coughed once or twice. His eyes sparkled. "You're my angel, Eva. My angel of hope. You've brought me hope."

April, *The Führerbunker*

The hope died around his ears. Then rose up like a daffodil in the snow. Then withered again. All before breakfast. His mood swung like a pendulum, an endless ticking that drew us nearer and nearer to the end. And I knew that was what I was waiting for. I'd known it from the moment I'd left the Berghof.

Blondi looked at me with her sad eyes. Her face rested on her paws, she yawned, giving off a small whine as she stretched her jaw. I ached to kick her. But what would the point have been? She wasn't getting out any more than I was. We watched each other, the last two facets of love he had left. She didn't blink, didn't break eye contact. My eyes watered. The more I thought about keeping them open the more they tried to close. I fought it. I tried to keep them wide so that I could win the little spar with his dog. And then the bombs began to fall.

They'd come daily, a rain of metal and fire. We were too deep to be bothered greatly by them. The lights would swing occasionally if one hit right above us, but mostly it was just the noise. Blondi smiled at me, seeing me pull my legs up tight around my body, squeezing myself into a little ball to keep safe. I knew they couldn't hurt me. But that didn't mean I liked that they were trying. I got up, anger swelling in me like a growing boil, and went to give the mutt a swift kick. The door swung open as I held my foot raised behind me.

"Traudl Junge," I said to the severe woman by the door. She clocked my raised foot and tutted.

"A dog, Fraulein Braun. You're jealous of a dog?"

"Jealous? I...no."

"The Führer has taken shelter in the Reich's Chancellory. They expect this to only be a short raid and he would like to finish his meeting on the surface before he comes back down here."

"He's not back in the bunker?"

"Please, Fraulein Braun, do not make me repeat myself again. I'm very tired."

"Thank you, Frau Junge," I said, dismissing her. She closed the door behind her as she left and I went back to my chair. All thoughts of kicking Blondi now gone. "Frau Junge," I called. She opened the door, her arm weighted in letters and papers. "Will you…" I gestured to the oversized couches and chairs that took up all the space in the room. "Please, I don't want to be alone."

She sighed, but took a seat on the large armchair nearest the door.

"You're from Bavaria, yes?" I said as the light shook and whipped frenzied shadows around our shoulders, peeking beneath our seats.

"Yes. That's why he chose me."

I almost said the same thing back to her, but bit my tongue at the last moment.

"Did you always want to be a secretary?" I asked, dumbly.

"Of course not," she laughed, her face brightening a little. "The war made me a secretary but my heart pines to be a dancer."

"A dancer? Oh Frau Junge, how exciting. Could you…" I looked around and saw how little space there was between the couch and arm chairs, a wooden sea of hard wood knocking at our knees. "I'd very much like to see you dance sometime."

"I'm not very good." She blushed. She was so young, I realised then. I'd never thought of her as a young woman before. In my head she was old and strict, a school mistress that liked to use the rod. But as she spoke about the few lessons in dancing she'd had before the war, the youth returned to her in spades, a glow flushing her cheeks. "And what about you, Fraulein Braun, what did you want to be before…"

"Before the Führer?" I finished for her. "An actress." It was a bomb all my own, one that buried me in rubble. I tried to breathe through it, I tried my best, but the weight of it was crippling. My lungs panted frantically, little shallow draws and intakes. My forehead was sweaty. I gripped the material beneath me as hard as I could. As if the brown table truly were a sea, desperate to drown me.

It was gone. That part of me. The part that could have been anything other than just his was gone. The canker had died, shrivelled and withered into nothing. I wouldn't ever be an actress. Not now. Not ever. And I knew, since I'd first picked up the gun all those years ago, that I wouldn't ever be an actress. I remembered that night so freshly that it could have been only days before. I remembered it because I felt then how I felt at that moment before Frau Junge – hopeless. As soon as I'd seen Addie walk into the photo shop, as soon as I'd pretended not to know who he was, I'd trapped myself in a wire net. Who would hire the Führer's whore? Who would make her their leading lady? The answer was clear, potent and visceral in my chest. It burned at my bones and soldered my flesh.

"Are you ok, Fraulein Braun?"

"Please don't ever stop dancing." My hands slipped in her own, hooking my nails into her knuckles. "Not ever. When you get out of here – when you leave this place," I tried to smile, but from how she grimaced I succeeded only in baring my teeth, "you'll keep dancing. Promise me that?"

"I'd like to go now, Fraulein. Please, let me go." She struggled against my grip. I felt her soft skin tear beneath my nails but I daren't let her go, not before she promised.

"Promise me? Promise me? Promise me."

"I promise, Fraulein. I'll never stop dancing. I won't, I swear," she was crying now. "Please let me go."

The strength in my hand dissipated like a hollow sail being betrayed by the wind. My wrist went limp and I slumped back into my chair. Frau Junge slammed the door as she left. And with it she took away the incessant bombing above and the bunker grew still. Silent. Smothering.

Blondi looked up at me again. Her ears stretched from her head, she listened for the sound of his footsteps. I could see the heartbreak plain on her muzzle. She strained to hear his footsteps coming towards her.

"Stupid dog," I said, not daring to see the parallel.

Heinz Lorenz burst in on us while we stood hugging closely. He'd been shaking so much that day, his heart was breaking in his chest and the strain of pretending otherwise was beginning to fracture the loose plates of his mind. I would hug him tightly, my arms straining against the soft fat of his body, praying that I could squeeze the plates back together long enough for him to make it through the day. *It's like we're still in the Berghof.*

"If only we could walk," he whispered into my ear, his breath moist on my lobe, as the door was first thrown open.

"Führer." He had the decency to blush. I let Addie go and sipped my wine as I sat by his large desk, the small portrait of Frederick the Great watching me closely. Even in the bunker, Addie needed the relic's watchful gaze. "Sorry, I need to speak with you at once, in private."

"Anything you have to say to me you may say in front of Fraulein Braun," he said, stunning us both. My tongue stopped moving and I began to splutter as the wine travelled down my wind pipe. Lorenz barely moved as he shut the door behind him, watching me as if I were a dangerous snake in the corner.

"As you wish, my Führer. The American President, Franklin Roosevelt, is dead."

His hand stopped trembling as if it had been the spectre of Roosevelt that had kept it moving. He cocked his head, like Blondi would when he began to speak. And, to both our astonishment, he began to dance around the room. He looked like a jester, a man in clown's clothing who had finally lost his mind.

"We've won the war! This is it. Our Victory. There is a chance now. A chance!" He clapped his hands together and spun around like a child around the Maypole. "Collect my generals. We must act. We must act. Rally them. Rally them and bring them all here."

Lorenz left at once.

"Addie, are you ok?" I said warily as he paused for breath, resting his small hands on the soft curves of his desk.

"This is great news. Fantastic news! God has answered me. He has, Eva. My little Tschapperl. He has sent me you and now he sends me this news."

"God?" I said, wondering where this affinity had come from suddenly. "You've never spoke about God before."

"I've never had to. Now, in my most desperate hour, He has come for me. Eva, He has listened to me, to my will, and He has provided it."

"Addie, this is wonderful," I said, smiling at his jubilation. The air felt cleaner for his happiness. The dark a little less menacing. For the first time since I'd nearly slipped down those four flights of stairs, I felt less like a caged beast and more like a burrowing mouse, waiting for my time to go out into the sun again. "Wonderful news. We are blessed, don't you see?

We are blessed. I always told you this. I always promised you would see it one day. And *voila!* Now you know it to be true."

"I have to go and get ready. I should run a toothbrush around my mouth. My teeth feel furry, it's been so long. For once that room won't feel like a coffin," he said, his eyes fearfully moving towards the tiny room just outside that fifteen men had to cram themselves into. "This is our chance, Eva."

"It is, Addie," I said nodding. "Go and revel in it. I'll be here. Waiting for you, my love."

He nodded like a child and ran from the room. I heard Frau Junge laughing as he grabbed her by the waist and spun her around.

I didn't ask. I didn't want to know. I didn't understand how this changed anything. It was the Bolsheviks at the door, the Red Army creeping through the streets – not the Americans. And although I didn't quite understand the fragile aspects of democracy, I was almost certain that the death of a president wasn't a precursor for a huge change in policy. Not like Germany. But he was happy, even if it was only on false hope. And every second he was happy was a second I could breathe properly.

"Eva," a familiar voice said. I could hear the glass tinkle on the floor as the momentary relief that had encased me shattered onto the floor.

"What are you doing here?" I asked, shocked.

"What am I doing here?" He slithered into the room, the heat around him a gravity drawing me closer to him. "I work here. I represent Himmler. What are you doing here?"

I'd never seen his face so worried, so marred with fright. I'd known him for two years and all I'd ever seen from him was passion and arrogance.

"I need to be with him."

"Eva, no. Stop this. Leave here. Is he making you stay? Is he forcing you to be here? I swear, Eva, if he is, I'll kill him. Is he?"

"No, Fegelein. No. I chose to come here."

"You…chose? Why? Don't you understand? The war is lost. Everyone can see it except him. He won't admit it, not even to himself. So, the generals, they…you don't need to know any of this. Come on, I'm getting you out of here."

"No." I pulled away from him but he reached out to grip me again. "No." I slapped his hand. He was on me in a second, stealing the breath form my lips as he pushed his own against mine. I melted into him, my hand riving the hard contours of his muscled body. The heat from him! And then, like a ghost, I smelt the faintest whiff of the perfume I'd sent Gretl for Christmas. "No." I pushed him away, tried to; he barely moved. He ground his erection into my thigh and the pressure made me quiver.

"No," I said, pushing more forcefully. Frederick the Great watching every second of us together. "No."

"Are you telling me no?" he smiled as he nibbled at my neck, "or are you telling yourself?"

"Does it matter? I won't do this to Gretl. I won't. She loves you."

"And I love you."

"No, you don't. You love you. You want me only because he has me."

The space between us was a gulf. A cold gulf of frustration. Loneliness.

"That's what you think? You think I am jealous of an old man? An insane old man? Really? Jeez, Eva, maybe you are as stupid as they say after all."

"Stupid?"

"You came here, didn't you? To the bunker, like an Angel of Death. Everyone knows the only reason you'd be here is to die. But you just had to come, didn't you? Fuck everyone else. Fuck how they feel, how you being here would make them feel. Fuck them, right? Gretl was right. You're selfish. So selfish. How could you do this to yourself? How could you come here?"

"Stop shouting, please," I said as I watched the door for someone rattling the handle. "Calm down."

"Calm down? Eva, you've signed your own death warrant by coming here. I can't watch it. I can't watch you do this to yourself. You could leave here. You could go to Gretl, to Ilse. They'd forgive you. You know they would forgive you. You can survive this. Do you know how many people would kill to have your privilege? To know they'd survive this apocalypse? And you're throwing your life away for a man that has abused and mistreated you for years. That's not the woman I love."

"You shouldn't love me at all. You're married to my sister. And life? What life would I have beyond him? Working in the photo shop? Being a secretary for the British? A whore to the Americans? A spy for the Bolsheviks? This is my chance to become history. To stitch myself to greatness. No one will cast me, not when they know who I was to him. This is my last chance to become somebody. To be something more than simply Eva Braun!"

"You've never had to be anything other than Eva Braun. You've just never could see it. That's so sad." He sighed, his face resigned. "You'll die here."

"I know. But I'll die with him."

The sound of children's laughter echoed down the hallways. At first, I thought it was leftovers of my dream. I'd been in a park full of children, each one in a pretty blue dress or a smart little suit. As the laughter had

346

grown, so too had the day went dark. And just before I opened my eyes, all of the children were dead, faces half burnt off and the laughter still ringing.

I got up from the bed. I was quick to dress, only applying a thin layer of make-up. And I wandered out into the hallways where I'd heard laughing. How he'd survived the months down here, I didn't know. I'd only been there for a few weeks and already the madness had crept in with the shadows. Morell's cocktails could only have been making things worse. But I had no solution better. I had no plan that I could execute to make him feel better. So, I had to let Morell poison him, infect him, inject him – just as I'd begged him to.

"Magda?" I said, seeing Frau Goebbels in a travelling coat, her children spread out behind her like the train of a wedding gown. "Why are you here?"

"Come on, children. We'll say hello to the Führer, wouldn't you all like that? Say hello to Uncle Adolf."

The two youngest were crying. Little Helmut had his finger wedged firmly in his mouth, his eyes gleaming at recognising me. The eldest girl stared at me with the eyes of a dead woman, her face painfully older than it should have been. Only she understood why her mother had brought her here.

"Frau Goebbels?"

347

"After," she said briskly as she ushered her children past me. "After, please, Eva. After."

I couldn't organise anything grand for his birthday. There was plenty of food, of alcohol and treats but nothing that I could give him as a gift. There were no flowers. No pretty cloths that I could at least try and make into a *Geburtstagstisch* for him. He'd once told me over the telephone how he would like to spend his birthday with me. I remembered the glee, the absorbent joy of those words, and marvelled at how different they seemed now. How our roles were changed. It wasn't him coming to spend his birthday with me but me choosing to be with him. If I had spent more time thinking about that, I'd have seen how far – how powerful – I had become. How vital to him I was. But, as it stood, I was more worried about finding a nice table cloth than I was about the philosophical reversal in our roles.

He came back down smelling of 'outside.' I had been buried for so long that the only way I could describe it was as a smell of 'outside.' Of space. Of air and smoke and dust and people. The scent of freedom, however dangerous that freedom was. It was all very well being able to see outside, but how much would that really matter if a bomb came down and tumbled your house down around about your ears?

He smiled and held me close as I wished him a happy birthday. We sat in his office as man after man, woman after girl came in and wished him a happy birthday. No one said it would be his last. The faces that had been at his side the year prior made no mention of it as they clasped his hand and genuinely wished him a long life. As I sat there, watching, ignored – largely – I saw in them the same thing that rotted in myself. I saw their devotion. Their belief that he was above a mere man, above angels even, he had turned 'Führer' into 'Lord' and it was plain on every person's face how grateful they were to be here with him. Only Magda, who had housed her children in the Vorbunker upstairs, closer to the surface, wept as she touched his hand. Her husband, for all his pomp and importance, said nothing and stood in the corner, silent as his wife cried.

"There's no need for tears, Magda," he said to her, his voice a gentle whisper.

"How can there be a world without you?" she said back.

"Magda," her husband's voice warned.

"It's fine. It's fine," Addie shushed him with a smile. He loved this. This naked devotion. He thrived on it. "Magda, no one has said I'm going to die." he lifted her face to look at his own. I itched for my camera, to take a photograph of their love. Its poignancy perfect, an embodiment of his hold on not just her as a woman, but on her as a German. "The war is not over yet."

"It's not?" she said, hopeful.

I saw myself in her. I saw the girl I had been. The infatuated, consumed girl that he had first met up a ladder organising shelves. I had been as plain as her, once. I had thrown myself towards him, bowing at his feet, and begged for his guidance. She'd seen it. She'd seen it the first moment she saw me and she'd sneered. The high and mighty Magda Goebbels would never allow a man to so wholly and easily possess her. We'd hated each other for it. I'd hated her sneering superiority and she'd hated my snivelling innocence. But as she wept at Addie's feet, no make-up on her face, her clothes dirty and unpolished, I could see inside her shell. Her hard marble shell. And within was the same naïve girl I had been.

"You reminded me of me," she admitted as the men left the room and we sat by ourselves, the wine bottle open between us. A pile of empty ones sat tucked behind the couch, hidden from Addie's eyes, as we both hoped he wouldn't notice the amount we were going through. "And I couldn't bare it. To see you so vulnerable. It made me sick. It made me hate you. And now look at me. Crying in a hole beneath the ground as the world around me ends. No amount of bravado could have saved me from this."

"But…" I hesitated, wondering if it was my place to comment on it. "Your children?"

"I know," she heaved in a calm breath. "You think I'm a monster, don't you? I would. But what's left for them out there? What would happen to them when they were discovered as my husband's children? I know. It happened to Marie Antoinette's son. It happened to the Tsar's daughters. You're lucky you have had no children of your own," she said like she could understand the pain that had caused me. As if it had been Sunday morning

decision made easily. "But that makes my children the first family of the

Reich. Odd, isn't it?" she said while laughing. "How much pride I took in

being a position above you, and now it's what will kill my darlings."

"You could…"

"No, Eva. No. You're not a mother. You couldn't possibly

understand. I can't be without them. I won't. There's no world beyond

Adolf. That's the deal I made. There's no life beyond him. Beyond the

party. Beyond National Socialism. And it's all falling down around us. At

least you didn't know. At least you were innocent of the horror. I'm not. I

knew. I knew everything. From that first time he said…well, it doesn't

matter now. But from that moment in a café a thousand years ago now, I

knew who I was committing myself too. This is my punishment." The

words broke her peace and she howled in agony, bent over, her head on my

lap. I stroked her hair. She was just a woman now. Not a great enemy, nor a

hateful bully, she was just a woman and so was I.

He stormed into his little office with a face filled with thunder. The black

clouds were his eyebrows, his face ashy grey like rolling mist. "We are lost,"

he said. "We are betrayed. We are lost. We are done for."

They spoke of suicide around me. They spoke of pills and guns and the alternatives of not dying. Tea was served around us as if we were still in the Berghof, still masters of our world. Magda hadn't brought a change of clothes. So, she sat in the same ones she'd came to the bunker in. I'd sent what little I had to her children, hoping that even the older ones may fit in some of the smaller garments.

"Herr Führer," Fegelein said, sticking his head around the door. "May I speak with Eva?"

The room noted the funny way his voice twanged at my name, but largely shrugged it off. Addie nodded a quick yes to me, so I got up and went to him. My cheeks burned. It was shameful. It was as if my place here in the bunker was only because my sister had married Fegelein. As if less than one year was more official than the fourteen I had spent by his side.

"We have to go," he said, dragging me towards the door that led up and out into the open.

"Go? What? No." I pulled at his hand and slipped free, I stopped to look at him but his fist came down so quickly that I couldn't move. It hit my neck, on the side where my little scar was and I fell to the floor. I didn't cry out. Didn't shout for help. I sat there, dazed, with my head against the wall.

"Look what you made me do. What you've made me become? Gretl's pregnant, Eva. She's pregnant, did you know that? And you're going to die here? And leave her with me? No, Eva. Get up. Get your arse up and come with me. I'm not asking you this time. I'm telling you. I've asked twice before for you to run away with me and both times you've chosen him. Not this time, Eva. Not this time."

"She's pregnant?" *Thank God. Thank God. Thank God. She'll be happy now. She's found her happiness. Someone to love who will love her back.*

He grabbed the soft flesh on my shoulders and hauled me up to my feet. I dug in, desperate that he wouldn't take me beyond the door. My resolve would waver. My dedication would crumble. I couldn't leave. Not after I had come so close. I wouldn't throw it all away. Not for a handsome man.

"You have to look after her. I'm trusting you, Fegelein. Promise me you'll keep her safe? She's pure. She's good. She's innocent and you have to look after her. Promise me?"

"Eva, you're not listening. We have to go. We have to leave, now. We can't stay here. You can't stay here." His mouth was on mine. But his lips were too rough and cracked, his stubble was scratching my chin. He moved his mouth with panic, not passion and his tongue was painful on my own.

"Get off. Stop this. Be a man, Fegelein. Be a man and look after my sister."

"I can't do it. She'll be better off without me."

"You're going to leave her?" I couldn't believe what I was hearing. He'd promised, before our Führer, to love her and care for her. I trusted him. I trusted him with her and now he was throwing her away like she was nothing.

"I can't stay with her. I love you, Eva. I can't look at her anymore. She's too much like you. I can't bear to be around her. I can't love her, Eva. I won't. She'll be better off without me. Without us. Come with me." He reached his hand out to mine. "Don't make me ask a third time, Eva. Come with me. The Americans aren't far off. We can make it. If we can get to them they'll treat us well. If the Russians find you here…"

"I'm not going anywhere, Fegelein. And neither are you. Go back to her, when this is all over, go back to her and keep her safe. Here," I took him to my room; he followed eagerly behind like a puppy. "Take these to her, for her and the baby," I said as I handed over jewelled bracelets, diamond necklaces and gold brooches. "I won't need these anymore. Take them. Take them to her, my dear, sweet sister, and make sure she'd looked after. And this…" I pulled the simple green bracelet from my wrist. It took the last little piece of me with it. Thin threads that clutched onto the final ounce of my humanity. "Tell her I love her. Tell her…" I couldn't speak. "Give her this. She'll understand. Hey, Fegelein." I pulled his chin up from his chest so that he looked at me. "Promise me? If you ever loved me, promise me this?"

He nodded, his pockets full, and twisted on his boots. He left me. Just walked away. And I don't know what I was expecting. But maybe if he'd fought a little harder...no.

"Eva?" I heard Addie call.

I wiped the tears from my cheeks and shook the image of Gretl swollen with her child from my head.

"Coming, my love."

Barely two hours had passed when Addie heard of Himmler's attempted betrayal.

"Peace? Successor? I'm buried beneath Berlin and he thinks he'll become Führer? Never! Not ever, I swear it! Never," he raged to Goebbels, who stood patiently beside him. He sent two guards to collect Fegelein when he discovered he'd left the bunker without his permission. "Bring him to me."

It took two attempts to bring him down into the bunker. But when he was, he wasn't the man he'd been only hours ago.

A huge wet patch covered his groin and reeked of urine. His eyes were glassy and his lip trickling blood.

"Alright Addie, how'ya?" he laughed as he spoke. "Things aren't going well, I see."

I couldn't move. I couldn't breathe. I couldn't do anything except bubble with hot anger. He'd promised. He'd promised me he would look after her and now he was here, drunk and useless. If he'd ran, if he'd taken the jewels and left at once, he'd have been too far away for Addie to catch. But instead he'd given into his weakness and festered within reach.

I turned to leave him to his fate.

"Eva?" Addie asked me. "Eva, you know what has to be done."

I think they expected me to beg. To try and save his life. I wondered if that is what they would say. When all this was over. "She'd begged for his life." But I didn't. I wouldn't.

"And what of the woman?" the solider who had brought him down said.

"What woman?" Addie asked.

The fine hairs on my back stood on end. I bristled like a cat.

"Gretl?" I whispered.

"No. Not Fraulein Braun's sister. Some other woman. What's to be done about her?"

I felt skeletal hands on me. They gripped my wrists as a black cloak – velvet, silk – whispered around my feet. His breath smelled of lilies. Of time. Of 'outside.' And he guided me back round to face Fegelein. "Give me the gun," the voice said through me.

The men at either side of Fegelein looked at each other uncertainly. But Addie didn't falter. He took the pistol from behind his desk and placed it in my hand. Its weight felt comfortable, familiar.

He sang to me – death – a lilting tune in my ear. I couldn't decipher the words but his intention was as plain as if it were written in blood on the walls.

Fegelein's eyes looked more sober now he saw the gun in my hand.

I love you, don't do this, they said to me.

I love you too, I admitted back.

"You promised," was all I said.

I pulled the trigger.

I put on my black sequined gown. I stood by his side. We both said 'I do.' He bent his head into mine, the wrinkles on his face more pronounced with the amount of weight he'd lost. There was no sense of time down there. I didn't want there to be. As he kissed my cheek, he whispered into my ear, as Fegelein never would again. "You won."

I looked at myself in the mirror. I changed again. This time into a black gown with white roses around the collar. I still had my glass of champagne from the little party we'd had to celebrate my great success. My penultimate victory. My hair was done, sitting in neat curls along my head. So, I watched my beautiful eyes as I painted the blood red onto my nails. I heard the faint sound of applause. It followed me around the bunker. A temptation of a different life and confirmation of my necessity in the one I was in. My lips were moving in the mirror, unbidden, though I knew what they were saying. I'd rehearsed it a thousand times in the bathtub, on long walks, even by his side as he napped after reading his book.

"And I'd like to thank Germany for helping me attain this most auspicious award. And my husband, the Führer." I stood up from the chair, knowing that I'd never see myself in the mirror again. I sat back down, panic in my chest, fluttering like a light butterfly. "You can do this, Eva B...Hitler."

I squelched through puddles of urine, through the smell of shit and death. The generals were singing in the common areas, unbothered by the stench of the ruptured sewage pipes. The Russians were above us. I could hear their boots on the mud upstairs. And the applause. And the sound of children's laughter.

"I want to be a beautiful corpse," I said to myself, stepping past the adjutant by my husband's door. He was smiling at me when I stepped in, Blondi by his side.

"You look wonderful," he said to me, a young man again. The man I had met in the photo shop. "How do I know this will work?" he barked at the man holding the cyanide capsule. "Prove it to me."

I sat down on the couch and smoothed out the curves of my dress. The dog barked and growled as the soldiers forced open its jaw. I laughed, lightly. All those kicks seemed so pointless now. I closed my eyes and thanked God. The capsule broke in the dog's mouth and slowly her whines grew quieter and quieter. He bent down and touched her face, one last farewell between the two friends.

Dogs don't go to heaven, I consoled myself with.

The gun sat squat and morbid on the coffee table. It would have been poignant to pick it up, to once again feel its dull weight between my fingers. In a way, the gun was more me than myself, its weight more real than I ever was – ever could be. But that would have signalled an end, a coming of a girl who no longer existed. Effie would have picked up that gun. She'd have been scared the capsule didn't work, as he was. She'd have been scared to be left behind. But I wasn't Effie anymore.

I promised Ilse I wouldn't.

The door came alive with the sound of pounding. It all sounded so distant, so far off. It swung open and there was Magda, her hair dishevelled and tears pouring from her eyes.

"Please, my Führer, don't make me do it. Stay alive. Escape. Please, Herr Führer. Please. I can't do it. I can't kill my own children. Survive. Please. Fight."

I shook my head and gave the "no," to his lips. The door slammed shut in her face. He came to me as she scratched at it with all her might. We were alone. Just him and me. Just the two of us. Together.

"I love you."

"You and me. You and me. Always, always. You and me," he said.

I took the capsule in my mouth. I kissed his own past his lips and considered his misty blue eyes one final time before I closed my own.

"Goodbye, Tschapperl."

ACKNOWLEDGMENTS

Writing a book about the Nazis was never going to be easy. Breathing life into people you revile, people that history shudders at the thought of, was both unpleasant and disturbing. But, as a writer, I am tremendously proud of what I've achieved with this novel, and it serves as a reminder that even the most evil of people are never *always* evil; that is to say, that we shouldn't only fear bogeymen who lurk beneath the bed – men who like dogs and adhere to a vegetarian diet can be the most monstrous of all, yet we don't recognise it until it's too late.

The works of Angela Lambert and Thomas Lundmark were seminal in the creation of what I dub as 'my Eva.' They take great pains to stress that we will never truly know who Eva Braun was as all the interviews that followed about her have been diluted by misogyny or were efforts to extricate the interviewee from the repercussions that befell those at the pinnacle of the Nazi regime. The Eva in this book is 'my Eva' because she's who I felt she was. Any missteps in historical fact are entirely my own and can be blamed upon a failure in research or a deliberate fabrication to enhance the narrative of the novel (i.e. Fegelein was actually executed in the Reich Chancellory's gardens, Eva was in Münich at the time of the 1939 plot against Hitler's life, and Gretl was married on June 3rd, not June 6th) but I have strived to work within what we know and build the day to day life of Eva as close to what history tells us as possible.

My thanks goes out to Amy Stirton who read this book and gave her honest feedback within days of receiving the manuscript – you've helped me more than you know.

To the faculty of the University of Dundee's WPS MLitt, I will be forever grateful for your tutelage and guidance in the early stages of this novel and hope, now it's completed, you'd grade it higher than a B1!

I'd be remiss if I didn't mention the Boaby Lovers, my ride or die Day Ones that have stood by me when I couldn't stand by myself. Your protection, your love and our silly memories have kept me afloat when I thought I would sink.

To Katherine Anderson and Emily Hakkinen – There. Are. No. Words. You've taken a novel that agents across the U.K. have refused to touch and brought it to life across the pond. Your encouragement, your love for this book, has kept my spirits high and my fingers typing when the wolf was at the door. Whatever this book achieves, it does so because of your belief in it. Thank You.

And to my gran. This books for you. As is the next one. And the next one. And everyone that follows those.

You know why.

And thank you, Reader. Thank you for coming on this journey with me. Thank you for sitting through scenes that made my stomach curl in on itself and for seeing what I saw in 'my Eva'…a message for everyone:

Love shouldn't cost you your life.

Follow me on social media.

facebook.com/ConnerMcAleese
@ ConnerMcAleese
@ conner_mcaleese